# all we left behind

# all we left behind

## Ingrid Sundberg

Simon Pulse

New York   London   Toronto   Sydney   New Delhi

SIMON PULSE

An imprint of Simon & Schuster Children's Publishing Division

1230 Avenue of the Americas, New York, New York 10020

First Simon Pulse hardcover edition December 2015

Text copyright © 2015 by Ingrid Sundberg

Jacket photograph copyright © 2015 by Getty Images/Tara Moore

All rights reserved, including the right of reproduction in whole or in part in any form.

SIMON PULSE and colophon are registered trademarks of Simon & Schuster, Inc.

For information about special discounts for bulk purchases, please contact

Simon & Schuster Special Sales at 1-866-506-1949 or business@simonandschuster.com.

The Simon & Schuster Speakers Bureau can bring authors to your live event.

For more information or to book an event contact the Simon & Schuster Speakers Bureau

at 1-866-248-3049 or visit our website at www.simonspeakers.com.

Jacket designed by Jessica Handelman and Karina Granda

Interior designed by Tom Daly

The text of this book was set in Adobe Garamond Pro.

Manufactured in the United States of America

2 4 6 8 10 9 7 5 3

Library of Congress Cataloging-in-Publication Data

Sundberg, Ingrid.

All we left behind / by Ingrid Sundberg. — First Simon Pulse hardcover edition.

p. cm.

Summary: "Marion is hiding a secret from her past and Kurt is trying to figure out how to recover from his mother's death as they both find solace in each other." —Provided by publisher.

[1. Secrets—Fiction. 2. Grief—Fiction. 3. Love—Fiction. 4. Sexual abuse—Fiction.] I. Title.

PZ7.1.S86Al 2015

[Fic]—dc23

2014036347

ISBN 978-1-4814-3742-4 (hc)

ISBN 978-1-4814-3744-8 (eBook)

*To Amanda*
*for forever changing the way I write*

# all we left behind

# one

# Marion

The sun parts the trees like lips, golden with half shadows and secrets. Dusk arches over the dirt road ahead, and I double-check the Post-it on my dash. It tells me to drive straight for another six miles out of town through this patchwork of New England trees. But the leaves are flamed orange-gold and so thick I can't imagine there's a lake, much less a lake house and a party, somewhere behind them.

"Are you sure this is the right way?" I ask Lilith, who bares her teeth in the mirror of my passenger-seat visor. Her red mouth fills the whole frame.

"Of course it is," Lilith practically snorts, tossing lipstick into her purse and fishing out a silver flask. She opens the cap and gulps back whatever's inside it, smearing red over the rim. "There is only one way, Marion!" Lilith bellows, rolling down the window and leaning into the wind. "Forward, my friend. Forward, into your future!"

The sun winks ominously through the trees, nearly set. The thin fabric of Lilith's tank top stretches over her cleavage, and I can't help but think about all the things Lilith knows. All the guys she's been with and the secrets her body understands, the same way a firefly knows to glow when night arrives, turning on in the dark.

"Marion, it's senior year!" Lilith hoots, nudging me as she leans out the window. "We're going to have the best year ever!" She laughs and her hair whips wildly, catching whispers of sun. And even though the trees angle in dark ahead of us, I can't help but smile and roll down my window with her. Because Lilith is so free, and so alive, and so radiant, that I know I'd follow her anywhere, for just a hint of that freedom.

At the end of the road the treetops open up to unveil the lake, and the final winks of gold shine over the mountain. It makes me forget we live near Boston, or that droves of tourists descend upon our small coastal town of Emerson in the summertime. It reminds me that once this land was nothing but virgin forest.

I park near the salt grass and Lilith drums her fingers on the dashboard, nodding to the bonfire by the shore. Two dozen kids from school already surround the flames, drinking and laughing.

"Let the mayhem begin!" Lilith says dramatically, checking her cleavage in the mirror and fluffing her hair like she's about to go onstage. My stomach grumbles from hunger or nerves, and I pull a McIntosh apple from my purse.

"Appetizer?" I offer, and Lilith looks at me like I'm holding a frog.

"Damn, Mar-i-doodle! You got a fruit stand in there?"

"Maybe," I shoot back, nodding to her flask. "You got a liquor store in yours?"

"Touché!" She grabs my apple and takes a dramatic bite, then shoves her flask in my hand. "Appetizers it is." She motions for me to drink.

I take a swig and the liquid is sweet, but then it hits my throat and burns. "Jesus!" I spit the rest out the window. "What is that!?"

"Sorry." Lilith laughs. "Okay, maybe you *do* need to eat before you drink." She hands me back the apple in exchange for her flask. "Finish that, fruit-girl, and remind me to find you some bread."

Cold air shoots up my skirt as we walk toward the lake, wind kissing my thighs. I grip the apple and tug at the fabric's hem.

"Be cool," Lilith says, dropping an arm over my shoulders and playing with the blond hair that flows down my back. "You got this."

She eyes my hands before throwing back another drink, and I'm not sure what she thinks I've got, only she's already skipping ahead through the reeds and motioning for me to follow. She heads for the bonfire, and from my angle the flames spark around her, wild and snapping.

That's Lilith.

Always on fire.

I hang by the water's edge as Lilith skips from one person to the next. She mentioned this party was exclusive, which sounded cool before, but now that we're here, it really means I don't know anyone. I don't even see the drama kids Lilith normally hangs out with. I could be mad at her for not introducing me, but I know better. Lilith bounces from person to person like a manic jumping bean, and I'd rather be a wallflower than get dragged around like a forgotten puppy. She'll find me when she's done. She always does.

The heat of the bonfire is surprising. It puffs up my skin like the flesh of a marshmallow. After lingering awhile I discover there's an invisible line around the fire. A heat line. On one side it's too hot to stand and on the other side it's too cold. The flames crackle, whispering secrets to the girls standing close to the blaze with their tan legs and low-cut shirts. They dig their toes into the sand, and the soccer players touch their elbows and waists and hair. I move closer to the fire but the heat feels like Lilith's breath, hot on my neck.

"What if you give yourself a deadline?" Lilith asked the other night, her brown hair lying against my white comforter in dark waves. "Like Halloween or Thanksgiving?"

"To find a boyfriend?" I shifted uncomfortably beside her.

She laughed. "He doesn't have to be your boyfriend."

I stared at the ceiling. I'd painted it sapphire a few years ago, but you could still see the outlines of the glow-in-the-dark stars and unicorn stickers beneath.

"Maybe I want a boyfriend," I threw back at her, and she rolled onto her elbow to face me.

"You're misunderstanding. I don't mean go out and screw the next guy that comes along. I mean . . ." She placed her index finger on my shoulder and started to draw swirls through the cotton of my shirt. She did that when she was thinking, as if the contact helped her to figure out what she meant to say. "It's not a promise you're making to *me*. It's a promise you're making to yourself. It's a promise to *your body*. Does that make sense?"

"Not really," I breathed. Lilith knew how to use her hands. She knew what boys wanted. What to do with them.

Her fingers hit my collarbone and goose bumps frilled over me. Cold then hot. Hot, forcing me to stare at the ceiling so she couldn't see all the things I couldn't tell her.

"You make the promise to yourself, Marion," Lilith said, her fingers tracing the hem of my skin. "Listen to your body."

Lilith dug her toes into the stretch of muscle above my ankle and I could tell she was tired. After ten years of sleepovers, I know the crook of Lilith's neck. I know the way her elbow bends. Those toes meant she was ready for bed. Or maybe she was just tired of rehashing this conversation.

"So, how does it work?" I asked, spreading my blond

hair over the pillow. I needed a map. Wanting to lose your virginity and *losing* it are two very different things. "If he's *not* my boyfriend? What are the rules?"

"There aren't any rules, Marion." Lilith rolled onto her side and began to braid my hair. "You trust your instincts. Let him take the lead. Your body knows what to do."

"But what if *I* don't?"

"You will." Her fingers moved effortlessly, her hands weaving the braid without even looking. "Your body knows things, Marion. Things you can't even imagine."

I didn't know what to say to that. Her words were like fog, untouchable and everywhere.

"Don't think about it," Lilith encouraged, eyeing my silence. "Just have fun."

"That's it?"

"Easy peasy!" Her voice got high, like maybe that was a lie, and I fixed my gaze outside on the empty sky, imagining it full of fireflies. "Hell, Mar-i-doodle, you're *hot*," Lilith continued. "So, it's not like it's going to be hard."

"Right." I nodded, wanting to believe her.

"Damn right!" she insisted, before sitting up dramatically and putting on her most obnoxious Catholic-nun voice. "Of course, you should always remember," she started, wagging her finger in the air. "Your body is a temple. You shouldn't defile it with one of those dirty, dirty boys. You should cherish it and keep your beautiful flower intact for your wedding day!"

I grabbed a pillow and smacked her in the face. We both doubled over laughing.

"You know, Marion . . . ," Lilith said quietly, as our laughter subsided and the smell of pine trees drifted in from the open window.

"Yeah?"

"You can . . ." She shook her head, her voice light and dismissive, and I thought maybe I could hear the paint peeling back to expose those plastic stars. "Like if you're working up to it and, I dunno, you're not into it or whatever . . . You know you can say *no*, right?"

My toes dug into the bedspread, squishy as mud.

"Of course I know that," I said quickly, shaking my head like she was crazy. "Who doesn't know that?"

"Sure," Lilith agreed, but then her eyes flicked to me like she wasn't sure I meant it. I pushed back the comforter and crawled underneath, ignoring the icy draft at the base of my sheets.

"Good night, Lilith," I said softly.

"Good night, Marion," she said, turning off the light, but in the dark I could still hear her voice echoing in my head. *Your body knows things*, it whispered as I stared up at my ceiling of sapphire-drowned stars. *Things you can't even imagine.*

# Kurt

There are black smudges all over my hands. It's charcoal from the fire pit that Conner and I are building for the party, trying to set it up before everyone gets here. But the dust is everywhere.

"We almost done?" I ask Conner, who unloads firewood from his SUV and is packing three bundles under each arm. It's impressive for someone who barely clears five foot five. But that's the thing about Conner, he's easy to underestimate.

"You got someplace to be?" he asks, dumping the wood, and I show him my hands. "There's a lake behind you, dumbass."

"Hey, I didn't even want to be here," I say, dropping my briquettes and walking to the shore. "Why didn't you get the freshmen to do this?"

"They're getting the beer. You think I'd trust those JV wimps with matches? You want to burn down my uncle's house?"

"What, and you trust *me* to light this thing?" I say, dunking my hands in the water.

"No, I trust you to shut up and do as you're told." I smile at that. Conner always knows how to cut through the bullshit. Especially mine.

This bonfire thing is Conner's idea. Kick off the season. Get laid. He's been on me all week about how I'm soccer captain and I better be here. So I am. Though he had to practically kidnap me to get me to show up, driving me here himself. I *should* be into it. It's senior year. Best damn year of your life. That's what my sister Josie would say. And what's not to like about being at a lake house in the middle of nowhere, drinking beer?

I scrub at the damn charcoal on my palms, but it won't come off. Fuck it. I wipe my hands on my pants, getting them dirty.

There's a holler and Rory and Troy drive up with coolers and bags of groceries in their backseat. I start helping them unload when Troy wrestles me into a headlock.

"Hey, Rory, you owe me ten bucks. I told you this douche would show up."

"Excuse me?" I twist out of Troy's grip and turn the tables so it's me with my arm hooked at *his* throat. "What's this? You two making bets on me?"

"Hey, I bet *on* you man, not against." Troy struggles and Rory laughs. "Lay off."

I don't let him go.

"You know, your chances of getting laid are better if I'm *not* here," I say to Troy.

"True," he agrees, still struggling. "But you're always so much *fun* when you're drunk." That's a dig. I rarely drink, and when I do, well, "fun" isn't not the word I'd use to describe it. I'm not mean. Not one of those raging assholes or anything. I'm just not . . . happy.

"You don't need to be drunk to get a little ass," I say. "Well, maybe *you* do, but—"

"Hey, not all of us were blessed with your pretty face." Troy jerks, taking a pretend swipe at my chin with the jab. "Some of us have to use our charm."

"Charm?" I press my weight into him, maybe more than I should. "Charm like making bets on who's going to show up and whose pants you're going to get into?"

"Well, I wasn't planning on getting into yours!"

I twist Troy just enough to make him stomp his foot on the ground and I wait for him to call uncle.

"Hey!" Conner stalks up to us with a giant bag of briquettes. He chucks it at me, forcing me let go of Troy in order to catch the bag and keep it from knocking us over. Black dust kicks up as it slams into my chest. "You two done making out? There's a fire that's not going to build itself."

"Jealous?" I smile at Conner, but he glares at me with his stop-fucking-around face.

"Sorry, Dad, geeez," Troy says, rolling his eyes and tossing me a look like we're both in on the joke. Only, Troy doesn't know when enough's enough. "Hey, Kurt," he continues. "Is Josie coming up from BU tonight?" He straightens his rumpled shirt and throws me a grin. "I mean, if there's one piece of ass you're not going to cockblock tonight, that'd be it."

The briquettes hit the dirt, and somehow Conner's forced his way between me and Troy before I can pummel him. Troy laughs loudly, thinking this is all part of the game we're playing. But if he could see how hard Conner's actually gripping me, how much effort it's taking him to hold me back, Troy would shut up.

"Forget him," Conner says in my ear. "He doesn't know what he's saying."

"Come on," Troy prods. "You two used to be the life of the party. Well, *she* used to be anyway."

I step off Conner and pull my weight back. "This is why I don't come to these things," I say to Conner under my breath.

"Fine," Conner says, and for the first time it looks like he regrets making me show up. "Why don't you go for a run. Blow off some steam."

My hands are fists. I'd rather break Troy's nose.

"What makes you think my sister would step out on her college education to hang out with you?" I throw at Troy, but he shrugs. He doesn't really care. He's just busting my balls.

"Once a cheerleader, always a cheerleader," he says.

Conner grips my shoulder and points to the woods.

"Run, Medford," he says. "We can set up the fire."

"Right." I laugh, only it's edged with sarcasm and Conner knows it. "You trust *them* with matches?"

"No." Conner looks me square in the eye. "I trust you to shut the fuck up and do as I say." He tosses me a water bottle and I head for the trees.

I follow the shoreline, so I don't get lost, and cut through the underbrush. My feet pound against the dirt and I forget Troy. Forget Conner. Forget all of them.

I put one foot in front of the other and run. I don't try. It just works. It's like there's something else in there that turns on and goes. Like it isn't me. Like it's some superhuman-fast me. I don't know where it comes from— God or something, that's what Mom would say. Not that I think I'm superhuman. Not that I think God has anything to do with it.

It's just sweat and grass, and digging in your heels, and running till your heart wants to burst. Running till you don't have to breathe anymore. They say that happens when you skydive, that the air around you goes so fast that you don't have to take a single breath. The oxygen goes right through your skin. It gets inside.

I look down at my hands. They're still covered in black. I dump the water from the water bottle all over them, but it doesn't help.

# Marion

**The bonfire crackles and I step closer to the blaze.**
My arms heat, but I force myself to stand with those other girls who let the flames singe the hairs from their skin. The back of my throat stings with alcohol and I wonder if I should get another drink, if all of this would be easier if I were drunk. If that's part of what makes Lilith able to dance with the fire.

I thumb the apple that's still in my hand, turning it to hide the bite Lilith took. I lift it to my nose, pretending it's untouched, pressing the waxy skin to my lips. I don't know what it is about apples, but they've always reminded me of Abe, my lab partner, and sitting next to him freshman year, under the tree in his backyard. An uneaten apple always feels like that moment—that perfect space before— waiting for him to kiss me. My lips part and I wonder if Abe will show up tonight, or if he's too smart for a party like this. I inhale the tawny apple scent and imagine what it will taste like.

Sweet. Slightly sour. Soft yet sharp.

Would it be like that to kiss Abe again? Not that I have a chance with Abe anymore. Not that I didn't ruin us a long time ago.

"Are you going to make out with that apple? Or eat it?" Lilith says, appearing from behind the flames. I chuck the apple at her playfully and she dodges it, the fruit rolling into the fire.

"Down, girl!" she mock scolds, sidling up beside me and hooking her arm through mine. "You got a crazy streak in you, lady!"

"You ain't seen nothin'," I joke back. "Imagine if that had been a papaya."

"I'd probably be dead."

"Be thankful we live in New England, where exotic fruit doesn't grow."

"Oh, I am." Lilith hands me her flask and I take a swig, forcing myself to keep the burning liquid down. I shake my head as my ears start to buzz. Lilith laughs and takes a drink herself, squeezing her eyes tight as she swallows. "Woooo!" she exclaims, raising her arms and twirling. Her skirt lights up like a parachute and the curve of her legs becomes silhouetted by fire. People watch. A few clap, and several boys stare at her legs. I want to join her. I want to kick off my shoes and twirl with her laughter, because somehow everything is easier if it's done with Lilith. She makes anything seem possible.

But then it would be my legs under those eyes. My broken flip-flops left in the sand.

I look past Lilith to the lake. It ripples silently, reflecting the dusky sky. Only, my gaze is drawn to the edge of the water where a reflection of black trees disrupts the surface. It's in that patch of darkness that you can see the slimy rocks and the mud and all that the lake is hiding. It's where one might fall in and silently drown.

Lilith loses interest in her performance and drapes herself against me, half-drunk and searching for balance. "I love you," she says, nuzzling my neck.

"I know," I say, holding on to her weight. She hums for a moment and I watch the skin of my uneaten apple curl back in the fire, turning black with the heat.

"I wasn't kidding," she says, her voice getting low. "When I said this should be our best year. I meant that. We've only got so much time left. We should drink. Have fun. Live it up. You know?"

"Absolutely," I agree, the sparks behind us blinking from orange to ash.

"Exactly!" She squeezes my arm, and the sentimentality in her voice is gone, replaced by her normal frisky charm. "So, seriously . . ." She turns us in one motion, like we're attached at the hip, and faces us in the direction of a group of soccer players. "Mar-i-doodle, this is the first big party of the year. And, I thought, you know . . ." She nods to the boys. They're the same group of soccer players that has been

17

touching elbows and waists and hair. "Well, I thought this could be a good *opportunity*."

My neck goes tight when she says the word "opportunity."

She's not talking apples.

She's talking cherries.

# Kurt

**The bonfire's blazing when I come out of the woods.**
I hear the clank of beer bottles and I'm surprised to see how many people have already shown up. I didn't think I was out in those woods for very long, but maybe I was.

The driveway's turned into a parking lot and I hear music up ahead. It's that angry metal crap Conner likes, where yelling is called singing, and the band can't play to save their lives. I've tried to educate Conner on good music, but he keeps insisting this shit's *the shit*. Well, at least he got one part right.

I snag a beer from a cooler along the way and halfway through it I see the golden eagle on the label. My stomach turns and everything in my mouth goes sour. Fucking freshmen! I curse under my breath and tip the bottle over, Mom's favorite seeping into the dirt. Guess, I'm *really* not drinking tonight.

"Medford!"

I turn to see Vanessa walking in my direction. Her

mouth is glossy and she deliberately tilts her head so her black hair slides off her shoulder. I chuck the eagle over the cars and into the woods, ignoring the crash of glass that echoes back.

"Where have you been?" she demands, moving in so close I could kiss her.

"Around," I say, checking out the front of her and remembering the way she moved when we skipped class last week. I took her to the dugout behind the baseball diamond, where her mouth had that waxy lipstick taste. The rest of her was soft though. The rest of her was worth enjoying.

"Well, good thing I found you, then," she says. "Getting *around* and all."

I roll my eyes. She likes this game, but I don't want to play it. She knows there's only one reason this works. And when it stops working . . . well, then it stops working. I thread a finger through her belt loop, pulling her in, and she hangs an arm over my shoulder.

"Geez!" She flinches, her arm hitting the sweat on my neck. "What did you do? Work out or something?" She sounds annoyed but her fingers play with my hair.

"What? You don't like me sweaty?"

She smiles mischievously. "I like being the one to *make* you sweaty."

I laugh and look over her shoulder to the row of parked cars. I could take her to Conner's SUV, but he's pissed at me.

"I don't have my car," I say, knowing we could find someplace else, but there's something in the air, and for whatever reason, I don't want the easy and the booze. Not tonight.

"Kelley has a car," she says, batting her lashes, and I smile at her persistence.

"Well, do you have the keys to Kelley's car?"

She tosses her hair again and the strap of her tank top falls from her shoulder. She probably just wants to go into the woods.

"No," she admits, moving in to kiss me, but I smell beer, and the last thing I want right now is lipstick and golden-eagle breath. I pull away as smooth as I can and throw on a teasing smile.

"Well," I say playfully, running a hand under her shirt, over her stomach, which makes her moan hungrily. "Why don't you find me when you have those keys?"

I inch my hand dangerously close to her breasts and she leans in for a kiss. I pull away, teasing, but she manages to pin me. The taste of wax spreads over my mouth, and I let her do it. It's not so bad, especially if I don't breathe.

"Keys," I repeat when she releases me. I drop my hands and smile sideways, heading for the fire without looking back to see if she's pissed or likes the challenge. All I know is that I don't want to deal with her right now.

I forget about Vanessa and walk to the lake and put my feet in the water. It's freezing. But the bonfire's behind me so I don't really mind. The water is flat. So flat it feels like it will go on forever. It makes me want to chuck a rock in it. Or ten rocks. Anything to cause a ripple.

"Hey!"

It's Conner behind me, followed by a smack at the back of my head that stings like my feet in the water.

"Stop being a douche and join the party!" He holds out a beer and I take it to humor him, ignoring the black label and gold wings.

"How far do you think that other shore is?" I ask. "Straight through. If I swim?"

Conner frowns at me like this is a trick. "I'll give you two football fields," he says, and I shake my head.

"No way, that wouldn't even get you to the center of the lake."

"I'm sorry, let me clarify." Conner smacks me again. "What part of 'don't be a douche' did you not understand?"

"Shit, all right." I step away from him.

"Two football fields," he repeats. "That's how far you're going to get with whatever chick you take out there. If I see you in that water *without* a girl, I will pound the shit out of you."

"All right. Point taken."

"Good. Now drink."

I look at the bottle and almost turn it over so the eagle is pointed at him. But I don't want to play the mom card.

"Bottoms up!" I say, raising the beer and tilting my head back. I down the whole thing. It's sour and cold, and tastes better than I want it to. I hand him the empty bottle when I'm done. Maybe he does see the eagle on it then, but if he does he doesn't say anything.

So much for not drinking.

# Marion

**Lilith scans the boys in the crowd, her eyes pur-**poseful and gleaming. She's serious about this.

"Lil, what are you—"

"This is going to be soooooo much fun," she interrupts, already bouncing up and down.

"I don't know." I eye the soccer team. "I can't say I'm into shin guards and sweaty jerseys."

"Oh, trust me." She leans in. "It's what's *under* the jersey that you'll be into. And bonus if it's sweaty!"

"Ew!"

"No, no!" She squeezes my side. "The correct answer is, please, sir, can I have another?" I squirm as she tickles me and we both laugh. But then she stops, zeroing in on a target. "Oh yes!" She claps her hands together, far too amused with herself. "Oh, girl, you are gonna *love* me."

"What? Who?" I look past her. There's Rory Hackett, who has ginger freckles and a canary nose. He's cute, if you focus on his legs, but I could say that about any of the soccer players. Next to him is Conner Aimes talking ten words a second. His baseball hat is flipped to the side, showing off a sweaty forehead of hair. Troy Beal is the best looking of the three. At least he's got that hot musician slouch, minus the cigarette.

I pinch Lilith. "Who?'

"Patience, grasshopper." She bats my hand away, laughing. "Your future awaits. Stay here." She skips off before I have a chance to stop her, and my stomach flutters like a hundred moths swarming a lamp. Only she walks right past the three soccer players and heads for the lake. Those moths in my stomach do a nosedive when I see who she's walking toward. All 150 of them fly straight for the bulb's hot pane of glass, burning their wings up in the light. I have to check myself, because she couldn't possibly be heading for—

Only she *is*.

She stops next to Kurt Medford.

He stands ankle deep in the water with his arms crossed over his chest, and the fabric of his T-shirt is so tight I can see the muscle definition underneath. Lilith offers her flask and he takes a drink, laughing, like they're old friends, and I wonder what she knows to say to him that makes him look so at ease.

Why would she pick Kurt Medford? Soccer captain. Gorgeous. Out of my league. Sure, I know who he is— *everyone* knows who he is. But he doesn't know *me*. He's the kind of guy you see from afar, tawny-haired, beautiful; he's not someone you actually speak to. I see him in the halls at school, sure, but there's something effortless about him. Intangible. He has that ability to slip in and out of the light, like a mirage you aren't sure you actually see. But when he's there in front of you, he's *there*—sort of sturdy and brilliant. On the soccer field, running, that's when you really see him. Every muscle moves with a purpose, every sinew wound tight and then released. It's his grace, startling and unexpected, that steals the ball out from under the other team's feet and scores when they aren't looking. It's as if you never really see Kurt, until he chooses to be seen.

Kurt's gaze flicks over Lilith's shoulders and my insides go hot. He looks at me longer than I know what to do with and I feel like I've swallowed a volcano of stars. The smell of smoke makes me cough and I look away, my hands sweating, and I want to pull my hair off my neck. I never wear it down and its weight is too hot. I twist the locks to one side and peek to the shore, only they're walking toward me.

"This is Marion," Lilith says a few seconds later, nudging Kurt. He frowns, tilting his head away from the fire, and I think about that heat line and which side I'm supposed to be on.

"Hi," he says, light sliding over his mouth, and all I can do is mumble a hello and extend a hand for him to shake. It hangs in the air for way too long and I realize no one shakes hands anymore. It's a stupid gesture I learned from watching my father at business meetings, only—

He takes it.

Kurt's hand is caramel soft and calloused at the same time. He grips me aggressively like the handshake itself is a dare and it catches me off guard. Only I rise to meet him, squeezing back, and I can hear my dad's words in the corner of my mind saying, *You only get one chance to make a first impression.*

"Nice," Kurt says, surprised, holding my grip. "Sturdy handshake. You don't usually see that in a girl."

"Oh?" I lift my chin to meet his gaze and his blue eyes flicker with fire. "What do you usually see?"

"Weakness." He smiles at me then. "I'm gonna like you."

Heat flames, and I can't tell if it's my cheeks or the pit's burning embers sparking hot. Only, I *want* to stand in it. Is this what Lilith meant when she said 'trust your body'?

"Have fun," Lilith whispers, kissing me on the cheek, and I reach out to make her stay. But she's too fast, slipping away through ribbons of smoke and light.

Kurt takes a seat on a blanket, and behind him the lake is camouflaged with stars, the water weaving into the sky and drowning the horizon. I line up my toes with the blanket's edge, needing a line that's clearly defined. I sit down next to him, and through the flames we watch Lilith drop herself into the lap of one of Kurt's teammates. The two start making out and her lipstick comes smearing off. A few of the guys whistle and I press my lips together, tasting the red chalk on my mouth as well, wanting to wipe it off on the back of my hand.

"You're in my chemistry class, right?" he says, his knee brushing my skirt.

"Have been all year," I say, even though all year is little more than a few weeks.

"You're lab partners with Abe Doyle."

I nod, surprised he noticed.

"Didn't you two used to date?"

"What?"

"Date. Like freshman year?"

I laugh, pulling at my hem, which exposes the light hairs on my thigh. I can't believe he knows that.

"Um . . . I guess." I stare at him, trying to figure out why he's asking. "I mean, that was forever ago. We're not together or—we're just friends—well, not really even friends, just lab partners. Do you know Abe?"

He turns his head away, inviting my eyes to the light that climbs his stubble-flecked chin. "Should I?"

"No, I mean . . ." I cough, pulling a strand of blond out of my face. Not sure what Abe has to do with any of this. After all, Abe's the smart, geeky type and Kurt's . . . well, he's all muscles and smolder, making my insides burn. He sits up and digs his toes in the sand. "Do you like chemistry?" I ask awkwardly, and he laughs.

"Not really."

"Right." I backpedal. "Who likes chemistry?"

"Well . . ." He looks at me, like he's about to make a joke, but then his gaze softens like he thinks better of it.

He shakes off whatever he was going to say and leans his head on his arm and looks at me, perplexed. Not meanly, just interested. I stare back and the heat of the fire slides up my legs. It's uncomfortable and way too intimate, and all I want is to look away, but I can't. I don't know what to say to him. Lilith's not here to make this easier, so I stare, and he stares back, with those quiet eyes, like he's searching for something.

I'm not sure I want him to find it.

"All right," he says, a flirty smile spreading over him. He stands up and sand sprinkles my legs.

"Uh . . ." I look up at him, confused. "All right what?"

He lifts his arms in a stretch, and a band of skin peeks out between his shorts and shirt.

"Let's do this," he says.

"Excuse me?" My voice squeaks, and I know my eyebrows have risen far too high on my forehead. "Let's do . . . ?"

He nods to the lake. "Go for a swim."

I squeeze my arms over my chest and look at the lake. "That water is going to be freezing."

Only I don't think he hears me, because he's already headed for the shore. I scramble to catch up with him.

"You're serious?" I call out as he wades in up to his knees.

"It's not that cold," he assures me, and I look back to Lilith for help, but she's still preoccupied by the fire.

"No one else is in the water."

"Marion." Kurt locks his eyes on me. They hold me

steady. Hold me firm. "Strong handshake, remember? A little water can't scare you."

Heat flushes my skin and I slip a foot in the water. It's cold—and yet so perfectly cold.

He doesn't look away. "You can swim, right?"

"Of course I can swim."

"Good."

He twists with that startling grace and dives under the water without a splash. He dives in with all his clothes on like he belongs to the water and it's a part of him. He dives in such a way that my legs move before I can think, and I'm underwater, in over my head, and under those stars before I know that I've done it. Before I even know I wanted to.

two

# Kurt

I dive into the lake and swim hard. I squeeze my breath inside me and swim far and fast. Not sure why I wanted Marion out in this water with me. Maybe to appease Conner. Maybe to get my fix of blond hair and soft legs.

My hands pull me through the water, but it takes more effort than running. My skin can't breathe. There's water all around me. More pressure. No air. And I can't shake that image of Marion staring back at me. Saying nothing, like she's okay with it. Like she's not going to ask. Other girls, they talk right through that, but this Marion girl—she shakes your hand like she's got the world figured out and she can stand in it. Like she's not afraid of the ash.

I swim till my lungs threaten to split. And then I swim farther.

Breaking the surface feels like fire, and my body throbs, almost too dizzy to breathe. I buzz. Drink air. Kick myself afloat and turn to see if she's followed.

I don't see her.

My stomach drops and I tell myself I'm wrong about her. That maybe she's not solid. That maybe she *is* one of those soft, wispy girls waiting for the world to save her. Only no one's going to do that. Especially not me.

But then there's a splash and her head breaks the surface thirty yards away. She spits and pulls hair from her eyes, and I can't help but smile and swim to her. The water's freezing and ridiculous, and if I hadn't asked her to swim out here with me, she wouldn't have.

"Does it get warmer?" she asks when I reach her. Teeth chattering. Arms pumping through the water.

"Just keep moving," I say, treading beside her. "Your body gets used to it and the cold wears off."

"Okay." She nods, watching me. Waiting. My shorts cling to my legs, awkward in all this wet, and I realize, I got her out here, so it's my move.

Only, I haven't got one.

Her lip trembles and I want to put my mouth on it. Kissing her would be easier than talking. That was the whole point of getting her out here anyway, wasn't it? To avoid talking. But something about her eyes and the way her arms cut through the water won't let me.

I like that they won't.

She's not like Vanessa. Vanessa would never swim in this water. She'd care too much about her hair or looking stupid or whatever. Marion wipes her nose, and lipstick comes off on her hand. I like it on her hand more than her mouth. It suits her better.

"I haven't seen you at one of these parties before," I say, inching closer.

"I've been to a few," she says. "With Lilith."

"I've seen Lilith. She comes to these all the time, but you . . ." I trail off, wondering why I haven't noticed her before.

"I know." She laughs. "It's hard to miss Lilith."

"I guess." I shrug, realizing it's her hair. I'm used to seeing it up, not down and spread out over the lake.

"No, she's . . ." Marion's voice gets low. "Well . . . she's Lilith."

I don't know what that means, but she stops treading water and the lake swallows her up to her chin.

"You're cuter than Lilith," I say, but she eyes me suspiciously. I meant it to be nice. But now that it's out there, I don't know what to do with the way she's staring at me. Like she isn't interested in the charm and the bullshit. Like she wants me to be something else.

I rack my brain for a joke, but it's freezing, and my balls tighten as we circle each other. Yeah, this was a real genius idea. I adjust my shorts, thinking about how much they're going to cling when we get out of this water, and how little they're going to show.

"You feeling warmer?" I ask, and her bottom lip distracts me, bobbing in and out of the water.

"Sure," she says, but it's a lie.

"It's fucking cold," I say, and she breaks into a smile. "I'm an asshole."

"Okay, a little," she says, and I can feel the pulse of the water beneath us. "I mean the cold part," she says, her teeth chattering. "You're only half an ass."

"Oh? Only half?" My hand finds the wet of her shirt, where she's soft under this water.

"Yeah, it—"

But she stiffens at my touch. Making me not sure. Like I should remove it. Like maybe I shouldn't be thinking about that bobbing lip and my mouth on it, or underwater skin. But I like the wet feel of her, and the cold buzz of the lake. Only, I can't read her. She strips me with that look, like she's waiting for something and I should know what it is.

"This was your idea," she breathes, her fingers fluttering against the surface. I want them. Her. I want the ripple, and this uncertain feeling, and her mouth in the water tasting of tin and sticks.

*Smack!*

Her foot whacks against my leg, and I grunt, surprised.

"Shit! Sorry!" she yelps, her arms cutting away from me. "Are you—?"

"It's fine," I say, reaching out.

"No. You just startled me—"

"Marion. It's fine." I find her under the water. Find her waist. "The guys kick me at practice every day."

"Right."

I squeeze her side, but that doesn't comfort her.

"It's no big thing," I say.

"Right, of course they do."

"They do."

"I know."

The ripples calm, and my hand is a rock against her hip.

"I, uh . . . ," I begin, but she's so quiet. Eyes on me, and I'm at a loss for what to say. Her skirt floats up against the back of my hand like the tentacle of a jellyfish, like it wants to wrap around me and pull me down. "It's um . . ." I look to the shore and keep my eyes off her blond hair snaked out over the surface. "We should . . ."

Only I fill my lungs with air and duck under the water without finishing. She mumbles something I don't hear because I'm already underwater. Swimming away from her.

Headed back to shore.

# Marion

**I don't know how to sit next to Kurt and be still.** He's been sitting next to me staring at the lake for what feels like an eternity—saying nothing.

His clothes cling to him from our swim and I can see his skin through the soaked cotton. I don't know what he's waiting for. The air to dry him? For me to say something?

I shiver, but he doesn't react.

I wait, but only the stars fill the quiet.

I should get up and leave. I want to.

He's the one who gets up and walks back to the lake house. He's the one who motions for me to follow.

And I do.

# Kurt

I walk Marion to the lake house and find her a towel. When she's not looking, I disappear into the crowd.

Conner finds me and asks why I'm all wet and gives me *that look*. I tell him I went skinny-dipping with *a girl* and he ignores the fact that my clothes are drenched. I ask him for his keys, wanting to bail, but I don't have a ride. Only this is his uncle's place and he's probably staying the night. I'm surprised when he hands them to me without a fight, and I almost say something, but he tells me to fuck off and pick him up in the morning.

I drive the ten-mile stretch that leads to the main road without the headlights on. I let my eyes adjust and push away that unsettling feeling that came from the brush of her skirt on my wrist. I focus on the road till I hear nothing but tires on gravel. Gravel on tires.

Slowly the dark turns to shape, and when I think I can trust what little I can see ahead of me, I close my eyes.

I coast, trusting the road will be beneath me as long as I drive straight.

I press the gas and rocks smack against the undercarriage. Rumbling.

Slapping.

Metal and dirt and fast.

And I wonder if this is what it's like to be out of your mind and drunk and barreling away from us.

Into dark.


When I get home the house is so quiet you'd think no one lives in it. The place smells of stale tobacco, and a yogurt cup on the coffee table overflows with ash and cigarette butts. A half-eaten sandwich sits on a paper plate in the sink, crumbs everywhere, and the microwave blinks 12:00 in bright red numbers. The way it does when the power goes off. Dad left for his shift hours ago, which means I get the house to myself. Just me and that damn wet plate he's not going to touch. It's the only evidence he's been here. He sleeps while I'm at school. Then works through the night. I can't complain. It's been four years since Mom. I'm used to it. The microwave always blinks twelve o'clock.

I chuck his plate in the trash and change out of my wet clothes. The dryer hums after I throw my pants in, and something metal whacks against the inside wall. Metal from my pants. The zipper maybe. Wham. Wham. It's too loud. It's the kind of thing Mom would use to start a song on her guitar. Only she's not here and that shit doesn't happen anymore.

I go outside and sit on the back porch step, my foot finding the divot where the paint's stripped bare from her cowboy boots tapping. Chipped gone from all those nights out here—Mom and me—like a couple of crazies with our guitars, howling at the wind.

Mom was made for music. Could have been famous if she'd ever left this town. Would have taken the country music scene by the balls, if she'd had enough money to record an album. She sat out here every night after waiting tables, curled over her guitar. Hair wild. Fingers ready. Once she started playing, that was it. Strumming. Bobbing her head. Slapping the side of her guitar to fill in the drumbeat. Playing with her fingers over the top of the neck, not under, like how Andy McKee does it. She'd forget my father on the couch with the TV drowning her out. Ignore Josie hovering behind the screen door. Hell, sometimes she wouldn't even see me playing right next to her.

If tonight had been Mom's, I know she'd've used the thump in the dryer to write a song. Not something for those pubs she played in on weekends, but a song for right now. For us. My fingertips itch and they want my guitar. They want to make sense of that girl with water up to her chin.

I go to my room and pull the two guitar cases out from under the bed. I miss running my hands over the strings.

Miss the first note that cuts through the silence so sharp you can taste the tang of metal in it. Miss searching through the messy notes of sound for one rib of pitch that makes sense. Speaks in ways you can't.

My pinkie runs against the side of her leather case like Marion's skirt on my arm, and I shove Mom's guitar back into the dust. Not sure I'll ever open it again. If I do, I'll smell the sour that sang on her breath, the one that came with gold wings printed on the bottle.

Lint kicks off with the latch, surprising me with how long it's been since I last played.

I sit on the floor, leaning against the bed, and try to remember. Three years? Four? A hint of beer hangs in the air and I almost shove my case into the dark with hers and forget this.

Only, I want to itch out this bunched-up feeling and go to bed. Thrum out the blonde. Sleep.

Inside the case, the guitar gleams, the cheap wood shining in its bed of black. I pick it up by the neck and cradle the body against my knee, letting my head hit the mattress. The strings feel good, the thin lines taut against my fingertips. I press through a series of chords, working my way down the neck. Remembering how the hollow wood feels, too light in my hands.

But I don't strum. I don't breathe. I don't make a sound.

# Marion

Lilith wants to know why I didn't jump Kurt when we were swimming.

"You two were out in the middle of the lake away from everyone," she says, sitting on my bed cross-legged, her legs sprinkled with sand. "It was private."

"I was treading water."

"You can kiss and tread water at the same time."

I pull my ponytail down and smell the lake behind its curtain of blond.

"If he wanted to kiss me he would have kissed me."

"Au contraire," Lilith says, crawling across my bed and wrapping her arms around me from behind. She nuzzles her head into the crook of my neck and I lean into her, wanting the safety of her touch. Touch that's not covered in water. "Sometimes boys need a little encouragement."

"Kurt strikes me as the kind of guy who doesn't need anything."

"Probably true." Her head nods against my neck. "But

not the point." She runs a finger over my collarbone. "Did you *want* to kiss him?"

I close my eyes and feel the swirl of her finger on my skin. It makes me think of that flush, that piece inside me that blossomed and stretched and pulled me into the water after him.

But then I was in it. Swimming, with my skirt floating up to my hips. Water touching under and over. I almost turned around and swam back to shore, where I could dry by the fire. Where I could breathe in the sparks and air and ash and forget that embarrassing thing I had done.

But then he saw me. Swam toward me, and I was up to my neck in it. With him. Swimming forward and into.

"Sure," I say to Lilith, her fingers spiraling over my collarbone. But my mind is on Kurt, on *his* shirt, *his* chest.

"Then don't hesitate," Lilith says, her hand blooming up my neck. Five fingers of softness cover my throat, making me shiver. I can't help it. "If you want it"—she traces a star over my windpipe—"then take it."

Her hand pulls away and I almost gasp at the separation.

My whole body is hot. Too hot. I stare at the ceiling, hating my skin for not asking permission. Lilith moves away, uncapping a pen from my nightstand, and starts to draw stars on the inside of her legs, near the hem of her dress. But my mind is on Kurt, swimming around me. My skin thrumming. On how I can't stop thinking about his hands. How I *want* his hands, but don't know how to ask for them.

*He* was supposed to make a move, wasn't he? In that water, when I was close enough to see his skin through his soaked shirt. Or on the shore maybe, with the lake water dripping down my legs. Or am *I* supposed to make the move? Is that where I went wrong? Is it *my job* to put his hands in my hair?

"How do you . . . ," I start, but then I fluff up my pillow to distract myself. This is all so easy for Lilith. Her lips may be bare now, but she had no trouble drawing red over the mouth of Kurt's teammate. *Taking it.* Not asking. As if there was an unspoken agreement beneath each of their tongues.

Ballpoint stars run the length of Lilith's leg, from knee and thigh, and I'm not sure she heard me start to ask—*how*. How her legs can give permission. How she can cover them with stars that burn up the night. How magically, without hesitation, she can take without a word, and wake in the morning to find those stars still intact. Not blue-smeared and rubbed off.

The summer before seventh grade, everything between Lilith and me changed. It was the summer of enchanting hair.

It was the summer of fire.

It had been an unusually rainy spring, and the wet ground became nested with larvae. The mosquitoes born in June pricked and welted us until we were swollen. But the price of June was worth the gift of August. August held magic. August gave birth to fireflies and set the night to flame.

There was a clearing behind Lilith's house. We found it one afternoon following a trail of wild blackberries. You couldn't see it from the road or even from Lilith's backyard because the trees hid it. I loved it because the grass grew so tall it hit my elbows, and when the sun set, the August night blinked to life.

It was our secret.

Lying side by side in the towering grass, we'd stare into the purple of dusk and see a single wink of gold, and then another, and then ten, and two hundred as the night yawned and fireflies poked holes in the sky.

Every night Lilith and I brought widemouthed jars to that clearing to harvest fire. I would wait in the weeds, catching each fly, one by one, in the palm of my hand. But not Lilith. Lilith would run. She'd dash, jar open, lid off, raking the glass through the air. More flies flew out of her jar than stayed, but she didn't mind. For her it wasn't about capturing the light, it was about falling through it.

I found them in that field.

Lilith and that high school boy.

I wasn't supposed to be there. I was supposed to be at dinner with my aunt, but she'd gotten a flat tire. I'd run down the hill to the field, after my dad left to help his sister, cursing under his breath that it would probably be a while.

The night was muggy, even with the sun down, but the fireflies were magic. When I got to the field, tiny lights covered every inch of grass and sky. There was no horizon. There was only gold and blinking starlight. But then I heard them, grunting, in the weeds. Saw them through the dark. Tangled, with him on top of her, Lilith's paisley sundress bunched at her hip with the white of her thigh exposed against the shadow.

I couldn't see her face. I couldn't tell if she liked it. There was only panting and snapping reeds and fireflies swarming, fireflies blinking, fireflies rubbing against the night.

I stepped forward and a branch cracked under my foot.

"Oh shit," I heard him say, rolling off her.

I didn't wait for them to see me. I ran and didn't look back. Ran all the way home and locked myself in my room, in the dark, where I yanked at my short hair and told myself—

It didn't happen.

In the morning, my father told me that Lilith was outside waiting. She sat crouched on the bottom step with her back to the door. I could see her flip-flops kicked off on the grass, and her bare toes curled tightly around the bottom step. Her arms were wrapped around the front of her, holding something I couldn't see.

"Hey," I said, inching open the screen door.

I waited to see her face.

Lilith unfolded her arms to place a mason jar on the step next to her. It sparkled blue in the morning light with black bugs crawling and slipping along the glass insides.

It was my jar. I must have dropped it.

I sat down next to her and stared at the jar, tracing the star pattern on the lid with my finger.

"Where'd you find it?" I whispered, pretending I hadn't been anywhere near our field last night.

She didn't answer. She searched my face and waited for me to admit it. But I looked away and stared into the sun that exposed too much of the sky. Her shadow passed over me as she stood up. She put on one flip-flop, then the other, and went home.

Later that afternoon, she called me and we went swimming. We spent the rest of the summer at the beach, splashing and laughing, and I hid that firefly jar in the back of my closet. I left it there in the dark. I let the bugs roll over onto their backs and put their legs in the air, in the dark—

Where I couldn't see them.

# three

# Marion

**Mornings before school are quiet.**

The kitchen is pristine and everything shines, full of expensive appliances like in a magazine. There's a Saran-wrapped casserole in the fridge with a note from my father that says he's going to be working late. He's always gone long before sunrise to catch the train to the firm, and now he comes home late too. He's like a vampire who exists in the dark. I want to tell him that Boston's not that far away and he doesn't have to leave for work so early. He could stay for breakfast and drive his car into the city. But there's always some excuse: parking, gas prices, life.

I'm not his little princess anymore.

I unwrap the casserole and eat it for breakfast, cold, and right out of the dish.

Outside, the wind is ruthless. It tangles hair over my eyes, even twisting up the longest strands from the middle of my back, having not seen the glint of scissors in five years. But inside my car the air doesn't move. It makes my skin itch with stillness.

I release the brake and pull off the curb, heading to Lilith's house. I listen to the wind, winding down the road with me, past the Georgian houses and pine trees that separate each estate. I crack open the window and smell the Atlantic, salty and crisp. Smell the bit of Emerson mornings that makes this part of town quaint and colonial, rather than new.

At the bottom of the hill, I park outside Lilith's two-garage estate and pull my blond hair into a ponytail, wondering if my mother's hair was blond like mine. I can't remember. When I was three, she swam across the ocean to be with another man, and Dad threw all the pictures of her away. After she left, Dad became the perfect father. He used to take me to Willow Park to ride the unicorns on the carousel or to the seashore to build a castle. He'd tuck me into bed at night and tell me stories about princes and kisses and magic spells. And when my father twirled his fingers in my blond hair, I thought I was Rapunzel with a secret.

Everyone loved that hair. Even strangers. They all wanted to touch it, crossing streets to give my father compliments.

"So lovely."

"So stunning."

"If only my daughter had hair like yours."

I liked it when people noticed, and Dad did too. I was his little princess with those long golden locks. It was powerful.

It could enchant.

That man tangled his fingers in my hair. That stranger who worked with my father.

It was a month before I found Lilith in our field. It was that same summer, the summer of fire. I had just turned twelve and the beach-rose bushes that lined the river grew rose hips as fat as cherries. Some were large like crab apples, weighing down the branches until the fruit touched the watery lip of the stream.

Before the fireworks, that man asked me to walk up the river with him, away from the company barbecue and the red-and-white paper plates. An hour before, he'd been my savior as I sat hunched over a burned hot dog listening to my father drone on and on about percentage points with his boss.

"D'you play horseshoes, Goldilocks?" he'd asked, holding out two rusty irons. There was dirt on his shirt, and the cuffs were rolled messily at the elbow. "Come on, Goldie, one game. It'll be fun."

I shrugged and said nothing.

He turned to my father. "Harold, I'm stealing your daughter to play horseshoes."

Dad looked up, nodded, and went back to his conversation.

"It's easy. All you do is—"

"I've played horseshoes before," I said, standing up.

"Great. I knew you'd be brilliant, Goldie." He dropped the two irons on the table in front of me. "You get the first throw."

I beat him three times. Not because I'm any good. My horseshoes kept rolling into the bushes. He let me win.

I took off my flip-flops and dipped my toes into the stream.

The creek water was cold.

He sat on a log and watched me from a distance as I waded into the water with my yellow skirt collected at my knees. It wasn't until I sat down next to him that I realized we'd gone around the bend and out of sight of the barbecue. We sat there a long time, watching the rose hips dip in and out of the water, and my legs itched where the ends of my wet skirt clung to my calves. The tiny embroidered daisies were soaked through to the skin. I wanted him to say something, to tell a joke, to fill the silence.

Instead, he spread his fingers wide and threaded them through the silk of my hair.

"You're beautiful," he whispered, his breath on my ear. "Golden."

It was the hair.

"Can I kiss you?" he asked.

It was powerful.

His fingers tangled. "Just one kiss, Goldilocks."

The air smelled sweet like beach peas and maple, with a light hint of smoke lolling down from the barbecue. His lips were round and smiling, his fingers soft and trapped against my skull.

He'd been enchanted.

In all the fairy tales, spells are broken with a kiss.

Just

one

kiss.

When Dad and I got home from the barbecue, I opened the medicine cabinet and found the scissors. The July heat made me sweat, and the evening was still damp with the smell of canary reeds and fire. But the scissors felt powerful in my hand.

The zip beside my ear was effortless. The cut was so soft and clean that my hair fell fast and quick. It fell like golden feathers in creek water—spilling its enchantments out, and off, and onto the floor.

Dad narrowed his eyes when he saw me, as if my lack of hair made me hard to find.

"What did you do?" he breathed, squinting, like the answer might be visible if he could only turn up the light.

"I, I—"

I almost told him.

But his eyes flicked away to the door.

"It's, well . . ." He picked up his papers, tapping them on the edge of his desk before walking up to me. "It's different."

His free hand found a missed curl behind my ear and he rubbed it between his fingers as a shadow washed between us.

"At least it will grow back," he said, forcing a smile as if that was all I deserved.

I became invisible then. Invisible without my hair.

# Kurt

**Smoke hangs in the living room, and Nick Drake's** *Pink Moon* aches out of the record player. The song's from the seventies but it's timeless. Drake wasn't famous in his lifetime. He wasn't discovered till after he overdosed at twenty-six. Of course, with a story like that, it'd be just like Mom to adore him. Which she did.

The record's scratched. Drake's voice skips every few rotations, and I look for Dad. Two of his cigarettes lie in the ashtray, but that's all I see of him. Probably already passed out.

I love Drake, but this shit's too sad for the morning. I switch it off and get some OJ.

I'm drinking straight from the carton when the kitchen phone rings. Mom's phone. The one she bought at a yard sale. She loved that dangling cord, always twisting it over her fingers, around the index finger, past the palm, and back again. I stare at the cheap piece of plastic but don't touch it. Only one person calls that phone.

I wait for Dad to come rushing out of his bedroom to answer it. But he doesn't. Probably pulled a double shift and is out cold. It doesn't matter. Nothing he says makes her come home.

It's too loud, the ringing. I try to ignore it, but the yellow cord is swinging against my elbow before I realize I've picked the damn thing up.

"Daddy? Is that you?" Josie's voice is weak, barely loud enough to hear behind a hiss of static. It's the same half-coked-out voice that leaves messages on the machine, always asking for money, sometimes just crying. I almost hang up and pretend I never touched this thing, only—

"Kurt?"

Her voice hooks into me.

"Dad's asleep," I say, starting to pace, only the cord chains me to this square of linoleum.

"Hey." Her tone brightens and I imagine her sitting cross-legged on the bleachers at school before cheer practice, her brown hair pulled up in a ponytail. I imagine her smile, soft and easy. Easy in a way nothing about her is anymore.

"How's it going, little brother?"

That's not what she really says. What she really says comes out mean and angry.

"Shit, why don't you call me back?" she accuses, and I want to tell her it's not me she's ever asking for in those messages.

"What do you want?" I ask, and a car alarm goes off in the distance behind her. It makes me wonder where she is now, if she's still living in that crappy apartment behind Fenway. The one she let me visit after she dropped out of BU, back when she had a cell phone and a number that worked. The place was small, made of cement, with a mattress on the floor and a kitchen faucet that rattled like a jackhammer.

"I miss you," she says softly, and I'm not sure if that's a trick. "D'you hear me? Kurt?"

Her voice sounds so much like Mom's I almost drop the phone.

"Are you okay?" I whisper, and she laughs.

It's a mean laugh.

"Do you think I'm okay?" she says, becoming full-fledged Josie again. "What the fuck do you care? Huh?"

She waits for me to say something, but this time I know it's a trap.

I look down and notice the cord wrapped over my hand. I've threaded it over the index finger, past the palm, and back again.

"Yeah, exactly," Josie says, and the line goes dead.

I grip the phone so hard I want to break it. I'm pissed I answered it and let her get in my head. I almost tear it off the wall, but suddenly Dad's here, standing a few feet away.

"Is that—?" he asks quietly, hair disheveled, wearing sweats and a hollow expression. I clutch the phone, the silence on the other end pressed to my ear, not sure what to say to him. But all I can see is Josie sitting on that dirty old mattress scratching her ankles. Scratching like there are bugs under her skin.

"Yeah," I say finally, not looking at him when he takes the phone. I head for the door and let that silence set in.

"Kurt," he calls after me, confused when she isn't there. But I can't look at him. I grab my practice bag and am out the door. "What'd she say?" He stumbles barefoot after me, but I'm already climbing into my car. "Kurt, what did Josie—?"

"She wasn't calling for me!" I interrupt, glaring at him. His lips purse together angrily, but I don't care. He can sit by the phone all day and wait for her to call back. Deserves as much. "It's your mess," I snap. "You fix it!"

His face goes dark, but I peel out of the driveway and don't look back. I point my car toward Emerson High School, crank up the music, roll down the windows, and drive. The radio plays that metal shit Conner loves, left from the last time he was in my car. The song's a bunch of screaming assholes grinding the bass, but it drowns out the thought of Josie at the other end of that phone line. Josie having dropped out of BU. Josie living in that shitty apartment in Boston with some hookup she met at a bar. It makes me want to punch something or someone, or just knock out all the colonial rich-kid mailboxes I have to pass on my way to school.

I turn up the music and let it pound me instead.

* * *

At school I duck through the hallway and keep my head down. Conner is standing by my locker with some girl I don't know, and I don't want to deal with him. I slip down the west hallway and skip it.

I consider going to Coach's office for a pass, but halfway down the corridor I see her. Button-down shirt. Blond hair. Her hair is up now, not down like at the party. It suits her. It makes her easier not to notice.

My feet slow as I watch Marion pile her books up one by one, and it strikes me that she's not the kind of girl I would ever pay attention to. She's good-looking, sure, but smart. The kind of smart that outweighs the good-looking part. The kind of smart you can see in her posture and in the upturn of her chin. Like life is easy and she's better than you for it.

Annoyance shoots through me and I have to resist the urge to go over and mess with her. To not lean against her locker and mention how I couldn't stop thinking about her wet, dripping body. I'd love to watch her face if I said that. *That* would get the smart to quiver right on out of her.

Not that it's the smart that scares me. Not that she's the type of girl who could—

"Medford!"

I spin to see Conner walking up with that girl I don't know. "This is Sarah," he says, half winking and all teeth.

"Sarah." I nod, checking out the rest of her. Bleached hair. Tight jeans. Some chunky necklace that would look better in a magazine. Conner waits for me to react. She's cute, but I'm not sure what he's up to.

"Sarah was at the bonfire the other night," Conner says, watching me like that means something.

"Uh-huh?" I stare at him.

"*And* she's a blonde."

"Wow, did you figure that out all on your own?" I mock. "Or did you need her to help you?"

Conner narrows his eyes, playing detective, and Sarah flips her hair like it might turn her hair more blond.

"*And* she likes to swim," he says.

"Does she?" Suddenly this makes sense. I steal a glance over his shoulder to Marion. Thankfully she has her back to us. "Blondes. Swimming. You on some crazy goose hunt, Conner?"

He grins like he won a prize.

"Wait, what is—?" Sarah's not quite following, her mouth hanging half-open, and I want to smack Conner for being a shit.

"Sarah, I don't know what he told you," I say, trying to apologize, "but don't believe a word he says. And please, as a personal favor to me, go tell all your friends he has a small dick."

Conner points at Sarah, and using his amazing powers of deduction, he says, "So not this one?" I roll my eyes and walk away. "Hey!" he calls as I start up the stairs. "Whoever she is, she's blond. I know that much."

I spin around to deny it, but Marion's staring at them.

At me.

I stumble on the step and Conner waves a finger in my direction like that was an admission.

"Blond hair, Medford." He laughs, and I kick myself for hesitating. "I've got witnesses."

Marion's eyebrows pinch together and I don't know what to make of her. I drop a shoulder and head up the stairs. Conner hoots as I turn my back on them and tell myself he doesn't know anything. Blond hair isn't much to go off of. And there's *no way* I'm telling him about Marion. Especially with her right behind him. Not that she's a secret. Not that she's anything.

Before the top of the stairs, I check down the hall for Marion, but what I see is all I wanted to see in the first place.

Empty hall.

# Marion

The afternoon sun shimmers in chemistry, sending silver light streaming through beakers of glass. Kurt's chair sits empty three stations behind me, and I haven't seen him since this morning, when he disappeared up those stairs without a second glance. When he shows up, will he look at me? Speak to me? Do I exist as anything more than a shadow splashing into the water behind him?

I open my notebook and hope he skips class.

"Do anything interesting this weekend?" a male voice asks, and I turn to sun in my eyes.

"Sorry?" I say, raising my hand.

"This weekend," he repeats, haloed in light. It's my lab partner, Abe. "Do anything interesting?" He sits down beside me and light bounces off his curls and for a second he looks like a knight in a Waterhouse painting, eyes and armor shining perfectly.

"Define 'interesting.'"

"Sex, drugs, and rock 'n' roll?" he offers, tapping his

thumb against my chemistry book. "Or maybe a cheap movie? A good book?" He flashes me his adorable boy-next-door smile, and I flush, happy he chose me to be his lab partner five weeks ago and we're talking again. I swear I smell apple in the air, and my eyes fall to his neck, where iridescent hairs glow like dandelion fluff. It reminds me of freshman year, when we sat under his apple tree and I made a wish before covering him in dandelion seeds. Just one wish before he kissed me with tiny parachutes in his hair. It was my first *real* kiss, nothing fancy, nothing uncomfortable; just two kids studying math under the apple tree in his backyard, learning the geometry of two and one.

"I'm boring," I say, finding my eyes on Kurt's empty chair.

"Did you go to that lake party?" Abe fishes, and I doodle in my notebook, trying to decide if I should tell him I went or not. Not that it should matter if I tell him. We broke up ages ago; *we* aren't anything anymore. It's been two years of silence since I went *Indiana Jones and the Temple of Doom* on his heart and we broke up. I don't want to say the wrong thing and mess this up again. "I heard Lilith talking about it this morning," he continues, and my pen gets slippery as I realize I'm glad he *wasn't* at that party. That he didn't see me in that water with Kurt. "Lilith said something about bonfires and—"

"Swimming?" It slips out and he looks up surprised.

"You went swimming at the party?"

"No, I just—" I stumble, flustered by how much I don't want him to know about this, and not sure if that means I still like him. The last thing I should be thinking about is us as an *us*. Only sometimes, I find myself wishing on invisible seeds and catching him stealing looks, like right now, like maybe, possibility . . .

"I, um . . . I heard some people went swimming," I continue, but then the classroom door opens, distracting me.

Abe follows my gaze, and I hate that he's noticed. But now I'm staring at my notebook and I don't know why I've covered the page in so many stars. I feel the heat of Abe's gaze, but my pen keeps on blotting out the ruled lines and white.

I don't look up as Kurt passes.

I don't want to admit that he unsettles me in a way I'm sure Abe never could.

I focus on the page and trace the outlines of the stars over and over, so I don't have to see Kurt look away and pretend he doesn't know me. Or worse, have him look into me, where he can see just how much I want to smell the lake in his hair.


In gym class we're sent outside to run the fitness trail around the school. The ground is covered in pine needles the color of rust and the air smells like mulch. Lilith lingers behind me, flirting with the four boys on the path near her.

Abe is one of them.

I could be a quarter of a mile ahead by now, but I've slowed to eavesdrop on Lilith, letting the orange needles stick to my sneakers. The fog hangs on the branches like tufts of cotton candy from the county fair, spun with weightlessness, and my mind drifts to Abe's fingers as we sat on the Ferris wheel freshman year, his lips stained sugar blue. His thumb rubbed the elastic strap of my bra, and my insides went queasy with the idea of him touching me, like he had the night before. How I didn't tell him not to. How I wasn't sure how to outline an invisible boundary, or if such a thing could even be drawn.

Abe didn't say anything about Kurt in chemistry class, and I'm thankful I've been able to avoid both of them. Not that I know what to do with either. Kurt doesn't look at me, and Abe, Abe is like the echo of something I started and ran away from before the fog could stick. Before the whisper of hands could ruin.

Kurt would be better. Kurt's a clean slate. His hands are distant, pumping through the water, less intimate.

"Marion." Lilith snaps me back to the present, only she's addressing the boys. "You have no idea," she says, laughing. "I kiss Marion all the time."

What? That isn't true! My neck warms and I pick up my pace, refusing to look back, like I didn't hear.

We've only kissed once. And it wasn't a real kiss. Nothing's a real kiss when you're ten. We used to stay up late at night watching our favorite romance movies. Only we didn't watch them so much as fast-forward through all the boring stuff until we got to the kisses: slow, hard, tongues, lips. It was a fascination. Only one night Lilith locked her bedroom door and asked if she could kiss me instead.

"You know, so we can understand how to do it," she explained. "Like practice."

I gripped my pillow, wanting to watch the movie and forget this.

"I don't know," I said, because I didn't. "You mean open our mouths and use our tongues?"

"Yeah." Lilith nodded, sitting on the bed beside me. "It'll be like a science experiment."

I didn't move.

"It'll be easy." She nodded again. "We'll just lean in and move our tongues around and see what happens."

"Just move our tongues around?"

"Like they do in the movies."

"And we won't tell anyone?"

"Of course not!" Lilith's eyes went wide.

I pressed my hands into her pink bedspread. I wanted kissing to be special, but I wanted to be good at it too. And this was Lilith.

If I could trust anybody, it would be her.

"Okay," I whispered, looking at the floor. "What do I do?"

"Close your eyes!" she squealed, and I shut my lids.

I felt the bed shift as she shuffled up next to me. It was quiet and I waited, but she didn't do anything. I held my breath and my body stiffened with the cold thought that she was playing a joke on me.

But then her mouth hit mine. It was solid and dry and I couldn't react before her lips opened up like a fish's, globing wide and rubbery. I opened my mouth and we twisted our faces back and forth, jabbing our tongues at each other. She moaned like the ladies in the movies and gasped for air before pressing her hand against my chest and pinching me through my shirt. She pushed the fabric up and rubbed her hand over my front and I think she wanted me to touch her, too. She'd already started to grow in that area. I had nothing but flatness and skin.

When she stopped kissing me we both sat at the end of her bed in the awkward quiet. I ran my toes against the zipper of my Disney princess sleeping bag on the floor. The metal felt jagged and grounding.

"Did you feel anything?" she asked.

I stiffened, not sure what she meant. "Did you?" Panic spread in my gut. I tried to think of a lie, something that wouldn't hurt her feelings despite the slobbering and the moaning and whatever that was.

"No," she said. "I guess it's different with boys."

She got up and unlocked the door, as if nothing had happened. As if I wasn't sitting at the edge of her bed with my shirt half off and my lips still bruised with the taste of her.

A branch smacks my face and I wipe it away, hearing Lilith behind me.

"Oh, you know it's true," she says, and I peek back to see they've caught up. "We're best friends," she continues, catching my eye and taking my hand. "We share everything."

"Yeah, right," says Mark, the tallest, egging her on. "I'll believe it when I see it."

"I'm sorry," I say, pretending I don't know what this is about, trying to untangle my fingers. "What are we—"

But Abe's look unsettles me. His eyes are dark and intrigued, like I've swallowed a secret and he wants to unfold it.

"Seeing is believing, you say?" Lilith says, fluttering her lashes at Mark. She ignores what I said and twirls me into a wooded nook.

"Lilith! What are you—?"

"Just play along!" she coos in my ear, and the boys fill up the space behind us. The whites in their eyes go wide and I can't look at Abe. I'm too embarrassed with Lilith mussing up my hair. Maybe he knows I'd rather her hands were his.

"Come on, Marion," Mark says. "Admit it. You've never kissed Lilith before."

My mouth is dry, but a hot pulse shoots through me from the eagerness in his voice. And I don't know if it's the safety that Lilith's a girl or the power to tease him that makes me brave.

"Oh?" I say, and the fact that it's true makes it easier to say. "I wouldn't be so sure about that. You want me to lie to you?"

The boys whoop and Lilith cackles, rubbing her thumb against my ear in approval. But it's the anticipation in the boys' eyes, pooled wet in their pupils, that makes me feel powerful.

"You want a show?" Lilith asks, and I almost tell her to stop. But it's the boys' eyes—*Abe's eyes*—on us, that flood me with heat, down to my stomach and below. I nuzzle my face in Lilith's neck and she purrs, pulling me closer as the air cinches tight.

One of the boys whistles and I hope it isn't Abe. I don't know if I like the idea that he's into this, even though it makes my skin prickle. Lilith laughs, and her neck smells of peppermint.

"You're just a tease," Mark says, but Lilith lifts my chin.

Our eyes meet and her breath is soft as she strokes my neck. She hesitates, perhaps wondering if I'm okay with this—but then her mouth is on mine. Lips blooming. She's gotten better at this. Much better.

Whistles flood my ears, singing fiercely and pushing us together. I shiver, like I'm being unfolded and don't want it to stop. But it's not Lilith and the taste of her that excites me.

It's *them* watching. It's *Abe* watching.

It's their eyes on our mouths and on our hips pressing one-two and against. It's the rush that comes with hearing the whistles and "hell yeahs" that rocks me, and scares me, and holds me hard against her—

Wishing I could do this with Abe. Or Kurt. Or anyone. But knowing I'm only brave enough when it's Lilith. Knowing her kiss isn't dangerous.

But I want to keep this heat. Want to keep this power, that Lilith can harness with a breath, that makes them pant and want and sweat. I press into Lilith, tasting the sweet of her mouth, knowing this power isn't mine, and that I've only temporarily borrowed it. Knowing that soon—

Soon—

Soon—

It will be over. And she'll take it back again.

Abe is in the hallway outside the locker room waiting for me. I catch him drumming his fingers against the painted cement and staring at the floor.

"Hey," he says as I come out of the girls' room, and we share an awkward smile.

"Hi," I say, remembering how he used to wait for me after classes when we were dating. Only Lilith's behind me, pushing her way through the door. She laughs when she sees Abe waiting.

"What's up, Babe-ra-ham?" she says obnoxiously, squeezing my side and nudging me toward him.

"Lilith," Abe acknowledges dryly, rolling his eyes.

"Just calling it as I see it, Mr. Lincoln," Lilith quips, but Abe shuffles his feet like he wishes she wasn't here. I nudge her to get the hint and she doesn't have to be told twice.

"Right, so, I have play practice," she announces, checking me. "I'll get a ride home from Jen." I nod for her to go and she squeezes me before leaving. "Later, Mr. President."

Abe jams his hands into his pockets as she stalks away, like this has turned into a much bigger moment than he intended.

"Hi," I say again.

"Hi," he repeats, and my stomach tickles, suddenly hoping he's about to ask me out. Maybe that kiss *has* made him see me differently, as not that girl on the Ferris wheel saying terrible things.

"I just, you know," he says awkwardly, looking to make sure Lilith's gone. "I know there was a bunch of us and all, but I want you to know you don't have to do that." He nods outside to the trail.

Mud crawls through me, squeezing mush between my toes.

"Do what?" I dig my fingernail into the cement to chip away the paint.

"Let Lilith do that," he says. "Kiss you."

My fingernail rams into a section of paint that's stuck hard; it won't flake off.

"It's not a thing," I say sharply. "We do it all the time. Plus, you all loved it?"

His eyes go dark, like outside, but I can't tell if that's an act or if he really enjoyed watching.

"Yeah, but I don't know if *you* like it," he says.

My insides squirm and I don't want to be here. I pound the flat of my palm against the cement like it might ground me.

"I'm not whoever you think I am," I say. "I'm not who I was when we—" I hate this conversation. I hate that I kissed Lilith and he could see right through it. "Just forget it, all right? It was a stupid Lilith thing. Like always."

"Sure." He nods, and I hate the straightforwardness in him, like he doesn't regret bringing this up and we're allowed to go back to being candid with each other after two years of silence. Like that silence hasn't changed me. "Hey." He smiles, breaking the tension, tossing hair from his eyes. "All I meant is Lilith likes the attention, being the drama queen and all. You . . . you don't have to do what she does."

"I'm not Lilith."

"Exactly."

"She's my friend," I say, looking for the exit. "It's just fun. I don't know why you're making this a thing."

"I'm not," he says quickly. Only, this *is* a thing. Nobody wants me to have this power. "You're just better than that," he says finally, and it feels like a slap.

I can't swallow and the air feels like it's gone. Abe looks at his feet.

"Right, so, I'll see you tomorrow in class," he mumbles awkwardly, before heading down the hall, and I want to scream as he goes. Doesn't he get it? I'm not better than Lilith. Sure, I don't have to be her, but I also can't be me.

Suddenly I wish it was Kurt in those woods watching me and Lilith, whooping with the others and playing along. Kurt, who doesn't know me. Kurt, who will let me reinvent myself. Kurt, who isn't afraid of this power.

# Kurt

**Running at practice feels like freedom.**

We do drills. Then Coach splits the team in half and we scrimmage, like boys on the playground. Field slick with dew. Mud on our shins. Troy pops the ball, high, clearing it from one side to the next, and I speed to reach it.

Sprint.

Remembering what it is to *want* something, even if that wanting is to let go, trust my feet, and not think. It isn't a choice. It's instinct. And it only happens if I give in to it, if I commit. It's the point when I accept that bones could break and shins could splint, and I don't care, because that little bit of freedom is all mine and I'm going to take it.

Hesitate and it's over. One second and the other team gets the ball. Two seconds and your kneecaps tear off. Three, forget three, it's only guilt and regret.

Don't think. Don't breathe. Charge.

I trap the ball and dribble up the line. The ease slides

over me, like a numbness, and everything else ceases to exist. I square up the shot and take it.

Like it's all I've got.

'Cause if I believe there's more—

I'll miss.

After practice I find Vanessa sitting on the hood of my car. She's got a basket of O'Dell's fries sitting in her lap and a Coke straw pinched between her lips. It's freezing out. But she doesn't seem to care with her tight shirt showing off just how cold it is. I think she likes the fact that it makes me stare.

"What do you want?" I say, snagging a fry.

"You're an asshole," she says, and I shrug. I walk past her and open the door to throw my bag in the back. She twists to look at me, her black hair slipping off her shoulders. "What the fuck was that at the lake? You ignore me, then take a swim? What's your deal?"

"I'm moody," I say, throwing her a half smile. She rolls her eyes and groans, the straw sliding from her mouth.

"A moody asshole," she says, finding the straw again with her tongue, which looks sexy and stupid at the same time.

"Are you gonna get in the car or not?" I nod to the passenger seat, and she glares at me. I wait and she rolls herself off the hood and climbs in, which I knew she'd do.

That's exactly why I like her.

It's why this works.

I take Vanessa to the lookout, where she climbs on top of me and I forget everything else. I forget about soccer, and school, and Josie, and Marion. I remember why I like my life the way it is.

Disposable like this.

Good like this.

# Marion

At home I lock my bedroom door and turn out the light. I climb under the covers and lean back, sliding my legs between the feather down and cotton.

Dad is still at work and everything's quiet.

It's just me, and this bed.

I think about Lilith and that power she has. That fire burning somewhere inside. Those boys reacted when I kissed her, but that energy, it was all her. Not me. I'm not sure such a thing could be mine. Or how to find it. That power is like my hair, it enchants, but it comes from someplace outside of me, and I have no control over who or why.

*If you want it, take it.*

The sheets are cold against my skin. I pull the covers up to my neck and think about being someone else. With someone else.

I think about the bonfire. I think about my skin, soft

and puffy. Think about Kurt's skin, his shoulders, his chest. I think about stretching, and limbs, and wet.

I reach down, over my belly, below. . .

Not sure if I should—

The water could drown me.

# Kurt

It's dark when I drop Vanessa off at her house. It's even darker when I drop my practice bag on the floor and notice how empty *my* house is. Quiet. It's the complete opposite of the way it was with Mom. No more music. No more Josie blasting the world out with her stereo set on high. Just silence and ash. I let it hum and don't disturb it with the TV or the record player. I like it like this.

The quiet's mine.

In my room, I flip through my chemistry book and attempt to do my homework. But chemistry makes me think of Marion sitting those three seats ahead of me with that lab partner of hers. The one she used to date, who makes her laugh like he's the funniest thing on earth. Not that I want to make Marion laugh. Or do anything with her. Except maybe unbutton that shirt of hers and get her out of my system.

I try to focus, but I can't. Blond-fire's got me annoyed. I get up. Circle the kitchen. Pick through the cabinets. I flip through Mom's records in the living room: Alison Krauss, Joni Mitchell, Waylon Jennings. Of course, I'm not going to listen to any of them. I chew through an energy bar and half a cup of ice, only to find myself in the bathroom, which is the only room in the house with a door that locks.

If I'm going to think about Marion, then I'm going to think about her like this.

I ease myself down onto the linoleum and I imagine her with her hair down. Biting her lip like Vanessa does. My feet hit the bathtub and my spine curls against the door. She inches up her skirt and—my head rolls back and I enjoy it. The thought of her hair rocking forward. Her hips. The hitch in her breath. My mouth, her—

The room smells like sweat when I'm finished. I open a window, but that lets in the hiss of the neighbor's sprinkler and the chatter of dogs yapping with their chains scraping against cement. I wash my hands and think I might go for a run or play my guitar, but I don't want any of it.

Instead, I go into Josie's room and lie on her bed. The sheets are straight and perfect. Waiting for her. If she wants back here.

I get out my cell phone, pull up her number, and hit send.

It rings and rings and rings. She doesn't pick up. There used to be a phone message after all that ringing, but there isn't even that anymore. Of course I know she isn't going to answer.

I call to listen to the silence. To remember what I can't change.

four

# Kurt

**I'm late for class.**

The afternoon bell rang five minutes ago and I take the stairs two at a time, counting my steps like I'm keeping rhythm on my guitar. I make a pattern of it—two-three, two-four, two-six—when I practically crash into her.

Marion.

I flinch and move to the side and we both find our balance. My hand catches the railing and Marion's grabs the wall, and we stand there looking at each other, half between steps. Not going up. Not going down.

Her mouth is part open, her hair up, and there's dust in the sun between us. I think I should say something, but the railing sticks to my palm and my neck starts to itch.

"Hi," she says, and I watch her mouth close. Swallow and don't say anything.

I wait for her to talk and she waits for me, and somewhere in the hall below us comes the clang of metal against the floor. It's probably one of the cafeteria workers unloading ketchup.

I push off the railing and walk away from her, regaining my balance enough to wipe my palms on my jeans. At the top platform, I can't help but look back. In the same way I can't help calling my sister. I want Marion to be there.

She is, sunned with dust in her hair.

"Hey," I say.

She perks up and kind of smiles. But this is like the lake, where I don't have anything to follow it.

So I just nod. And go to class.

# Marion

My eyes scan the soccer field. It's been forty minutes since the last bell and the parking lot's deserted.

Yet here I am, watching.

That hello in the stairwell wasn't an invitation, but it was *something*. And I don't know how much time that hello will grant me before this small door of space slams shut again. *If I want it—*

Kurt's number eleven. He's easy to pick out because he's fast, slipping past his teammates like a trick of the light. It keeps me glued to this patch of grass, with my hands finger-hooked through the chain link, trying to kindle that power Lilith has. Not sure if I even know how. If it takes flint or skin. But here I am, because I don't want to be the girl Abe thinks I am.

*Take it . . .*

Kurt's wet from running. His shirt's soaked like when he sat next to me at the party, after the swimming, when the fire was out of reach and there was nothing but silence and wetness between us.

Wanting.

But having nothing to say.

Kurt clears the ball and I catch him stealing a look at me, but then he spends the next five minutes focused on the ball. Reacts. Runs.

Their coach yells for a water break and that swiftness in him catches me off guard, because he strides right past the water cooler and heads for me.

I straighten up, but my hair gets caught in the fence. I mess with it, my head tilted awkwardly as I try to get it unhooked, when suddenly he's here.

In front of me.

Chain link between us.

"Hey," he says, but the word slides out of him, more like an exhale of breath than something actually said. His cleats dig into the mud and I bite my lip, trying to make my head tilt look natural. His fingers curl through the fence, and his thumb grazes the thin strip of my hair.

"So . . ." He squints, looking to the sun, and gold light rims his lashes. "We've got another hour, or whatever."

I nod. My insides tight, watching his thumb tracing the bow of my hair.

"You can wait here, I guess," he says, dropping his hand. "It'll um . . ." The whistle blows. "It'll be a while."

I nod and he heads back to the field, where he runs, and stops, and slows. I unknot my hair from the metal, my fingers threaded over the thin strips of the fence where he stood. Here, where he's told me to wait.

After practice he showers and I stay by the field watching the sun, counting the minutes and the seconds till there's no more chain link between us.

He walks up, eclipsed in light, and I'm not sure I believe this is actually happening, if he's really in front of me. The sun sets behind him and I'm glad he's half-shadowed and I can't see his eyes.

*If you want it—*

"Coffee?" I sputter. "Do you like coffee?"

He frowns before nodding to the parking lot.

"Coffee, sure," he says, walking me to his car and opening the door.

The seats are stained and there's a half-eaten bag of popcorn on the floor. It makes me think of his buttery hands covered in salt. Loud music screams from the speakers when he turns the car on, angry metal music, which he quickly turns off. He drives us away from school and over the hill.

My fingers wrap around the seat belt when we reach the stoplight at the center of town. The street is lined with unopened tourist shops, closed for the winter season, and I dig my fingernail into the nylon belt at my neck.

He turns left.

Orange leaves cover the pavement, blooming into a

ribbon that leads past the post office, and the bed-and-breakfast, and the red oak at the edge of town.

Right would have taken us to the coffee shop.

The coffee shop we aren't going to.

My neck goes taut, because I know where we're headed.

After half a mile, Kurt turns off the main road and his tires dig into the mulch—soft—where the asphalt ends and the dirt road opens up. The tires spit mud and lurch us forward. Kurt cranks the gears, turning his car through the woods and winding us over the hill to the ridgetop—where people go, people like Lilith—to go and do what you do in cars like this one.

I crack open the window to slip in some air, just enough to know I'm still breathing. Kurt wets his lips and I go hot with the idea of his mouth, his tongue. I pull my hair down and let it spill over my shoulders, hoping it might harness some of that power I'm not sure I have.

Lilith says it hurts the first time.

Hurts more than I could ever imagine.

The car rattles as the road gets rougher. I roll down the window and cold rushes over me, shooting goose bumps up my arms and turning my nipples hard. I feel the heat of Kurt's gaze and I hunch forward to loosen the fabric of my shirt, trying to hide the parts of me I can't control.

He reaches over and touches my elbow, softly pinching the skin, and my body clenches—only not in that bad way. It's in this other way, where my insides go tight and something stretches, and for a second I think maybe, actually, I'll be able to do this.

Be gentle, I think. Like a gentleman.

I look at Kurt and wonder if he knows my last name. I wonder if he'll ask me my favorite color, or the name of my favorite book, or if I like chocolate more than vanilla. But the trees curl back ahead of us, exposing the ridge and sky, and I know none of those questions will matter.

Because the road has ended.

And his hand is already in my hair.

He cuts the engine, and the thrum of the car rumbles out beneath us. His fingers tease my neck and I look out the window at the view. It's breathtaking. Water stretches all the way to the horizon, ocean against dusk, and the last thread of sun dips behind the tide.

His thumb hits my earlobe, and it's me—turning to him, wanting what I don't know how to ask for or take.

I close my eyes, and for a moment I'm not inside myself. I'm not here at all. It scares me, because I know this is all happening too fast, and I want him to know my last name and my favorite subject and that I miss my mother sometimes, and that I'm not Lilith. That *this* isn't easy for me.

But I'm sure he thinks I've already said yes.

"Kurt, I—"

But his hands cup my neck and we're kissing. His lips press against mine with a rush of breath, and he opens my mouth and finds the inside of me.

His hands are hot, wrists at my collarbone, elbows brushing the fabric on my chest, and I don't know what to do with him. I don't know how to do any of this. I don't know *him*.

His mouth tugs on my lip, the bottom one, and I try to concentrate on his warmness and spit, but his hands are in my hair. He pulls me close, and hard, and against. And all I can think about are flip-flops broken between my toes, and mud, and creek water, and—

Hands that touch.

Hands I can't trust.

Kurt unhooks my bra and his fingers slide over my breasts, making me shake. Only this isn't the good kind of tremble.

My seat falls back with a clunk, and he's reclined the chair. He climbs on top and I can't keep track of his hands, his lips. He peels my shirt up, over my head, and his touch is everywhere—hot, wet—and this doesn't feel powerful. This is small and dark as his weight digs into my hip.

My skin shudders, my arms lifted high above my head, where they drape naked over the backrest. My hands dangle and I want to cut my hair off and get rid of this blond fanned out over the seat. The smell of barbecue and mud clogs in my throat and I don't know how to tell him to stop.

He's on top of me.

His hands are in my hair.

I got in his car and wanted him to kiss me and—

My body trembles as his hands slide down my front to the top of my jeans. His fingers undo my buttons and start unzipping—and I *know* this is it.

Everything shudders. My insides unhook, rumbling up like an earthquake unleashed from the pit of me. My shoulders heave and I can't stop it.

I can't force it down.

There are things my body knows—

Things it wants to scream that I can't say.

Things—

Things my body has to say for me.

# Kurt

I shift my weight and what I see makes me want to fucking die.

Marion's not trembling, she's crying. And she's not just crying, she's *crying*. Like somebody died.

"Shit, are you . . ." But I freeze. I don't know what to do. My elbows lock and I hover over her. Not daring to move. "Um, do you . . ."

But her whole body shakes. Her shoulders rock and that blond hair of hers falls to the side, exposing her chest. I force my eyes out the back window, cursing the fact that I'm still hard, which she must know, because I'm freaking on top of her.

"Uh, do . . ." I grip the seat, panic squirming in my gut, and I see her shirt in the back. The tag sticks up and the whole thing is turned inside out, and it's too far to reach without touching her. "Look, uh . . . here."

I pull my shirt off and lay it over the front of her. The crumpled fabric makes her flinch, and her eyes hollow me. Her arm wraps over her chest and I can't shake her expression.

It looks exactly like Josie's did when we found out about Mom. Eyes puffy. Red. Like the world fell out, and it's all my fault.

"I'm gonna move," I say, adjusting my weight. "I'm going to—" But I stop explaining and just do it, crawling into the driver's seat and ignoring the fact that I simply *have* to touch her because there really isn't enough room.

She puts my shirt on and uses it like a tent to fix her bra, then looks in the back for the shirt that's inside out. I stare through the windshield and I don't move. I want to ask her if she's all right. But *obviously* she's not.

If she were Josie, she'd be telling me to fuck off right now. She'd yell at me to get out of the car and leave her alone. But Marion doesn't do any of that. She doesn't say anything.

Air crawls over my back from the open window and I think about the extra jersey in my practice bag. But I don't move. I don't dare do anything. Not till she tells me to.

"Thanks," she whispers, placing my shirt on the dash.

I grab it and stretch it over my head as fast as I can. My hands shake and I need to get off this ridge. We shouldn't be here. I throw the key in the ignition, click on my seat belt, and turn us back around. The gearshift rumbles and the trees blur as I pick up speed. The road spits rocks and dirt at me, but I don't ease up on the gas.

I peek over at Marion and she isn't wearing a seat belt. She's curled up with her arms around her knees, and I want to ask her to buckle up. But I can't.

There's no way I'm asking this girl for anything.

# Marion

Kurt guns it down the road, accidentally hitting the horn, which blasts, shaking the car and the trees. I feel like I *am* that sound, loud and hollow and screaming through.

I squeeze my eyes shut. My face is wet and everything is caught in my throat. Mud in my toes.

Creek water under my toes.

All I can think about is that man from the barbecue with his wrinkled shirt and untidy shoes. His mouth was no longer on mine, but his hand was in my hair.

There was a jangle of metal and buckles, and the rose hips on the other side of the creek dipped in and out of the water, halfway between holding on and drowning under.

My toes were cold, dug into the sand.

Metal jangled and that man's shadow crawled over me. He stood up with me sitting beside him on the log, the taste of his tongue still in my mouth. His belt was open and the top button of his pants undone. The leather strap of his belt curled forward and the metal buckle tapped against my face as he breathed.

His hand in my hair.

Tangled.

As he unzipped himself.

"Are you all right?" It's Kurt's voice in the car beside me, and my hands shake as I grab the door handle beside me.

"I'm fine," I whisper, but I can't bring myself to look at him because I'm not fine. "Pull over," I say, shoving the door with my shoulder. "Please, stop the car!"

He slams on the breaks and I spill out of his car. I gobble down breath after breath, but everything's caught in my throat, being up here, his hands, my skin, the throbbing, all of it.

I walk into the woods, because being in that car with him reminds me too much of my dad driving me home after the barbecue yammering on and on about what a nice time he had.

I wasn't listening to my father. My eyes were glued to the plate of leftovers on my lap, wrapped in tinfoil with the sharp edges poking my thighs. It smelled rotten, like pork-belly meat, slathered in barbecue sauce, caught in my throat.

I gagged.

Vomit burned my mouth. But I clenched my jaw tight and forced it back down.

I opened the window for some air, but everything was

sticky-meat-smell, and I chucked the entire plate into the street.

"Jesus Christ, Marion!" Dad slammed on the brake like I threw out a child. "What are you doing?"

The car lurched to a stop and someone honked, swerving past.

"I'm going to be sick," I said.

"All right, okay." He pulled over. "What did you eat?"

My left flip-flop was torn, the strap snapped by the big toe.

"Do you think it's food poisoning, or do you have a temperature?"

I saw his hand come toward me, but I was already yanking the door open and throwing off my seat belt. I rushed into the tall grass beside the road. My broken flip-flop tripped me and threw me to my knees.

"Marion?" he called after me, and I pretended to throw up.

My shoulders heaved and there was vomit in the grass and on my feet and in my hair—

But nothing really came out.

# Kurt

My door hangs open and there are kernels of popcorn all over the seat. Exploded from the microwave bag when I slammed on the brake. Through the door I can see Marion. Standing in the woods. Back to me.

She stares into the dark and I don't know what to do. All I know is this is bad. Bad like Josie scratching her legs and crying on the other end of that phone line. Crying and too far away from me. I don't want to get out of the car, but she's out there for so long, I don't think she's ever going to get back in.

"Marion?" I say, warning her so she knows I'm coming up behind her. "It's pretty dark. We should get going."

She shakes like some piece of her is broke, and I know this is something I shouldn't see. Something private. Like Mom. Like Josie. I walk into her periphery and her eyes make me hate myself for taking her here.

"Hey . . ." I inch closer and reach my hand out, even

though the instinct is all kinds of unnatural. But this is what you do, right? You comfort people.

"Please don't touch me," she snaps, and I drop the hand so fast she shudders. "I'm fine," she whispers, but there's no way I believe that.

She stares into the forest, like she wants to walk into it, and more than anything I want to take her hand and tell her this is going to be okay. Even if I don't know *how* it's going to be okay. Just that it is. So she knows she's not alone.

But I'm not that guy.

The parking lot is practically empty when I pull in and slow down. There are a few cars near the gym and I'm sure one of them is hers, but I don't ask. She hasn't said a word, and I haven't said a word, and I'm not going to start now.

The car isn't stopped when she opens the passenger door again. I slam on the brake and she shoots forward, throwing a hand out against the dash.

"Hold on, geez," I say. "I can take you to your—"

"This is fine."

She doesn't leave, despite the fact that everything about her says she wants to. I swallow, with the door half-open as she strains her neck to look at me.

"Which car is your—?"

"My last name," she says, cutting me off.

"What?"

"What's my last name?" She says it quietly, barely above a whisper, and I notice her hair is up. At some point she pinned it away and all that's left is this raw question in her eyes.

And for some reason I want to answer it. But . . .

"Are you the Honda?" I say, nodding to the closest car.

"Sure. Why not," she says, which means it's not, and now I really don't know what to do. I could drive her to the Honda, even though it's not her car. Or I could sit here and let her get out, which somehow seems worse.

"Medford," she says, forcing me to look at her. I expect her to smack me, but there's this weird resign in her eyes instead. She's not angry, which I hate, because I could deal with this if she were angry. Only she's not. She's whatever this is, with my name dead in her mouth.

Medford.

And I wish more than anything that, right now, I could tell her hers.

But she already knows that I can't.

five

# Marion

**Two blocks from my house I pull over and throw** open the door. I can't be in this car right now.

Any car.

Not even my own.

Streetlamps slash light over the pavement, and I walk—run—up the sidewalk to my house. I don't go inside. Instead, I head into the backyard, where a giant oak rakes a thousand branches against the sky.

I kick off my shoes, and the leaves are too soft beneath me. The tree tall above. The scent of bark enticing me up, away from this ground. I grab a branch and pull myself to the first bough, and then the second, my feet finding the niches of the tree without looking. My feet remembering this bark, knowing its roughness and skin, carrying me higher, to where the boughs are thinner; higher, to where the leaves are wider; higher, to a place where it feels like I might be able to fly up beyond everything below me and never fall back down.

Near the top, the wind is fierce and screaming through.

My hands shake, and I grab the tree, gulping down breath after breath, despite everything that's caught in my throat. His hands. My skin. All of it. My heart pounds from climbing this tree, showing me that this body is meant to be physical, made to move and climb and sweat and run, and I hate it for reminding me of that.

I tuck myself into a top branch and I pull out my cell phone. I try to punch in the numbers, but they're a blur, and I can barely grip the thing.

Breathe. Swallow.

My keys jangle in my pocket and I chuck them to the ground.

"Mar-i-doodle, what's up?" Lilith's voice jolts me, and I realize somehow my fingers have managed to dial.

When in doubt, call Lilith.

"Hey," I wheeze, but the words are pinecones in my throat. I don't want to talk about Kurt, but I can't imagine not telling her either. "I . . . um . . ."

In front of me I see my initials, carved into the tree. A lump lodges in my throat and I remember hacking them out in quick, careful jabs, peeling back the bark till it exposed the flesh below. Only now the bark is a puckered black scar.

"Marion? Hello? You there?"

"Hey." I try again, coughing and looking up at the sky, punctured with stars. "Did you DVR that new vampire show?" I manage. "Ours didn't record it."

That does the trick. Lilith starts blabbing ten words a second about how stupid and awesome the show was, and I can breathe again. I press my feet into the bark and listen to the steady in her voice. It's like a drug anchoring me in the fine and the normal, as if nothing happened today. As if all that exists is high school and homework and the ever-important debate between the hotness of vampires versus werewolves. And I wonder if she can hear the fact that I'm crying. If she can, she doesn't stop and ask.

Later, I walk into the house and see a light on in Dad's home office. I peek in the doorway to see him sitting behind his desk, rubbing his temples like the papers in front of him make no sense. The skin is loose around his eyes, showing off his wrinkles. He doesn't seem that old to me, but then, I guess he is. His hair is peppered with gray and trimmed perfect, like everything else in this room, having its place.

"Dad?" I inch into the doorway, not hiding my wet face, but he doesn't look up. "Hey," I say a little louder, and his eyes find me. He glances at the clock, but doesn't say anything. He doesn't ask where I was or with whom. He doesn't ask why I'm not wearing my shoes.

I grew back all my hair, but I'm still invisible.

"I'm going to be up late," he says, picking up his stack of papers and tapping them against his desk. It's his way of showing me how much work is left to be done, and dismissing me. "There's supper in the fridge." He nods to the door. "If you could . . ."

I reach for the silver knob and it feels as cold as those scissors in my little-girl hands, always shutting doors instead of opening them.

# Kurt

Dad's pickup is sitting in the driveway when I pull in. He should be at work. Not here. Not at this hour.

The house is dark when I unlock the door, but I can smell fresh ash. The TV flickers and I see him on the couch, sucking on a cigarette with his back to me. For a second, I think we've put Mom's box in the ground again, and he won't move from that couch for days.

"Where've you been?" he says, not looking up.

"Out."

"Out?" He lifts the cigarette to his lips. "What's that supposed to mean?"

"It means I wasn't *here*."

"Oh, you're funny." He looks at me, face in shadow, and all I can see is smoke streaming from his nostrils. "Fun-ny man." He flicks his ash and turns back to the show.

The only thing moving is a spray of hair next to his ear, caught in the light of the television. I decide he's done with me.

"Popcorn?" He holds up a plastic bowl. "It's that kettle-corn shit you like." He lowers it and nods for me to join him. "Sit down, they're running that James Bond flick."

I don't move. Popcorn makes me think of all those kernels spread out on the floor of my car. Under Marion's feet.

"Come on." He pats the seat next to him. "I don't ever see you. Sit down."

I don't go near the couch. It smells like mildew and the left seat is busted on the inside, the springs twist wrong so they poke into you. I've learned not to sit there. I stay away from that couch. Dad's couch after all.

I take the recliner near the door.

"How's school?" he asks, handing me the bowl. "You passing math?"

I scrunch a handful of the corn in my fist.

"Sure."

I could fail math and he wouldn't even blink.

"What about soccer? How's it looking for state?" He follows it with a string of others. Girls. Grades. Whatever he thinks a good parent is supposed to ask.

"You ever think about going to get her? Josie," I say, and he coughs—ash in his throat. He hacks, trying to clear it, as smoke billows against the ceiling. "I know where her apartment is." Only that's not really true. I visited her that one time, but she probably doesn't live there anymore.

"It's not that simple," he says, stubbing out his cigarette.

"She's nineteen. I can't force her to do something she doesn't want to."

I squeeze my fistful of popcorn.

"Do you even call her back?"

"Of course I do," he snaps, glaring at me. "What kind of father do you think I am?"

He doesn't want to know the answer to that.

"So, this—" I stand up and nod to the couch, throwing the corn in the trash. "Is this the new thing? Your schedule change?"

He slumps back and starts flipping channels.

"Maybe." The word comes out deflated. "That going to be a problem?"

He looks small. The TV flickers and I want to ask him what happened—if he got fired or whatever—but instead I head for my room.

I flick on the overhead lights as I leave, flooding the space, and hoping he'll yell at me.

He doesn't.

I go into my room and flop onto my bed, annoyed that he shrugs everything off like it doesn't matter, like if he pretends it doesn't exist, it will go away. Only there's a problem with wanting things to go away. Sometimes they do.

The curtains blow over my head and a light from the street makes them glow. That image of Marion standing in those woods fills my head. Her staring at the dark like there's something in that emptiness. I saw Mom look like that. On our back porch, gripping her guitar, drinking. Not playing. Like there wasn't any music left.

I heard the tires grinding the gravel of our driveway before I saw the lights—that morning—red and blue lights on my curtains. I almost laughed. I'd thought about calling the cops the night before, but I didn't have the nerve. Yet here they were anyway.

The steps against the gravel were steady. Slow. Cop footsteps. Not Mom's.

The door latch snapped open and there was a creak of hinges before those footsteps got out a single knock.

"Officer?"

It was Dad's voice, and it was the only word I heard clearly. The rest came in a jumble, too low for me to understand. But I could imagine the lecture those footsteps were giving my Dad. Drunk driving. Jail cells. Threats about fines and reckless behavior and body bags.

We'd done this before.

The officer would tell Dad that Mom was in a cell at the station and he could pick her up. But Dad would leave her there for the rest of the day. He'd clean out the house, taking all the empty bottles to the firing range, where he'd explode them into the dirt. Once it got dark, once she was sober, he'd go and get her.

I stood in the door frame waiting to hear the clank of glass, but Dad was empty-handed when he padded down the hallway.

"You know she deserved it," I said, imagining her in that station cell. Curled up. Hungover. I stepped into the hall. "You know that—"

*Crack!*

I was on the floor. Fire in my face. Erupting through my jaw.

He shook out his wrist, like it hurt, but I couldn't focus. There was too much pain to register.

"Dad?"

It wasn't my voice. He'd slashed out my air.

Josie's foot came into view.

"What did you do to him?"

Stars danced in my vision.

"God, you're just as bad as sh—"

"Don't say something you'll regret," he spat, storming past her and slamming the door behind him.

Josie pulled me into the bathroom and pressed a cold washcloth to my cheek.

"What's his problem?" she asked, her eyes bloodshot.

My face throbbed and I looked away from her, not wanting to think about her white-stripped eyes or what Josie might be coming down from. I nodded to the front door, where the officer had been. "They got Mom."

"Figures," she said. "She was a mess. What did you say to him?"

"Nothing that isn't true." A smile crept up my face. I

didn't know yet. "The truth hurts," I joked, and she laughed, shaking her head.

"No shit."

My cheek throbbed and I kicked myself for not finding those damn keys the night before. In the dirt. I kicked myself for not keeping her home.

"I'm glad he hit me," I said quietly, looking at Josie to see how she'd react. But she kept dabbing at my face with the cloth.

"Better you than her," she said finally.

"What's that supposed to mean?"

She tossed the cloth in the sink and walked to the door.

"It means you know how to take it."

Dad didn't collect any bottles that day.

He didn't collect any bottles ever again.

six

# Marion

I sit behind Lilith in English class. We're supposed to be reading, but I can't stop looking at the fallen strap of her tank top. It dangles over the curve of her shoulder like an invitation, and I'm not the only one who's noticed. To my left, Sean Cole presses the paper edge of his book against his bottom lip. He's reading the freckles of her skin like they're printed in ink.

I want Lilith to explain it to me.

How she does it.

How she closes her eyes, takes off her clothes, and comes back intact.

I want to tell her about Kurt, and understand how it's possible for her to do what she does. How after, she can still be 100 percent Lilith—maybe even more Lilith than before.

But I can't ask.

After the firefly field, a rumor started in middle school about an eighth grader who'd lost her virginity. Pretty quickly

Lilith's name started to circulate, and then she outright claimed it. It made her popular with the girls who wanted to know about sex and even more popular with the boys.

At lunch the girls would crowd around Lilith and ask questions.

"Did he tell you he loved you?"

"Were you embarrassed taking off your clothes?"

"What does it look like? You know, his thingy?"

She held nothing back.

"No, he didn't tell me he loved me. That's stupid."

"Go somewhere dark if you're embarrassed. And trust me, you don't have to take off *all* your clothes."

"It's called a penis, not a thingy. And it looks like—"

I plugged my ears. I didn't want to hear her talk about what it looked like. What it felt like. I hummed to blot it all out and ignored the other girls' faces flushing pink.

"What about you, Marion?" Lilith turned to me one afternoon and asked point-blank. "What do *you* want to know?"

I ran a hand through my chopped-off hair, and the other girls waited. In the distance I could hear the rush of creek water, and a hint of smoke filled my nostrils.

I didn't want to know anything.

"Did it hurt?" one of the other girls asked, breaking the silence, and Lilith looked straight at me.

"Of course it did," she said, and my feet went cold. "It hurts more than you can imagine."

* * *

At lunch Lilith drags me outside to the bleachers by the soccer field, where the metal is edged in frost. She hands me half of an uncooked Pop-Tart, and I pick at the frosting.

The field is empty. Ice crystals hang on the grass and I kick a mud print of cleat marks, but the ground is frozen. Lilith flops down on the bench and I look at the chain link where I stood yesterday, before I got in his car. It makes me wonder if she deliberately brought us out here because this *is* the soccer field. Does Lilith have a sixth sense about this sort of thing? Can she look at me and just *know*?

Of course she can't. I cut off all my hair after the bar-becue and she didn't think that was abnormal, just like my father. And then there was the firefly field and the mason jars and the things we don't talk about. A lie with Lilith isn't really a lie. Not if it's something no one brings up. If I don't tell her about Kurt, it's just an omission. It becomes the negative space between two rungs of a chair. I think that's where our friendship lies. In that space where no one has to see the invisible parts of me.

"What if I can't do it?" I say quietly, scratching my nail into the tin grooves of the bleacher. "The whole boy sex thing." I eye Lilith, thinking maybe I can get her to lay off this hookup business. "I mean, let's face it . . ." I try to make this sound lighthearted, like a joke. "I'll probably freak out and cry or something."

"God, I hope you don't cry," she says, dropping her

Pop-Tart back on her plate, midchew. Her tone crawls through me, barbed with how disastrous that would be, and how miserably I've already failed at this.

"Exactly, that's my point," I say, coughing to cover the quake in my voice. "I mean, it's going to end badly anyway."

I toss the crumbs of my pastry onto the dirt and they fall into the tiny mud holes frozen into the ground.

"No, it's not," Lilith says. "No, really, Marion. It's not." She touches the ridge of my ear, and her fingers are so warm I pull away.

"I'm not you," I say, my voice only a whisper.

"I know that," she says, dropping her hands to her knees. But I don't think she gets it. Fire isn't afraid of the fire. Fire thinks it's easy to burn and spark and take control.

"I just . . . I think we should drop it. That's all." I take a bite of the Pop-Tart but all the sweet crumbles feel like sand.

"Okay," she says quietly, and I don't look at her because I can hear the reluctance in her voice. "But when you and Abe broke up," she says, fidgeting with her bracelets, "it was because of this, right? Because he wanted to fool around and have sex?"

My jaw tightens and I stare at the ground. I don't know how to tell her that what happened with Kurt happened with Abe. That it all turns to mud. The chime of her bracelets tangles with the wind, and I wish she'd drop this and be on my side for once.

"Look, I get that you're not me," she says, raising her hands quickly as if she can feel my annoyance. "And you don't have to be me. You can wait as long as you want. But . . ."

"What part of 'drop it' do you not understand?"

She waves her hands like white flags. "Sorry, sorry. It's just . . . I *know* you liked Abe. And hell, Marion, you *still* like him."

"I—"

"You do, Marion! I saw that look in your eye when he was waiting for you after gym class. So . . ." Her shoulders raise to her ears like the solution is as plain as day, and I hate that everything feels so simple to her.

"So what?"

"So, forget the hookup and pick the guy you *like*. You're never going to surprise yourself if you don't try. And that's the thing, Marion—" Her arms rise in excitement. "You are *amazing*. You're beautiful and sensitive, and the second you try, the second you give this a real shot, you're going to realize just how awesome you are. And then you'll knock the socks off whatever guy you want to be with."

I shake my head and laugh. It's a fast and hasty laugh that comes out my nostrils, because she doesn't understand. *She* can fall into firefly fields and lift her skirt to the shadows. *She* can skip back to the light with stars drawn all over her thighs. There aren't fingers of mud dragging her down.

"I can't wait till you realize you can do that," Lilith says, ignoring my laugh, and I press my knuckles into the ice of the bench.

"Yeah, me too," I force out, knowing I *can't* tell her about Kurt now. Because telling her one thing means telling her everything—Kurt, the creek, that man—and she thinks there is this other part of me, something solid that isn't negative space, something that knows how to shine in a jar with no air, like all those fireflies. I can't tell her I was half-naked and I freaked out. I can't tell her I cried. Lilith doesn't understand that it takes air to keep those fireflies alive. It takes air to kindle a fire. And somewhere in the middle of this conversation, I stopped breathing.

# Kurt

There's popcorn all over my car. Stupid fucking popcorn on top of everything.

I swing open my door and start throwing kernels onto the driveway, crawling over the damn seats till every damn kernel is out. It makes me hate Marion. Hate her for making me feel like this. For making the ridge not okay, and my car not okay. And for existing. And I hate that too. That I want her not to exist, like my father doesn't want me or Mom or Josie. And the last fucking thing I want to be is my father. Ignoring *everything*.

But there's nothing I can do. I can't fix the fact that I took Marion up there. I can't change the fact that I wanted her and that was supposed to be okay. And I don't know why she got in my car in the first place if it wasn't okay with her.

But people get in cars all the time when they shouldn't. People drive into the dark.

\* \* \*

Josie's eyes were always bloodshot after Mom died. Maybe they always were before. I don't know. They were definitely bloodshot that night I took out the trash and found her sitting on the front porch waiting for someone. It was Friday, a date maybe. She looked nice. Short skirt. Hair down.

"You going out?" I asked, sitting beside her on the stoop. It was her senior year, so it was a stupid question. She went out every weekend. She took a drag off her cigarette and handed it to me before nodding.

"Yeah," she said quiet, like it was something she didn't want to talk about.

"This one of Dad's?" I asked, turning over the rolled paper. He was at work, like always.

"He won't miss it," she said, wiping her eye, and I couldn't tell if she had something in it or not. The porch light was burned out.

"You gonna give me a lecture about how I'll ruin my soccer career with this thing?" I waved the cigarette at her before taking a drag. She laughed.

"That thing's harmless."

I couldn't see her smile, but I imagined it. Josie had the best smile.

"You got a party to go to, with Madeline or something?" I asked, and she shook her head.

"Just a party," she said, taking the cigarette back like she was annoyed at sharing it. "Not with Madeline." She took a drag. "Do you still have a crush on that girl?"

"No."

"Good."

"Why's that good?"

"She's an asshole."

I squinted at her, trying to make out her face. I thought they were best friends.

"Hey." Josie laughed and nudged me with her shoulder. "Don't take anything I say too seriously, little brother." I liked it when she called me that. It made me feel like I had a big sister again. "The world's full of bullshit, all right, the least you can do is see through mine."

I didn't know what that meant.

She reached down and started scratching her ankle, and there were a pair of high-heeled shoes on the bottom stair. Fancy shoes. Too fancy for a high school party.

"You want to go bowling?" I asked, and she laughed again before taking a drag.

"What, like when you were ten?"

"Yeah, exactly like that. Just you and me. Forget the party."

She checked her watch and looked up the street. "I would totally destroy you at bowling." She pointed the cigarette at me. "Did you forget how good I am?"

"No," I said. "I like how good you are."

She smiled for real this time. My eyes were starting to adjust. This smile I actually saw.

"You're adorable," she said, mussing up my hair. "No wonder the girls love you."

"I don't take girls bowling."

"You should." She laughs. "God, remember that fake baseball move you had?"

"I didn't know how to hold the ball!"

"You kept knocking over the guy's pins in the next lane. Man, you're shit at bowling!"

"It'd be fun."

"It'd be *something*," she said, still scratching that ankle. "I'd obliterate you."

"Bring it on."

She smiled again.

"Put on some jeans." I motioned to the house. "Forget the party and let's see if you still got it?"

A car honked.

We looked up to see a dark vehicle pulling up to the curb. Josie stood quickly and handed me the cigarette, slipping into those heeled shoes on the bottom step. They made her taller than I was used to. I didn't like how they made me look at her legs.

"Kurt, hey." She bent down and put a hand on my cheek. "You should go out yourself, okay? Forget bowling. You made varsity. The girls think you're adorable. You run like nothing can catch you. Get out there and enjoy it. Okay?"

She said that in a way that made it sound like it wouldn't last.

She turned her back on me and got in that car. I ignored the fact that I was pretty sure that car wasn't taking her to a high school party. And I ignored the fact that two days later I saw bruises all over her legs.

# Marion

I put my books into my locker and afternoon light pours down the hallway. Abe leans against the locker next to mine, his fingers drumming along the metal, not impatiently; it's something he's always done, like his brain clicking its way to order. Only it makes me think of the other day, after Lilith kissed me, and how he thinks I'm better than her. Whatever that means.

"So I'll do the charts and you'll write the paper?" he says, holding up his notebook.

We've been nothing but business in class. Theorems, solutions, charts. We haven't quite returned to the tight-lipped silence after we broke up, but it's close, and I don't know how to navigate this unspoken space between us.

"I didn't appreciate what you said the other day," I blurt out. Abe's hand drops from the locker and his face gets serious.

"Okay."

"Lilith's my friend," I start, pretending to organize my

locker. "I'm not *better* than her. I don't even know why you said that. She expresses herself the way she expresses herself, and that's just Lilith. And I love Lilith. And you shouldn't shame her, okay?"

"I didn't mean it that way."

"Well, that's how it came off."

"All right, I'm sorry."

"If there's something you need to say to me, about—"

Abe looks at me so seriously, I almost drop my books. I shove them into the back of my locker with a clang.

"About me, or us . . ." I swallow hard. "Before, or whatever. Then say it to *me*. Okay? Don't go backhand and make it about Lilith."

"All right, I didn't mean to make it about her. I—" His hand runs through his curls and his fingers drum against his skull like he's unsure what to say. But then he suddenly breaks into this adorable smile and his hand drops, the tension falling with it. "I missed you."

"What?"

"This." He motions between us. "You, busting my balls."

"I'm serious about the Lilith thing."

"I know you are, that's the point." He smiles like he used to under the apple tree. "I miss how you can call me on my shit, and that you don't let me get away with it because I'm smart."

"You're not that smart."

"Exactly."

"Okay, maybe a little smart."

"See. I love that *that's* your idea of flattery. A *little* smart. I am going to be valedictorian, you know."

"I know."

"And you don't want to reconsider that 'little' comment?"

"Would you like me to call *other* things little?"

"Maybe not."

"Like your vocabulary?"

"'Coruscating' is not a little word."

"You don't even know what that means."

"But I *said* it like I did. Only someone like you would know I don't."

"Someone like me?"

"Yes, exactly," he says with a quirk. "Precisely, unquestionably, unequivocally, certainly, sure."

Suddenly we're both grinning at each other and my eyes catch the whisper of curls at his neck. They glow like the fluff of a dandelion, and I want to lean in and smell the sunblock he wears year-round. It temps me to blow on the fluff of his hair and make a wish.

"*This* is what I meant the other day," he says seriously. "This is better than kissing Lilith. This—" My smile drops and he immediately backpedals through my silence. "Never mind, forget that. Would you like to get out of here? Work on this paper?" He holds up his notebook again.

"I, uh—"

"I swear I'll stop being a shithead. Plus this is brand-new

graph paper. Completely untouched." He flips the pages under his nose like he's smelling a stack of hundred-dollar bills.

"Are you really trying to bribe me with graph paper?"

"I am." He flips through the pages again and I can't help but smile. He's such a dork.

"Okay," I agree.

"Brilliant. Shall we library or coffee shop?"

"Does the library serve lattes?"

"My kind of girl." He winks, swinging a ring of keys around his finger. "I'll drive."

The thought of his car makes me want to puke.

I turn to my locker and swing open the door so he can't see my face.

"I forgot . . . ," I mumble, pretending to search for something important. Only my mind is suddenly on that empty chair in chemistry class. Kurt's empty chair—the one that sat vacant for fifty minutes without him in it. I dig through my notebooks, annoyed that something that takes up no space—the absence of him—is actually worse than him being in class. Because if he'd shown up, I could at least get it over with—the seeing-each-other part. The ignoring each other. The—

"Did you find it?"

"Yeah." I shove a book into my bag like it's what I was looking for. "Did you say *you'll* drive? Is it possible that the state actually gave you a driver's license? Remind me how many points there are in a three-point turn?"

"That was a special circumstance!" Abe launches into a detailed defense, and I love how riled up he gets over nothing. I love that we're joking and talking to each other again. It makes those two years of silence seem less awkward and not in the way. I shut my locker and turn, when—

I see Kurt.

Walking straight for us, with that grace, swift and certain. Before I can blink or think or react, he's in front of me. Abe stops midsentence, and all the energy shifts to Kurt. Kurt's gaze flicks from me to Abe and back again, and I'm not sure what to do. I can't move or breathe or—

"What's up, Medford?" Abe asks, yanking Kurt's eyes to his smiling face. He sizes up Abe, but only for a second before he's back on me.

I open my mouth to . . . I don't know, speak, breathe, throw up.

"Taylor."

That's it. That's all he says. One word—my last name—and he's gone as fast as he came, disappearing through the light.

"What was that?" Abe asks, and I shake my head.

"Nothing," I lie, looking into the sun, not sure if he was a mirage, half-real or just gone.

"Are you two . . ." Abe fishes, his eyebrows rising, and I attempt to swallow the flutter in my throat.

"Are we . . . ?" I deflect back at him, buttoning my coat, but the snaps are sweaty.

"I dunno." He looks down the hallway where Kurt slipped away. "Are you guys friends?"

I shake my head and clutch the strap of my bag. This next part's easy, because it's true. It *isn't* a lie.

"No, we're not friends," I say, busting open that unspoken space all over again.

## Kurt

**I walk away and don't look back.**

I feel lighter now that I've done it. Now that I've said her name and she can't hold it over me—like I don't know, like it was wrong of me not to know it. Well, I know it now, and she knows I know it. So . . .

Good.

I go outside and take the long way around the building.

I jog toward the soccer field.

I run.

Then sprint.

Mom used to tell me there was no reason to tell anyone you were sorry if you didn't mean it. And Mom never said sorry to anyone.

# Marion

My latte steams and Abe hunches over our homework, his pen tapping our chemistry chart. Curls dangle in his eyes, whispering to me, dandelion tufts waiting for me to disturb them. I almost brush them back, wishing the gesture could take us back to his apple tree, where a kiss could be innocent and unpoisoned.

Only I'm not allowed that snug bit of his skin. I'm not allowed to touch those curls and ask for a kiss. The sting of cotton candy burns at the back of my throat, and I can't stop thinking about how I ended us. It was the week before sophomore year and Abe and I had been dating all summer. We were at the top of the Ferris wheel, and the carnival lights blinked red and yellow below us. The hair of Abe's leg brushed against my knee and I stared at the horizon as his arm slid over my shoulders. The seat rocked and I wondered how many times we'd have to go up and down and around on that ride before they'd let us off again.

Before I'd tell him.

Curls hung in his eyes, the ends frayed and in need of a haircut. Without thinking, I tucked the brown whorls behind his ear. But when he leaned in to kiss me, I looked away, forcing my gaze over the ring toss and dart balloons, to the forest that cradled that funny carnival of lights. Wishing we weren't up there alone, so far from the ground.

"Are you all right?" he whispered in my ear, and I shook my head.

"Too much sugar," I lied.

He pulled back to give me some air and *that's* the moment I wanted to kiss him. But one of his hands still touched my shoulder, where the strap of my bra dented the skin. My whole neck prickled, remembering the release of that elastic the night before. Of how our breath had been hot, and our lips inseparable, but then hooks were unsnapped and this cotton layer of me was on the floor and his hands were on my breasts.

"Do you need some water?" he asked. I took the cup he offered, which was tucked next to him by the bag of cotton candy.

"Thanks." But there were only a few sips left before the straw gurgled with air. Abe faked a smile and I felt the slow of the Ferris wheel as the bucket swayed and the machine began its pattern of start and stop.

"What's wrong?" Abe asked, his lips sugar blue. He tilted his head so those curls fell back in his face, but I didn't touch them. I pressed myself into the far side of the bucket, feeling the sway of the night and the weight of what I'd spent the whole evening avoiding.

"I, uh . . . ," I started, my back sweating, and I grabbed that cotton candy and started to pull out the fragile puffs. The sugar melted on my tongue, too sweet and dissolving. I shivered, thinking of the ghostly echo of his fingers that had been just as light on my skin. "I can't be *that girl*," I whispered, and he looked at me confused.

"What kind of girl do you think I want?" he said, the copper bulbs lining the bucket blinking distractingly. I folded my arms over my chest, thinking of his bedroom and the movie ending. Of the credits rolling and him laying me back on his flannel comforter. His hands under my shirt. His hands in my hair.

"The kind that you kiss and . . ." I think about caramel apples, covered in too much sweet, dripping sticky gold onto wax paper. How was I supposed to tell him I didn't want his hands? "I just, I can't . . ."

"Why not?" he said, and I shuddered, because he wanted an explanation to something that didn't have shape. "Don't you like me?"

"It isn't you," I said, wanting off this ride. "It's *me*. I'm the—"

"Don't say that," Abe interrupted, suddenly furious. "You're going to sit there and break up with me with some shitty TV line!"

"No, it's . . ." I dug my toe into the metal bucket. But that was the problem.

It *was* me.

"Is this about last night?" he asked, hooking fingers into his curls and pulling them from his eyes. "Because we—"

"Some other girl is going to make you really happy," I said, trying to smile. Only my chin wobbled and the muscles couldn't hold up the corners of my mouth.

"I don't want another girl."

"You do," I insisted, staring down at the controller below. He was helping another couple out of their bucket and I was suddenly envious of their chair, swinging free and empty of them.

"Marion, I—"

"Abe, I will never have sex with you!"

It came out so fast and I couldn't stop it. His mouth dropped open and I knew that was it. Eight words and there was no more cotton candy. No more carnival rides. No more dandelion wishes. Eight words followed by two years of silence, and I deserved every unspoken word of it.

The espresso machine hisses and I can't believe Abe is speaking to me again. Flirting even. It feels good to joke with him again and return to something that feels so easy.

But then, nothing's really easy, is it? I *know* Abe hasn't forgotten that carnival ride. I can't erase what I said. I can't explain to him that I felt trapped on that Ferris wheel and I couldn't breathe. That I needed those eight words to make space, to give me air, to create the room to run. And I did. I ran away from Abe as fast as I could so he couldn't touch me. I ran away from Lilith in the firefly field, because I didn't want to see her underneath that boy.

I ran because I *could* run.

Because some things you can't run from. Some things tangle, and hold you down by your hair.

The foam of my latte clings to the inside of my cup. It creates a sticky residue that hangs on the porcelain. I look around the shop and wonder what would have happened if I'd actually come *here* yesterday, if Kurt had taken me out for coffee, instead of to the ridge. Would it have been different? Would we have had . . . I don't know, *anything*, a connection? Something more than those woods. Or is this all I can be? Like with Abe and Kurt and the few half-assed attempts in between that were nothing but sloppy kisses and hands tangled in my hair. Will my toes always be slick with mud and unable? Always running scared?

"Taylor." Abe's voice jolts me back to the shop and he slides the chemistry chart across the table.

"Yeah?" I pretend to be fascinated by it.

"Do you like the column weighted on the left?" he asks, but all I can hear is my last name—Taylor—on Kurt's lips, echoing down the hall, off lockers and light, like my name is worth knowing. Like there's something there. Anything.

More to us.

The air is wet and rimmed with a fog that cradles the soccer field. It's been a few days since the lookout and his car, yet here I am again, watching Kurt practice. Chain link between us.

He didn't ask me to come and I don't know why I'm here, other than that one word in the hallway—my last name on his lips. One word and I'm all spun up and standing here, needing him. Or rather, needing to know why he even bothered to find out. To know if learning my name was an apology or an invitation or . . . *anything.*

Or maybe I simply can't ignore one word spoken, and how brave it is, when all I want to do is run toward the quiet.

The team breaks for water and Kurt walks up to the fence. I grip the chain link, unnerved by the parts of me he's touched and watched and seen me shed. I'm suddenly furious that he hasn't said more than that one word, like he's allowed to touch and kiss and forget.

"What are you doing here?" he says, and I smell the dregs of mud under his cleats, mixing the scent of the earth with the scent of the sky. I don't have an answer, because after his car, I don't want to be alone with him. Yet I'm still here and I don't know what this is.

If *this* is anything.

"We never did have coffee," I say, and he raises his eyebrows like I've asked for a date. My neck burns and it seems stupid to be concerned with such a little thing, considering his car.

"I don't drink coffee," he says, and I'm happy he says it. Cold rushes through me, clean as a single bird flying through the sky, because maybe a date is all I wanted in the first place. And if he doesn't do that, then . . .

"That's cool," I say, dropping my hands from the chain link and looking at my feet. His cleats hook the edge of the fence with their teeth clotted with dirt. I stare at the bloated grass between the spikes and a lump starts to rise in my throat.

I think about all the other girls he's pinned against that seat and I don't want to be one of them, and at the same time I do. Just not like that. Not so fast. Not so disposable.

I pound the heel of my hand against the top of the fence and bite my lip so it will goddamn stop quivering. I force myself to look at him, though I'm afraid of what his eyes will hold.

But I don't find any meanness in him. He's quiet and still as the October water that swallowed me up to my neck.

"The swim at the lake was nice," I say, and I'm not sure where the words come from. "But the rest of it was pretty shitty."

He flinches, and I can't explain how *good* it feels to see him flinch. To see him feel anything, especially after he's seen so much of me, under him.

I turn before he can respond and walk as fast as I can without looking back. There are too many pieces of me that he's touched and kissed and unearthed with his hands, and I hold that one little piece of him firm in my palm, knowing I shook it out of him.

Knowing this one little splinter of Kurt—

Is mine.

# Kurt

I hear the whistle and my feet carry me back to the field. My teammates return to the scrimmage, but I'm not thinking about them or the ball. I'm thinking about that little bead of spit on Marion's lip.

I run up the field, but I'm not paying attention and the ball blasts me in the face. I taste the copper of blood, and the impact stings like the back of my father's hand.

"Daydreaming about pussy, Medford?" Conner hoots, running up the line.

"Get your head in the game!" Coach yells, and I spit blood and run.

Ahead, Conner's faking out our fullback. Only he gets cocky, thinking he's clear to frame up a shot.

I slide tackle the ball right out from under him.

"Jesus fuck!" he curses, kicking empty air. The momentum throws off his balance, and he hits the dirt.

"I can daydream about pussy *and* school your ass," I say, clearing the ball before offering him a hand.

He bats it away, but there's a smirk on his face.

"That's why I like you on our team, bitch," he says, getting up. "Oh, and—who's *that*?" He nods to the parking lot, where Marion is a blond fleck getting into a purple car.

"No one," I say, and Conner laughs.

"No shit." He grins. "A *blond* no one."

I shake my head and he wags his eyebrows before heading for the goalpost.

"Uh-huh," he yells back. "I need to get me some no one, too."

seven

# Marion

The next morning I pull into a parking spot behind the gym where gray clouds block out the sun. Before I have a chance to put the car in park, my passenger door opens. The sight of Conner Aimes looking in at me is something out of the *Twilight Zone*. For a second he looks surprised and I'm sure he's got the wrong car. Only he flips on a smile and slaps my roof with a playful *bang!*

"Purple Nissan," he says like it means something. I stare at him, because there's no universe where it makes sense that Conner Aimes is talking to me.

"What?" I say, and he takes that as an invitation to sit in the passenger seat. My hands tighten around the steering wheel, but he leaves the door open, propping his foot up against the frame.

"You're not what I expected," he says, giving me a once-over, and my body goes stiff.

"Excuse me?"

He pulls off his Red Sox cap and ruffles his hair, before

replacing it backward on his head. "But I can see it." He winks, leaning toward me. "You're Lilith's friend, right? Marie?"

"No. I'm—" I cross my arms over my chest, not liking the way his eyes walk over me. "Yes, I'm Lilith's friend. But no, I'm not Marie." He squints, like I'm not making sense. "It's Marion. Not—" I shake my head. "Conner, why are you here?"

Conner smiles. I *hate* the way he smiles, crooked with the things he's not saying.

"Did Kurt tell you—" I start, but Conner stifles a laugh and slaps a hand on my shoulder.

"Don't sweat it, Marion. You're golden." He squeezes my shoulder, which is sort of brotherly, though I can't tell if he's mocking me or being nice. He unhooks his foot from the door and for a second that perplexed look slides over him again, showing just how hard he's trying to fit *me* into whatever Kurt's told him. "Golden," he repeats, handing me a piece of lined paper, before stepping out the door. "See you around, Marion." He taps the roof again, shuts the door, and struts off.

I stare at the paper in my hand, not sure if that just happened. Only, I'm holding the evidence. I unfold the note and find three bits of information scrawled in half-legible writing.

*Saturday. 10 p.m. 114 E. Macnamara St.*

That's it.

My door opens again and I'm about to grill Conner for

more information, but it's Lilith who slides in beside me.

"Was that Conner Aimes I just saw getting out of your car?" The excitement in her voice bounces with the rest of her.

"I guess." I crumple the paper into my fist. "I think it was a mix-up."

"Mix-up, my ass. What did he want?"

"Nothing." I shove the paper into my pocket, wanting to keep this my secret. If I tell her about this then she'll ask about Kurt. And I'm *not* telling her about the ridge. I can't trust her with that. And I don't want to hear it, whatever she'll say. I already know how horribly I handled it, and some things should never be said out loud.

"Marion?"

I reach for my coat, shoving the paper deeper into my pocket. "It's nothing," I say. "I have no idea what he wanted."

"Well, what did he say?"

I shake my head, running our conversation through my mind. Out the windshield, I can see the soccer field. A low fog covers the grass, hiding the painted lines below, but a gust of wind is all it would take to expose them. It makes me shiver with how transparent I might be. Of what I can't hide. Of what Kurt has probably told Conner.

"He said . . ." My fingers run the jagged line of my zipper, the sharp edge catching a nail. I should trust Lilith. Maybe she can explain it to me. "He said I'm golden."

Lilith wrinkles her nose. "Golden?"

"Right?" I punch an arm through the sleeve of my coat. I've said too much.

"Is this about Kurt?"

I try to find the second sleeve, but the coat is tangled behind me.

"Marion?"

"No." I struggle another second, only to give up. "Maybe. I mean . . . it's possible he told Conner—"

My throat clogs with the idea of Kurt's hands, of my hair, of his calluses on my—

"Possible he told Conner what?"

Red leaves streak over the windshield. The wind has picked up, tossing maple stars through the lot. Lilith squeezes my arm and the warmth of her touch makes me want to tell her everything. But if I do that then all these things will be real.

"I have no idea," I say, the leaves swarming.

"*Is* there something to tell Conner?" Lilith asks. "You and Kurt just went swimming, right?"

I toss my coat to the floor.

"Right."

"So, what's there to tell?"

I open my door and crimson stars flood me.

"Nothing," I say, heading for the building and ignoring the wind. Ignoring how it lifts up the fog, how it pulls at my hair, how it swallows my lies.

# Kurt

I pull the laces of my cleats tight. Tie them once, wrap the extra around my foot, and tie them again. Conner opens his locker next to me and smirks.

"So," he says. "Marion Taylor, huh?"

I don't look at him. How has he figured that out already? I was pretty sure he couldn't tell who she was yesterday when she was by the fence, but damn. I should know better. I stare at the bench and switch feet.

"Right, so when exactly did that happen?" He changes out his T-shirt for his practice jersey.

"Nothing happened," I say. "Don't know her."

"You're a shitty liar, Medford." Conner chucks a sock in my direction. I bat it away. "So was this some divine inspiration that struck you at the bonfire, or have you and Miss Goody Two-shoes been at this for a while?"

I shove my clothes into the locker as calmly as I can and say nothing.

"Play quiet all you want, Medford, but *Marion* seemed

pretty concerned about what *you* told me about her."

"You talked to her?"

Conner lifts an eyebrow. "Who, Marion? You mean that girl you don't know anything about? I repeat, *when* did that happen?"

I shut my locker and head for the door. What did he say to her?

"So, you wouldn't care if I asked her out, right? You two aren't a thing?" Conner calls after me. I flip him the bird and he starts to cackle. I'm halfway out the door and he starts to sing, "Like a virgin. Oooh! Touched for the very first time. Like a viiiiir-gin. When your—"

I let the door slam behind me. Conner can be such a dick.

I immediately start running when I get to the field, doing two laps to get my muscles working. I shouldn't be as pissed at Conner as I am. But fuck, he didn't see her in my car. Crying in that way no one's supposed to cry.

I promise myself I won't let this show in practice. But when Conner jogs up to me I pull him into a headlock. "Look, Con," I say. "If you want my sloppy seconds, you can have 'em." But that only makes him laugh harder.

"Not my type, Medford," he says, squirming out of my grip. "Not that I would have pegged Taylor as your type. But if you've got the itch, scratch it."

He makes an obscene gesture and I want to smack him. Tell him it's not like that. I don't know why I keep defending her. She *should* just be an itch I want to scratch. And part of me still wants her. But that's the problem. I can't touch this girl. Not after seeing her cry in my car. And I don't know what it means that I *like* that I can't touch her. I don't know why that scares me more.

After practice Vanessa is sitting on my car. Conner smiles when he sees her, and I open the passenger door. I make sure Conner is watching, so he gets it and will lay off on the Marion thing. Or maybe I do it to convince myself there *is* no Marion thing.

We go to the ridge and fool around in my backseat. Everything with Vanessa is easy, and I like easy. I like that I don't have to think. I like that her shirt's so tight it reminds me of Madeline wearing that snug V-neck that was mostly see-through. Madeline was Josie's friend and I met her at my first high school party, which Josie took me to my sophomore year. I'd just made varsity, and Josie gave me a bottle of vodka to celebrate. When we arrived, everyone at the party noticed Josie. Not because I was with her, but because Josie had a presence all her own. Something they couldn't ignore.

"Welcome to the playground, little brother," she said, unscrewing the top of my vodka bottle and nodding for me to drink. "Let's make you a king."

The liquid burned.

It was crowded and people sat on couches and each other's laps. Out the window was a red barn and a keg, but we didn't have to move. The party came to Josie. She introduced me to everyone, her eyes lighting up when she told them about how I'd just made the team.

"It's not surprising," she said, her arm around my shoulders. "Have you seen how fast this fucker can run?"

I was a shiny penny she was showing off—but not in some shit way, like she needed attention. This was different. Like she was proud. It was different than at home. She didn't retreat into her room or tiptoe around Mom. She didn't scowl at me or bitch about how Mom never taught her how to play guitar. This was another world for Josie. Where she was someone else. Someone better.

The party had been raging for a while, and I was sufficiently drunk, when Josie introduced me to her friend Madeline. Madeline had black hair and wore a white shirt that was so thin I could see her bra through it. I don't know how it happened, exactly, but Josie disappeared, and Madeline took me out to the barn.

She hooked her fingers through my belt loops and we went behind the hay bales, where she put my hands on her tits and started kissing me. I was so confused and excited, I just went with it. I mean, she was gorgeous and she let me touch her everywhere. She moaned and nibbled my neck as if she liked it. Which I guess she did, because she pushed me onto the ground and started losing clothes. Before I knew it she pulled me out of my pants, slid a condom on me, and we were having sex.

I don't know if she was drunk or if she had planned this. All I knew was that I was having sex and it felt so fucking good and then it was over.

Straw poked my legs, and I didn't know what to do after, so I said—

"I love you."

Madeline laughed.

"Gawd!" she said, pulling that tight shirt over her breasts. "Don't tell a girl you love her unless you mean it."

I looked away and grabbed my jeans to cover myself.

"It's just sex, Kurt." She leaned over and kissed me, hot and wet. My hands touched her through her shirt, and she pressed into me and moaned. I thought we were about to have a second round, but she rolled off me and pulled up her pants.

"Trust me, you'll get better," she said, before leaving the barn. "I'll tell your sister it was awesome."

I shifted away from her and pulled off the condom. I didn't want her to tell my sister anything. I clawed through the straw and shoved the condom under it, not sure what else I was supposed to do with it, then I put on my clothes.

I went back to the party and found Madeline by the keg. She was laughing with her friends and one of the seniors from my team. I came up next to her, not sure if I should put my arm around her or play it cool, but she didn't look at me. I touched her elbow and she pulled away, dropping herself into the senior's arms and pressing her tits against him.

I went into the house to look for that bottle of vodka my sister had given me. Most of it was gone when I found it, but I spent the rest of the night nursing it anyway.

Later when Josie was driving us home, I asked her about Madeline, if she'd said anything about me.

"No," Josie said, looking at me funny. "Why?"

"No reason," I lied.

"Oh my God!" She laughed. "You totally have a crush on Madeline!"

"No, I don't."

"You do! God, you'd better get over that quick, because Madds is totally in love with Jackson. And you're cute, little brother, but trust me, you haven't got a chance."

"I don't want a chance. I don't care."

"Good." Josie eyed me before reaching over and pinching my elbow. It was a weird big-sister thing, that pinch, like she knew I was lying but it was okay. "It's for the best. She'll break your heart anyway."

I shrugged and looked out the window. So Madeline didn't want me to love her. Fine. She didn't want me to be her boyfriend or even her date. She just wanted to screw me and that to be the end of it.

And oddly, I was okay with that.

# Marion

After school I head into my kitchen and dig through a stack of papers by the phone. I find the paper I'm looking for near the bottom, yellowed with coffee stains. It's the phone tree from elementary school. Printed at the top, under "A," is Conner Aimes. I enter his number into my cell, go upstairs, and lock my door.

I pace through my room, holding the note Conner gave me. This number is from elementary school. It probably doesn't even work anymore. But I still click open the number and hit send.

"Hello?" a gruff voice barks on the other end.

"Um, yes. Hello." I swallow. "Could I please speak to Conner Aimes?"

There's a silence and I'm sure I've got the wrong number.

"You don't have his cell?" the voice asks, and I sit up.

"Um, no, sir. I—"

"Let me give it to you. Do you have a pen?"

"Of course, yes." I scramble for the first thing I can find, because he's already reciting numbers.

"You got that?"

"Yes, sir. Thank—"

"Don't call this number again, use his cell."

"Of course not—"

But he's already hung up.

My heart pounds as I stare at the number, certain I shouldn't even bother with the second call. But I type it into my phone anyway and hit send.

"Who's this?"

For a second I think I've hit redial because Conner's voice sounds just like his dad's.

"Um—" I stand up and start to pace. "Conner, hi. This is Marion."

Silence.

"Marion Taylor," I repeat, pressing the paper note he gave me under my fingernail.

"How did you get this number?"

I stop by the window and play with the latch, realizing how dumb this is going to sound. "Your dad."

"My what?"

"At least I think he was your dad," I say, backpedaling. "I called the number on a phone tree from like fourth grade. Is that—"

Conner starts to laugh and I shut up. "Marion, you are something else."

I bite my lip, not sure how to take that.

"So, how can I help you?" he asks.

I latch and unlatch the window.

"Um, well, I was calling about this thing on Saturday."

"Okay."

"Yeah, so . . . what is it?"

Conner laughs again. "It's—" He pauses, clearly amused. "Look, it just means you're *in*. Don't sweat it."

"In for what?"

"In for nothing. Just *in*."

"What does—?"

"It's a *party*."

I want to hang up the phone. Of course it's a party. What else would it be?

"Right," I say, releasing the latch. It snaps back violently, stabbing my thumb.

"Look." Conner pauses, and I put the bruised finger in my mouth. "Just come, all right?" His voice is kind, almost genuine. "Just come."

He hangs up before I have a chance to ask about Kurt and find out if he put him up to this. I consider inviting Lilith to the party, not sure if that would be okay. It probably is, but the thought of Lilith being there feels wrong. I don't want her in my head. I don't want the advice and the sideways glances, like she's all grown up and not sure why we're still friends.

A knock clicks lightly against my door.

"Marion?" It's Dad, only his voice is soft and uncomfortable, like he isn't sure he's allowed to knock.

"Yeah?" I say, hiding my phone under my pillow, along with the paper Conner gave me.

There's a pause and then he tries the knob, but it jangles and thuds. Locked. There's an awkward pause before he tries the knob again, twisting the metal back and forth like he wasn't sure he did it correctly the first time. I started locking that door after the barbecue, not sure what I was trying to keep out or in. It didn't erase the memory of belt buckles against my chin.

"Are you okay in there?" he asks, but the question sounds more like an apology for knocking and I'm sick of him always tiptoeing around me. I swing open the door, with my throbbing finger pressed to my lip.

"What's up?"

He squints at my hand but doesn't ask. He never asks. Instead he peeks over my head like he's looking to see if someone else is in the room with me. I lean against the door so it opens.

"Just me," I say indignantly, the room in view. It's a joke, but his eyebrows arch.

"Should I be worried about that?" he asks, his eyes focused deliberately on me, and not on what might be in my room.

I almost say yes, to see how he'll react. God, what would he do if there *was* a boy in this room? Would he see me then?

"I trust you," he says, his voice serious, and cold reeds through me. I hate it when he says that, like it's all up to me. Did he say the same thing to my mother, before she left with that lawyer guy? Did he *trust* her? Shut the door? Refuse to see?

"I know," I say quietly, pushing the door open completely, so he *can* look if he wants to.

"You're a good kid," he says, stepping back and pulling off his glasses. He cleans them on the front of his shirt and looks to the kitchen. "Do you want pizza?"

Hot, sticky pizza sliding down my throat? No, not really.

"Sure," I say, slipping past him and heading for the kitchen. I'll pick off the cheese.

I leave my door open behind me in case he wants to look and see if anyone's there. I secretly hope he *will* look. But when I glance back, he pulls the door shut.


A week after the Fourth of July barbecue, Dad came into my bedroom without knocking.

I didn't have a lock then.

My hair was gone, cut off and thrown in the Dumpster, and there were crumpled tissues littering the floor. The pink wastebasket next to my bed didn't smell pink anymore and my whole body ached from puking. I couldn't get rid of the taste of meat and muddy water under my tongue.

Dad's weight sank into the mattress as he sat next to me, and I pulled my vomit-stained comforter up to my chin.

Slats of sunlight peeked in through the blinds, and my broken flip-flop lay on the carpet. The thong between the toes torn free from the rubber.

"Lilith's been calling," Dad said, pressing a hand against my forehead to check for a fever. "She wants to know if you want to go to the beach."

I closed my eyes and felt the warmth of his hand. I didn't want to go anywhere.

"You don't have a temperature," he said. "You should call her back."

"I—"

"Nope," he interrupted, removing his hand from my cheek. "I know you're embarrassed you cut your hair off, but it's time to stop pretending you're sick."

"But—" I pointed to the pink belly of my trash can.

"No buts." He stood up and took the end of my comforter. "This needs to be washed."

He swept away the fabric in one quick motion and air flooded me.

"Lunch is in the kitchen," he said, crumpling the blanket into a ball and heading for the door. "I expect you to join me in ten minutes."

Something caught his foot. He looked down and a yellow clump of fabric was wrapped against his shoe. My skirt. The one with embroidered daisies along the hem. Drenched daisies that dipped in and—

Rose hips caught in my throat.

Did he recognize it? It was the same yellow fabric that had stuck to my legs. Flip-flop broken. Meat wrapped in foil.

He clutched the puffy-white comforter in his hand, the fabric pillowing through his fingers like dough.

"Ten minutes," he repeated, shaking the yellow fabric off his shoe. "You're not sick and this is the last I want to hear of it."

He kicked the yellow skirt under the bed, into the dark, and after that day he never once barged into my room again. In my mind I could see that man at the barbecue smiling, with my kiss hidden under his tongue—

Where no one could see it.

# Kurt

It's dark when I drop Vanessa off at her house and drive home. I pull up to find Dad's truck parked diagonally across the driveway. I park by the curb and think about the unemployment form I saw sitting on the counter this morning. It answers the big question. The fact that his truck's moved means at least he got off the couch.

On the front step, I pull out my keys, but my practice bag hits the door and it inches open. Unlocked.

That isn't like Dad. That's a Mom thing to do. I cringe at his carelessness and wonder how long this unemployment bullshit is going to last. How I'm going to put up with sharing this place with him.

"Get off me!" a woman's voice shrieks from inside the house, and my stomach drops. "Get your fucking hands off me!"

I drop my keys and I throw open the door. Voices argue, but everything's dark, and I can't tell where the voices come from. There's a rushing sound, like the shower is on, or a pipe's busted. A dim light glows down the hall and a scream pounds my stomach to my throat.

I run toward the light, shadows slashing against the wall.

"Come on! You have to—"

It's Dad's voice.

But the woman shrieks and drowns him out. The noise is feral, like an animal. And then there's a *crash!*

I speed forward.

"Dad?" The word shoots out of me like vomit and the yelling stops.

"KURT!!!"

*Her* voice curdles the silence. *Josie's* voice—tearing through me like a thousand razors.

She can't—

This can't—

It's not possible.

But what I see through the door frame tells me different.

The bathroom mirror is smashed. The shower head roars and beneath it is my sister. Hunched over. Fully clothed. Wet.

Behind her is my father, clutching her wrists, holding her under the water with all his weight. He's fully clothed too, and it almost looks like he's hugging her. Almost.

I don't move. Not sure what to make of this.

Josie's black eyes glare at me, mascara streaking her cheeks, and when I don't come to her rescue she starts to buck against my father. She screams, trying to dislodge him, and that animal noise—*it's her.*

"Help me!" my dad hisses. "She's detoxing, Kurt! Get over here and help me hold her down."

Josie's hand slips from his grip and she claws at his face. "I hate you," she screams. "I fucking hate you! I hate *both* of you!"

Her palm smacks his nose and red smears over Dad's cheek.

I'm moving now.

Josie swings at me, but I wrap myself around her, pushing down with all my might. Dad does the same. I'm half in the tub and half out when she screams. Bites my ear.

Hot pain flashes through me.

White pain.

"Jesus fuck!" I stumble, but I don't let go.

Water thrashes. Pounds over us. It floods the floor and the tile and the hall. We don't stop. We squeeze tight and hold. Hold all that we have.

The lights are off in the hallway. Dad's in the bathroom mopping up the water from holding Josie down, and I'm on the floor, sitting across from Josie's room.

The screaming has stopped. Even after we got her to calm down in the shower, she started again. Made sounds behind that door like there were bugs hatching out of her skin. Sounds I won't ever forget.

Light creeps up the hall and Dad steps out of the bathroom, two bloodstained tissues hanging from his nostrils.

I'm surprised he isn't holding a cigarette. I consider getting him one, but I don't dare leave this door. He glances at me from the door frame and I can't tell if he's angry or sad. Mostly he looks tired.

"Where did you find her?" I ask, and he removes one of the tissues and breathes deep, dabbing his nostril with the back of his hand.

"Nowhere good."

My jaw tightens with the implication and I glare at the padlock on Josie's door. The one on the *outside*. Our side.

"What's that supposed to mean?"

"It means, be happy she's here." He shoves the tissue back in his nose and slaps the mop on the tile.

I stand up and grab the padlock. I yank the metal and it bangs, making the door smack against the frame. But I don't have the key.

"Hey!" Dad rushes me. "She needs her sleep. Let her rest."

"How long are you going to keep her in there?" I get in his face. "Why isn't she in the hospital?"

He snorts and a bitter laugh drops out of him. One of his tissues falls to the floor, and I smell dried blood.

"You got money for that?"

"I could get a job," I offer, but he shakes his head, not bothering to pick up the tissue.

I smack the padlock, hating this.

"So that's it?" I say. "We lock her up, like a prisoner?"

He nods at me calmly and I want to hit him.

"That's it."

I curse under my breath and he walks away, tossing the mop into the bathroom, where it smacks loudly against the tile. So much for quiet.

I slump onto the floorboards and wonder if he gets that *he's* the reason she stays away. The last time Josie was in this house it was Christmas Eve. She came home from BU after her first semester, only she looked like shit. She hadn't gained the freshman fifteen. She'd lost it. She and Dad were decorating the tree when I heard a loud *bang!* I came out of my room to find them screaming at each other. Broken ornaments all over the floor. It was dark, except they both had fists full of glowing tree lights, strung taut between them.

"I'm a fucking adult," she hissed.

"Yeah? Who's paying for those classes you're not attending?"

"You can't tell me—"

"No, I can tell you *exactly* what to—"

"Fuck those classes." She yanked on the lights and the tree wobbled like it might fall down. "I didn't sign up for next term. So keep your money!"

"You what?" He yanked on the string and the lights ripped from her hands.

"You're impossible!" She threw her arms in the air and stalked away from the mess.

I could barely make out her eyes when she looked up and saw me. But they went dark.

"What?" I glared at her, standing my ground.

"God, you love having this house to yourself, don't you?" she snapped.

"I don't miss this," I said, pointing to the shattered glass.

"No, but you would have loved picking up the pieces if I was *Mom*."

"Fuck you."

"You thought she was such a saint!" She shook her head at me. "You do know she was only ever nice to you when she was drunk. You know that, right? You know that being drunk was the only way she could pretend she wanted this life!"

"Knock it off!" Dad boomed, moving forward in a shadow of anger. I cowered against the wall, but Josie glared at him. Unflinching.

"You think that scares me anymore?" Her voice was eerie calm. "You think the *truth* scares me anymore? At least I can look at it." His fist clenched and she laughed. A mean laugh, gutted from some dark place inside her. "Why don't we all admit that we *loved* it when Mom was drunk. She was fun. It was easier."

"You're full of shit," I snapped, but she looked at me so hard it felt like she'd kicked my kneecaps in.

"Am I?" she said, and I wanted to punch her for all those lies. "You're so naive, Kurt. I bet you didn't even know she was fucking around on Dad, or that he kept on handing her beers so she'd keep on laughing and playing music on the back porch. Like that music was going to fix anything!"

Dad slammed the lights to the ground. They sparked violently and slashed out. Cold crawled up my arms and darkness cast over both of them.

"Get out." His voice was so black I stopped breathing.

"You think—"

"Get out!"

I couldn't tell if she was scared, only that she shut up.

I heard footsteps against broken glass—hers—walking away from him.

"You don't live here anymore," he said, and my throat felt thick with ash. "Get your things and don't come back."

She didn't take a suitcase, or even her coat. There was only a black shape walking out the door.

On Christmas Day she called. But when he heard her voice on the other end of the line, he hung up.

In the morning I wake up in the hall. I must have fallen asleep outside her room. It's quiet and I don't hear Dad or Josie. But when I look at that padlock—

It's open.

I shoot up. Push through the door, but there's no one in there. Fear streaks through me, but a hand grabs my side.

"Hey—" It's my father.

"Where's Josie?"

"She's in the kitchen," he says, holding up his hands to calm me. "She's eating breakfast. Give her some space."

I shove past him, but when I get to the kitchen I slow. Not sure I'm ready. Where has she been? Will she be that animal I saw last night?

Through the door I see her hunched over a bowl of Froot Loops. Her legs poke out from baggy shorts revealing skin over bone, and the oversized sweatshirt she wears doesn't hide how little of her is underneath. Scabs cover her legs. Her hair is chopped short on one side, and I swear there's a bald spot above her ear.

Her spoon scrapes against the bowl. Scrapes again, going round, chasing the last Froot Loop. Only she never catches it. Never raises the spoon to her mouth.

She's only been gone ten months, but I would have walked right past this person on the street and never have known it was her. *My* sister. I would have been looking for someone else. I hate how that makes me think of Mom. How I liked seeing Mom happy and playing her guitar. How I didn't want to see her when she wasn't drinking.

"You gonna stand there like a pervert and stare? Or you gonna come in?"

Her body's thin, but her voice isn't.

I walk to the fridge. She tilts her chin up at me, and yellow skin stretches over the tendons of her neck. I yank open the fridge and force my eyes inside. Rotted KFC. Green Powerade. Bread.

She's got a carton of milk on the table, but I'm not going near her.

"You look good," she says, as I pull out the bread and untie the bag. "Big-boy soccer champ, taking on the world." She opens her mouth, like she's trying to smile, but her tongue juts into an empty space between her teeth. It writhes around like it knows the tooth is missing, but looks for it anyway.

"You—" I start, but I pull out slices of bread.

"Me what?" she fishes.

I keep pulling out slices until I have five in front of me and nothing to do with them. I grab them all and head for the door.

"Kurt."

Her voice catches me. I scrunch all the bread in my fist and don't want to look back at her. Everything she says is a trick.

But when I do, she doesn't say anything mean. She just looks tired.

"It's good to see you," she says, and it's not a joke.

I nod, but my throat is tight. "Yeah," I say. Not sure I know how to look at her. How to see her this way. "It's good to see you, too."

"Yeah," she agrees, and I want to ask her about the scabs and where she's been. But maybe those things are too personal. Maybe they're none of my business. She shakes herself suddenly, like a reflex, and her hand flies to her nose. She starts huffing through her nostrils like she's trying to blow her nose without actually blowing it. It's rhythmic. Again and again and again.

I watch her, but she's lost in it. Like she can't make it stop.

I go to my room and change my clothes. I need to run. Get out of this house and—

But I hear Dad padlock Josie in her room. I lean against the wall and try to hear her through the wall. I listen for wheezing like in the kitchen, wheezing like I was watching something already broken. Something that can't be fixed.

But I don't hear a thing.

No screaming. No scratching. No nothing.

I listen harder, knowing this wall is thin. When Josie was in high school, I could hear her talking to her girl-friends through this wall, or playing music. I even heard her having sex with her boyfriend once when our parents weren't home. But after Mom died, things got different.

Muffled.

I knew something was wrong. I could hear her, crying. But I wasn't going to knock on her door. There was a wall between us.

Josie came out of her room one night with her face puffy and red, and I started to ask, but she told me to fuck off for even looking at her. She didn't want me to see her like that, and what would I have said anyway? Nothing I ever said to Mom made a difference. Josie would be exactly the same.

Josie didn't need me. Josie never needed anyone.

# eight

# Marion

I arrive at 114 E. Macnamara Street and the front door is open. The house is huge and I knock politely on the door frame, unsure if I'm supposed to walk in or not. I don't see a single person despite all the cars parked in the driveway.

I pad down a hall, my shoes sparkling with sequins that seem too dressed up. I look for Conner or Kurt or anyone, but all the main rooms are empty. I should have brought Lilith. She would yell loudly and storm this silence to find out where everyone is hiding. I run a hand through my blond ringlets, which I spent way too much time curling, and tell myself I don't need Lilith. I can do this without her.

Laughter cuts through an open window and there are lights in the backyard. Conner didn't mention that this was going to be a pool party, but it is. I find everyone in the pool house out back, wearing bathing suits and shorts. It's so humid inside that I start to flush, the ceiling covered in a hundred panes of glass, all fogged with breath.

I take off my coat to deal with the heat, and a dizzy smell of coconut and marijuana seeds the air. Music plays, which sounds vaguely tropical, and people linger with tiny pink umbrellas in their drinks. One umbrella has fallen into the pool and is floating on the surface with its thin tissue paper soaked wet.

My dress is already damp, sweaty under my arms, and I lift my hair momentarily to get it off my neck. The hairspray lacquered all over the curls makes them sticky with frizz. I look for Conner, but he's nowhere to be found, Kurt either, and I make a deal with myself to stay for at least half an hour. Or at least till Conner gets here. But the more I look around, the more I feel like I've crashed the party. And maybe that's the gag. I show up uninvited and the joke's on me.

No one's in the pool, which I'm happy about. Only I overhear a girl behind me mention that it's so hot that she and her friend ought to go skinny-dipping. I run a finger along the strap of my dress, not sure I should have worn it. I'd thought it was pretty when I put it on, with its off-white color and swirled rosettes. But the fabric is thin, layered with cheap chiffon that makes it soft and ruffled. If I did jump in that water with this dress on, all those layers would lie flat. They'd become pink as skin, and transparent.

Someone opens a side door to deal with the heat. It doesn't help.

"I don't think the AC's really broken," the girl behind

me says with a snicker. "It's a plot to get everyone naked." I peek over my shoulder and she's smiling like she thinks that would be fun. Her friend grabs a towel from a stack and tosses it at her, and the two stumble off giggling.

The surface of the pool is smooth, as still as the lake before Kurt and I dove under it with all our clothes on, like there was something beneath needing us to disturb it. I slip off my sequin shoe and dip a toe in the water. It's warm, as hot as the room, and definitely heated. Only Kurt's not here, and there's no way I'm going into that pool.

"You need a beer."

I turn to see Tommy Rhodes from the soccer team walking my way. He eyes my legs and smiles, but his lips are so thin they almost disappear. A group of soccer players hangs by the far side of the room, and I scan them for Conner and Kurt.

"What's your poison?" Tommy asks, flashing yellow teeth, and I almost decline the drink, but no one else is talking to me.

"A beer's fine," I say, pulling my toes from the balmy water to follow him to the keg.

"You here with someone?" he asks, shooting liquid froth into a cup, only the whole thing overflows as he hands it to me, foam oozing over the rim and covering my knuckles. "Careful there," he says, wiping the drippage, and somehow his other arm finds its way around me. I get a whiff of his BO laced with chlorine, and I adjust, trying to move out of his grip without being rude. But his arm squeezes my shoulders.

"Conner invited me to the party," I say, hoping that makes him back off, but he nods like that make sense, and beer slops from my cup. It hits his shoe, beading up like globs of sweat. "Have you seen him?"

"Nah, I don't think he's here yet. Which is good for me." He winks, and I don't know how to untangle myself from him politely.

"Have you seen Kurt?" I try, hoping Kurt holds more clout than Conner, but Tommy shakes his head, or at least I think he does. It's hard to tell, because his hand is on my neck.

I take a drink and look out the windows, but all the panes of glass are covered in steam. The beer is bitter and I consider spitting it on Tommy just to get him off me.

"Are you a natural blonde?" he asks, his hand in my hair.

I can't breathe. It's too hot and there's creek water under my toes. I close my eyes and try to swallow but my breathing is unsteady and all I can see in my mind is that man from the barbecue. Beside me. Wrinkled shirt. Untidy shoes.

# Kurt

The house is huge, with too many mirrors and ugly pieces of art. The house belongs to Carrie, one of the cheerleaders, and as he leads me down the hall, Conner explains to me that her parents are in Spain or Portugal.

I want to bail. I'd rather go to the quarry and shoot some bottles, tell Conner about Josie. But he insisted we come to this party. Not that it matters. What would I tell him anyway? That my father locked Josie up? Fuck that.

We find the party in the back. Everyone's hanging around a pool so small it looks like a parking space for water. Someone forgot to turn on the air, and it's damn muggy. And everyone's got stupid umbrellas in their cups.

"Hey, would you look at that," Conner says, nodding to the pool and showing me his shit-eating grin. "A body of water. How interesting." He grabs my shoulder and I glare at him. "Do you think later you might get inspired," Conner teases, "and, I don't know, go *swimming*?"

"What did you do?" I scan the room.

"Nothing." Conner laughs, shaking his head. "I just heard that water gets you wet."

"You're a fuckhead."

"I'm your fuckhead, baby," he says, checking the crowd. "Only, I think pre-swim you might want to visit the keg." He swings a finger to the corner and pulls it against the air like it's a trigger. "Because Tommy's poaching the party favor I worked real hard to get here for you."

I look to the keg and Tommy's leaning over a pretty blonde.

I don't know who I'm more pissed at, Conner for pulling this stunt or Tommy with his arm around Marion's neck.

"Happy swimming," Conner says, and I elbow him in the gut.

"Oh, I'm sorry—" I turn to him. "Did you run into my elbow?"

He clutches his stomach and grins through the pain. "You're welcome," he says, before limping away.

I stand there watching them. I should leave, but Marion's hair is down and Tommy's hand is in it. It makes me wish she'd worn it up, like at school.

The smell of pot and chlorine makes my head throb and I'm walking before I even know what I'll do.

I want his hand out of her hair.

"Tommy." My voice comes out low.

Direct.

He looks up and I want to smile at the way he cowers.

I stare him down, keeping my face cold, and I can feel Marion looking at me. Her breath gets shallow, and I want to tell her I got this, but I have to deal with Tommy first.

"Hey, man," Tommy says, laughing a little, but I don't move.

"Hey," I say flatly, and he knows that's a challenge. His arm tightens around Marion's neck and it reminds me of the bruised arms on that guy Josie was dating, when I visited her in Boston. His arm hung over my sister like he owned her. Tommy better play this right or I'm going to take off his head.

I glare and the stink of marijuana closes in on Tommy. His Adam's apple slides up and down his throat and there's a clicking sound when he swallows. But he doesn't back down. I'm so close to both of them I can't tell if other people are watching, but I count to five and tell myself to breathe.

"I think you should get me a beer," I say finally, and Tommy nods.

"Sure, man." He turns to the keg. "No problem."

But his arm is still hooked around Marion. His weight bends her neck, causing her to hunch, and he pulls her with him. Her eyes hit mine, and I see that hollowed expression in them. Like when she looked at me in my car. Maybe worse.

He's fucking done.

I shift my weight, wedging myself between Tommy and Marion. He feels me behind him and twists, but he can't move because of how close I am. My hand is on the back of his neck, forcing his head forward so he can't look at me.

"Let her go," I say quietly, leaning in to make this as uncomfortable for him as I can. So he knows I'm gonna lose my shit if he doesn't do it. He instantly releases her and Marion exhales sharply. She moves behind me and I grab the beer from Tommy's hand, not giving him any space. He cowers. Body hunched toward the ground like a fucking dog. Tail between his legs.

Good.

I keep him there.

I stand over him long enough so that he understands just how much more uncomfortable this *could* be.

I step back and turn to Marion.

"Outside," I say, pressing three fingertips into the small of her back and moving her to the door. I don't care who's watching.

The air is so fucking cold outside it slaps me awake. It tastes bitter and I don't know if I'm riled up because of Tommy or because it's her or if it's the fact that I'm out here under the stars—again—with *this* girl.

I drop my hand from Marion's back and I walk ahead of her, moving so fast I'm already at the tree line where the grass is damp. She catches my eye and I'm so jumpy I dump out my beer and chuck the cup into the darkness. I'm not sure what it is about this girl, why she riles me up so much, or what I'm supposed to do with her.

She inches up beside me and I don't say anything, because whatever comes out of my mouth right now is going to be messed-up and wrong.

"You don't drink?" she asks, holding her cup away from her like a bum asking for money, and I shake my head.

"Not tonight."

She stands there a moment before tipping her cup over and throwing it out to meet mine. She smiles irreverently and that urge rushes through me. Damn, if she was *anyone* else, Vanessa or one of the cheerleaders or . . . I kick the ground, but it's slippery and unsatisfying.

"Tommy's a jerk," I say, and she looks at her feet. She's got on glittery shoes that catch the pool house lights. They shoot flecks up her ankles, and my eyes slide higher to the dots on her knees and thighs and—*shit*! I've got to stop thinking about this girl like this.

"Thanks for helping with Tommy," she says, picking at the manicured grass with the point of her shoe. I stare into the woods and realize we've stood here long enough for my eyes to adjust. I can see twenty feet ahead of me.

"So, uh . . . ," I start, but my palms sweat and I steal a glance at her. She's watching the dark like it's something we can stand in, and for a moment I want to tell her things I don't tell anyone. About how I'm scared to death because Josie's home, looking worse than I ever imagined she would be. And how I don't want to look at my sister because it means she's not okay, like really not okay. Like Mom. And

I want to ask Marion how she can cry the way she did and still stand here next to me. 'Cause I don't know what I'm supposed to fucking do.

I really don't.

Suddenly I need us to not be standing here, saying nothing.

"You like music?" I say, and she squints like that was a stupid question, because it was. But it's the only thing I could think of.

I *want* music.

"Right, so . . ." I run a hand through my hair and wish I still had my beer. *Something* to occupy my hands. I'm not used to doing this. The talking part. It's not what I do. But there's no way I'm letting her back in that pool house with Tommy.

"I like music," she says, bailing me out, and I laugh nervously. I look to the side of the house, toward the driveway, and I know this is a stupid idea. I shouldn't. I don't have my guitar.

"Right. Who doesn't like music?" I joke, brushing my palms against the sides of my jeans. "So, do you want to—"

There's a distant laugh. I look to the pool house and a group is lingering by the doors. A few people are smoking and one chugs a beer with gold wings on the label.

I should walk away right now. Leave her here by the trees. Disappear into the crowd. Like at the lake. Forget—

"Do I want to what?" she asks shyly, and the softness in

her voice kills me. It's stupid. So damn stupid. It makes me want to trust her.

"You want to hear something?" I say, jamming a hand in my pocket like that might make this easier. "A song, I mean."

"Like your favorite band?"

I roll onto my heels. What am I doing?

"No, like—" I shake my head. Legs going weak. I kick my foot into the earth and dig the toe in, like when I switch directions in a game. Commit. Trust gravity. Trust the inertia and the dirt. "No, something else."

I don't know how to explain this. I just want her to hear it.

"Come with me." I take her hand and lead her around the house. She squeezes my palm like that first handshake at the bonfire, and now I'm sure I have to do this.

In front of the house there are at least twenty cars parked and double parked in the U-shaped driveway. I weave through them, spotting my car, when—

She lets go.

I turn to see what's wrong, but then I get it. My car. She thinks—

"Hey." I raise my hands like a criminal, adrenaline surging. This isn't *that*. "We're not getting in my car, okay?"

Her eyes are wide.

"Stay here, all right? I'm going to get my player. I'll be right back."

I head for my car and hope she doesn't bolt. I pick up my pace, wanting her to hear the music. Mine. Mom's and mine. Music I haven't listened to in four years. I don't know why this feels so important, but something about her eyes in my car and the fact that she's still standing here not running away makes me think that if she heard it, she might get it. Like how she knew to dive into that lake after me.

I grab my iPod from the glove compartment and weave my way back to her. She stands by a blue SUV running her finger over the back of the passenger mirror, tracing invisible constellations in the stars.

"Here," I say, holding out two earbuds and the iPod. "This is, well . . ." I don't want to explain it. "Just listen."

A curious smile quirks her lip and it makes me more sure of this. She puts in the earphones and it takes me a second to cue up the song.

I hit play and her gaze softens over me. I jam my hands in my pockets, because I'm going to need a straitjacket if she's going to look at me like that. Especially while listening to Mom's song. But then she closes her eyes and tilts her head to the side and I can't take my eyes off her. She's serious. Really listening. Not just bobbing her head. Not pretending.

I hear the hum of an acoustic guitar, and her head sways. Blond curls brushing her collarbone. But it's the dimple that tugs her left cheek that fascinates me. It presses in as her mouth tips in an almost smile, but not quite getting there.

Then her lips part with a quick breath, like she discovered something. And I want to ask—*What? What was that?* It makes me anxious and reckless at the same time, like before a game, when the field's untouched and nothing's determined yet.

Like anything's possible.

# Marion

**I don't know what I expected.**

Not this.

The song in my ears is quiet, acoustic and voiceless. It's just a strum and a melody, and after a moment a second guitar layers in over the first. I stare at the ground trying to focus, even though I can feel Kurt watching me.

I close my eyes and listen, because he's sharing something, and it's pretty. Which is a word I'd never associate with Kurt, and yet that's exactly what it is.

It's pretty.

It's simple.

It's a harmony that folds and whispers, with both guitars calling out for each other. Haunting. I press my hand into the pad of his chest and feel the cotton of his shirt, his muscle.

The guitar thrums and I pull him closer till his breath is snared with music. His hands drop to my waist, barely touching, and with three fingertips at the small of my back, he nudges me forward—

And into.

# Kurt

**Her fingers spread against the cotton of my shirt,** wide over the muscle, and the urge to—

Only I *can't* touch this girl. Not after what happened in my car.

I pull away, but she grabs my collar like she's the hot and lustful one. And the smell of girl overwhelms me because she's so close. And it's not just the smell of girl but *this* girl, who I can practically taste, and want to taste, but don't taste. And I don't know why I'm fighting this but I am.

Through the earbuds I hear the faint thrum of my guitar. Strumming. And my hands go weak. They drop to her waist, barely touching. I can fight part of this, but I can't fight all of it. If she was just a little closer, instinct might kick in. She might go back to being any girl, and not the one who won't get in my car. Not the one who—

Lips.

My lips. Her lips.

*God, she tastes good.*

My hands clutch the fabric of her dress, and someone trembles. Fuck! That better not be me. That better be *her*, under me.

I press my weight into her, leaning us against the car. Not fast. Not hungry. Not like normal—but slow—because she tastes so damn good, and I don't want it to stop.

In fact, I'm not sure I *can* stop with how good this feels. Like crazy good. Like better than running or breathing. I press my hip into her and she moans softly, and holy shit, I want to take her into my car right now.

But I can't.

I fucked that up already, which is why none of this makes sense.

I nibble on her bottom lip and I don't stop kissing her. I should. I *really* should. This is going to be a mistake and not just because of my car. I shouldn't want this so much. And I don't know why I do.

I feel drunk. But not the bad kind of drunk that numbs everything. It's the good kind. The kind where I don't want to be anywhere but right here, right now, and the world could end and I wouldn't care. And it seems stupid to have spent so much time being numb, when I could feel like this.

I should stop kissing her.

I really should.

But I don't.

# Marion

Kurt's mouth is warm and soft and nothing like when we were in his car. The curve of the SUV behind me is cold, perfect with the heat of him against me. My mouth responds to his, listening to this melody blooming, his music in my ears. And I know he's sharing something with me. This song. This secret.

The music turns bold and I pull him close till our lips are snared between harmonies and breath. My hands buzz, running over the velvet of his chest, and I'm not sure if that's his heart, beating, or the music, beating, or me—

My fingers curl around the collar of him, pulling him closer, and I'm overwhelmed with the almostness of him. Drifting. Barely there. His fingers tease, like those guitar strings thrumming, and I want him. This. This power clenching in me, hot and damp. His breath on my chin, and my throat, and—

Hands.

Like the tide, it rips the current.

Hands. Kurt's hands.

And my hair.

I pull back, refusing to let that earthquake surface again. Not allowing it out and up. Not when his kiss is so kind, and this is so—

Hands.

Kurt presses against me. Hips and hard and I can't breathe. I turn my head to the side so he'll stop kissing me, and those two guitars ring in my ears. My mouth buzzes, and I'm dizzy from this heat. His breath fans against my neck, his pants coming in short hot bursts—like orange buds bobbing in and out of the stream.

I don't want this to be about—

He steps away from me and the separation of him, the weight of him—off of me—makes my whole body ache with the suddenness of it.

The weightlessness of it.

"Marion, I, I—" He looks at me with that same fear from the ridge, like all this is broken. And I'm desperate to tell him it's not like that.

"Kurt, it's . . . It's—"

But it *is* like that. It *is* creek water and cars and *still* wanting the nearness of him.

I pull out the earbuds, needing the silence. I coil the wires into the shape of a small white nest, cradled in my palm, and that song, this moment, it all seems too precious and rare.

I give it back to him.

"The guitar, that music . . . ," I say, placing the cord in his hands. "Was that you?"

He nods, his fingertips curling over the wires, and I want to ask him about the second guitar. Who it was and why it sang so hauntingly. But I brush a strand of hair out of his face instead, allowing my fingers to land at the edge of his neck.

"It was beautiful."

He nods, stuffing the player in his pocket, and I miss the weight of his lips. My thumb grazes the line of his chin. Barely a touch. Barely anything.

He looks up. Tenderly. And I hate how much it scares me.

nine

# Marion

**Orange tea warms my cup. Sunrise peeks through** the mist covering the backyard oak and I'm not sure why I ever stopped climbing that tree. Dad opens the porch door and sits beside me, his own cup scented with orange steam.

"Morning," he says, glancing at the sequin shoes left on the bottom step. The soles edged in brown, dirty from the grass behind the pool house. Dad doesn't ask where I was last night or who I've been kissing.

Am I different now, because of that kiss? Does it make me more visible?

Dad stirs his tea, pinching the paper square attached to the string, and I want to ask him about boys. Am I allowed to bring up sequins and kisses? Water and skin?

One year after the barbecue, Dad and I stood on this porch lighting sparklers. Mine flamed gold against the purple sky, and the embers nicked my wrist as he lit the tip of his from mine. We stared at the looming oak, our sparklers burning down the metal straws toward our fingertips, like an hourglass counting the sand.

"I'm sorry I had to work today," he said, nodding to the burned hamburger on my paper plate. "I know we usually spend the Fourth of July together. . . ." He leaned against the porch railing and dangled his sparkler over his cup of apple juice. "You should have gone to Lilith's. You didn't have to stay here all day."

I moved my fingers closer to the sparkler's needles of heat.

"It's fine," I said.

"Next year go to Lilith's," he said. "You should be out having fun with your friends."

There was a sizzle, and he dropped his sparkler in his juice, drowning out the gold.

Dad blows on his tea before sipping it, careful not to burn his lip, careful to only look at me from the edge of his eye, where I'm allowed to exist, in his periphery.

I imagine myself saying, "I met a boy," but the dawn is thin, the light hardly strong enough to cross this distance between us. If I had a mother, she'd ask me about this. Wouldn't she? She'd care where I'd been. She'd know by instinct about the moths in my stomach, and the lingering salt of a kiss. She'd know what to do with the mud and how to clean those sequin shoes so they sparkled again. He sips his tea and I want to scream at him for thinking this is a conversation.

"Lilith called," Dad says, nodding to the landline in the kitchen. "She left you a bunch of messages, and mentioned your cell was off."

"This morning?" I ask.

"No." The steam stirs as he shakes his head. "Last night." He eyes my muddy shoes.

A woodpecker hammers the oak tree, poking out holes and fishing for bugs. Slurping down its wormy breakfast of mud. I can't swallow. I wait for him to say something. To ask.

"You should call her back," he says, standing up and pouring his tea over the railing. "And please charge your battery. I want to know your cell phone works in case there's ever an emergency."

"An emergency?" I press hot ceramic to my lip.

"You never know," he says.

And I agree with that. You never ever know.

# Kurt

**I pull out my guitar and the weight of it feels good.** I lean against my bed and play one single chord. The sound fills the whole damn room. Loud sound. Possible sound.

The quiet settles back in and I remember being eleven and Mom's footsteps padding into this room. Strappy thrift-store sandals hung from her hand as she stumbled down beside me smelling hot with eagle fire.

"You gotta put your hand like this," Mom said, taking my guitar and showing me where my fingers should be bent. A run split her stockings and a scratch of blood was dried where the hole began. I think she'd been at an open mic night at the pub. She'd gotten into the habit of going to those events when there weren't paying gigs to play at.

She held my guitar tight, like it was the only thing holding gravity in place, as if letting go meant there'd be nowhere left to land. She hit the strings and played nothing in particular. Chords, a string of noise, riffing her way through the morning till my little room of space opened up and sang.

She stank of beer and stopped abruptly midsong. She wrapped her arms around me and put the guitar in my hands. Showed me where my fingers went.

"Okay, now you," she said, holding my fingers down. "You gotta learn this, Kurt. You gotta know how to play so you got something to hold on to. Got that? This is your anchor, when all the rest is shit."

I didn't know what was shit exactly, or if that was the booze talking.

"There's always music. Don't forget that. Now play me something."

"I'm no good," I said, but she covered my fingers with her hands. Breathing hard against my neck and trying to be patient. She showed me the chords. Again. Again. Then told me to strum.

"That's it," she said. Nodding her head. Eagle on her breath. Me in her lap. "Just like that. Keep at it. It don't matter if it's no good. It's just got to be real. Hear me? Whatever's in you. Play that. Even if you don't got the notes yet. You'll find them."

She leaned back and stroked my head. Her short fingernails massaged my skull as stubby fingers swept through my hair. Eagle breath kissing my head.

I tried. I played what I could, awkward, and plucked half-wrong. But she kept whispering, "Good, that's it. You got it. There ain't no note that's bad. What you're playing, right now, this is the most beautiful song."

It wasn't a song. It was messy sound. Any sound. Filling my room so whatever she was chasing away had no space to come in. Her body started to shake behind me and I knew she was crying. She sniffed hard, rocking me with her sobs, and half humming as she stroked my hair. I played her a song, and somewhere in the middle of those awkward notes she told me that I was an angel. That God had sent me right on down from heaven to save her. And then her voice got strong as she wrapped her arms around me and she held me so tight I couldn't breathe.

"You're the one thing keeping me here, Kurt," she said, holding me. The weight of her arm was pinning me, and I could only play one chord, over and over. It filled the whole room. "You're the one thing keeping me here. The *one* thing."

But there's a box in the ground now, telling me different. There's a box in the ground filled with whatever's left of her. Maybe nothing. It was a closed casket. Maybe nothing is all she felt I deserved to have.

# Marion

Lilith sits across from me at the Firehouse coffee shop. Her eyes dart through the ugly wall art as she nips her brownie.

"Is that supposed to be a sunflower?" she says. "I mean, do they let anyone show artwork in here? Two hundred bucks for that piece of crap!"

I cup both sides of my porcelain mug as she reapplies her lip gloss and pretends to play with her phone. She's deliberately avoiding the topic of last night. Yes, she's taken me to every party I've ever been to, and I should have returned the favor, but . . . How would I explain it? The invitation? Kurt?

"So, there was this party last night . . ." I venture. "At—"

"Carrie's house," she interrupts. "Yeah, I know."

She grabs a handful of sugar packets and tears them open, dumping them in her drink. I count six packets before she tosses the rest aside and takes a sip without stirring.

"Look, I didn't know if I could invite—"

"I thought this was supposed to be our best year ever," she interrupts again. "Remember? You and me."

"Yeah, I know . . ."

"So?" She stares at me and I don't know how to tell her that I wanted this for myself. That I needed the space. That this is one of those invisible places I'm not ready to show her.

"You're right, I should have . . ." But then I think of that kiss and Kurt, and I don't want to apologize for making room for that. I roll my shoulders and try again. "I kissed Kurt," I say, taking a sip of my drink and hoping that will satiate her.

Lilith doesn't react and coffee burns my tongue.

She's supposed to be excited about this. Wasn't that the whole point of her pushing me to lose my virginity? So we could talk about these things?

I drag my spoon across the table and punch my foam. "I like him," I admit. But all I get is red fingernails wrapped around porcelain. "Or—" I backpedal. "Maybe I got caught up in . . . Maybe it's nothing."

"Don't do that," she says, putting down her drink. "You're allowed to like him."

My cup rattles against the saucer and I realize I *want* her permission. That telling her I kissed Kurt is a notch on my bedpost that I've been waiting to tell her I have. Thinking it might bring us closer, and make me more like her.

Only, I really do like him.

Lilith pulls my hand away from the rattling mug and flattens my palm against hers. It's soft and soothing.

"It's good that you like him," she says, tracing the lines of my palm like a fortune-teller, her fingers swirling. Waking the skin. Our eyes meet and her gaze is kind. I *need* this part of her. I need someone I can trust with this. "What was it like?" she asks, fingers tracing the belly of my wrist. "To kiss *the* Kurt Medford."

"Soft," I whisper, trying to be brave and share this with her.

"Did you like it?" A machine hisses beside us, exhaling froth and steam.

I nod.

"What did he taste like?"

"Salt," I whisper. "And skin."

I close my eyes and hear the music. Hear the guitar. His, and then that second one laying in on top of the first.

"Did you want to touch him?"

Lilith's fingertips flutter like the wings of a firefly. Yawning open. Beating in. And in my mind I see her in the firefly field with that boy on top of her. Suddenly her hands on me feel too daring.

"Lie with him? Open your le—"

I pull away and her hand smacks against the table, her fingers curling up like the legs of a bug.

"What?" She looks at me sharply.

My eyes jet through the coffee shop, embarrassed that someone might be watching. Not sure what kind of voyeuristic stunt Lilith is pulling. There are things we don't talk about and things we *shouldn't* talk about.

"What are you doing?" I pull my arms back, and she shakes her head.

"Nothing," she says defensively. "I do that shit all the time. When did touching you become a thing?"

I stare at her, realizing how much she doesn't know me. How much she'll never know about me. How the space we don't talk about defines us.

"You weren't just *friendly* touching me." I try to keep my voice down. "You were *touching* me."

This weird smile crawls over Lilith, and suddenly I feel manipulated. Everything seems heightened somehow, that kiss in front of Abe, the one when we were young, every time she's touched my hair.

"Seriously?" she says, her eyes becoming dark slits. "You've been more than happy to let me be your surrogate boyfriend for the last four years. And what, now that you've actually kissed a boy, it's a problem?"

"You've been my surrogate *what*?"

"Get over yourself, Marion! You think the way I touch you is something normal friends do?"

Cold reeds though me, and this feels like a trap.

"We've been friends for—"

"Forever. Yeah, I know," she says. "Why do you think I keep pushing this whole virginity thing? Because you're in desperate need of affection."

"What are you talking about?"

She looks at me boldly. "You *like* the way I touch you."

"What?"

She shakes her head, a miffed laugh escaping from her throat. "Go ahead and deny it, Marion, like you deny everything. Be my guest. But don't for a second pretend that you didn't like it."

"Are you a lesbian or something?" I ask, and she shakes her head calmly.

"No, but maybe *you* are."

"What?" I cough, my head buzzing. She isn't actually saying this right now, is she? I grip my coffee mug, and hot liquid spills onto my fingers.

"Or maybe you're not," Lilith says, raising her hands defensively. "All I know is nobody touches you, Marion. Nobody but me. I'm the only person *you let* do that." She lowers her voice. "Look, touching isn't an issue for me. But it *is* for you. Why else would you break up with Abe? You two were perfect for each other. If you wanted a nice, innocent romance, you could have had it, but you kicked him to the curb. Why do you think you did that?"

"I, I . . ." My brain is spinning. "I wasn't ready."

"Which is exactly why I do it, Marion. For *you*. So you can figure out how to *be* ready. Only it's not some kinky sex thing for me, okay?" Her eyebrows pinch and she looks at me thoughtfully. "Though, it might be for you."

"Kinky what?"

"It turns you on."

"No, it doesn't!" I look around sharply. No one's looking at us, but it feels like we're under a microscope. "That doesn't make any sense." I lean in to whisper. "Why would you do that?"

"Because you *need* to be touched, Marion. We all do. I thought if you realized you *could* be turned on, you would go out and get it from a guy or whomever . . ."

"I'm not into girls."

"Fine, you're not into girls. I don't care. The point is, eventually you've got to lose your virginity and get this from someone who isn't me."

"I'm not like you, Lilith!"

"You mean someone who can actually deal with her own sexuality? Yeah, I know that."

I glare at her, furious.

"What were you doing just now?" I demand. "Asking me about Kurt?"

Her lips stretch tight like she can't believe she has to keep explaining this to me. "You want him, don't you? You can tell me you don't all you want, but your skin, your body, it wants him. Doesn't it?"

I can't breathe. I feel like she's thrown me inside my mason jar with the dead bugs and screwed the lid. Tight and suffocating.

"That desire is *in you!*"

"You kissed me in front of Abe and those—"

"Because that gets boys hot, Marion. It got you hot too, but not because you were kissing me. Because you want to be kissing Abe."

That isn't true! Only, it is. I *did* want to be kissing Abe. I'm so confused and I don't know what to make of any of this.

"That's fucked-up," I say finally.

"Yeah, it is." She looks at me plainly.

"You're—"

"Oh no." She cuts me off before I can blame her again. "It takes two." She purses her lips, but then her gaze softens. "Look, I understand that you don't have anyone else. And as fucked-up as you may think it is, I *want* someone else to touch you. I want you to know how good that can be. I was just trying to be someone you could explore with until you figured out whatever it is you need to figure out."

"I didn't need you to—"

"You did." She pushes her chair back to stand up. "You do."

The room feels like it's full of steam and I'm drowning in dead bugs and foam. Lilith grabs her coat and pushes away her chair.

"If you don't want to be touched anymore, fine," she says. "If you think this"—she gestures to the table and my hands—"crossed some kind of line, fine. You just had to say so."

I stare at her, and this whole conversation feels too loud. It's too public and exposed. I'm furious at her. Furious that she thinks this is about me. Coffee spills onto my napkin, the brown spreading over the white, bleeding.

"I can't believe—"

"Don't," she interrupts, and I clench my hands into fists. "Just go home and . . ." She clutches her purse to her chest. "I don't know, just, figure out what you want. And figure out how to ask for it."

My mouth falls open, and I notice people staring.

"I'll see you at school," she says, walking to the exit. The door chimes as she goes, leaving a shrill echo with her disappearing footsteps.

I blot the spilled coffee on my tabletop with the soiled napkin. The effort is fruitless, but it's the only thing I can do. Everything Lilith has said makes my head spin. I didn't want her to touch me. Did I? Not like she implies I did. It was just something safe, part of the intimacy of knowing her my whole life. I didn't want more.

I never want more. I don't want anyone to touch me.

No one.

I swallow and know that isn't true. I wanted that kiss with Kurt. I like Lilith's touch when it's a comfort and she's not pushing boundaries. Only that's not what Lilith does. She likes to cross every boundary she can find, and *this* is another one of her games, manipulating everything. She didn't do this for me.

She doesn't do anything for me.

# ten

# Marion

It's Monday in chemistry, and there have been no calls, no contact, no Kurt. A few people looked at me funny in the halls, but I haven't seen Conner since the party either.

Maybe nobody knows.

Abe drops his notebook on the desk and slides in beside me.

"So, Kurt Medford, huh?"

Or everyone knows.

I tuck my hair behind my ear and shrug.

"Maybe," I say, but my hands are damp. The look of disapproval on his face makes my skin prickle. "Maybe it's nothing," I say, thrown off by how much I want him to believe that. Or maybe I'm trying to convince myself, so I don't feel so guilty about the way he's looking at me. Abe stifles a laugh, digging his knuckles into our desk. "Really," I continue, trying to shake the waver in my voice. "It's nothing."

"Oh, I *know* it's nothing." He looks at me hard. "The problem is I don't think *you* know it's nothing."

The air punches out of me. I look back at Kurt's empty chair and try to breathe. What does Abe know? He wasn't there.

"Why do you care?" I shoot back, trying to stay calm, and Abe scoffs. But then the confrontation shakes right out of him. He looks at me seriously and three soft curls fall onto his forehead. I reach out and tuck them behind his ear. I do it without thinking, caressing the dimple behind his ear. It's not until my fingers are in his hair that I realize how personal it is.

"That's why," he says, and my whole body goes hot.

He looks at me and my belly curls tight with realization. I *always* want to put my hands in Abe's hair. Always. It's not just that kiss under the apple tree, and all the other fragile beginnings. It's so much more than that. It's all the things that weren't about kissing. It's how we used to walk through the forest and make up stories about my mother, or have root-beer-drinking contests at the creamery. It's theater hopping on Sundays, and debating the evolutionary use of opposable thumbs, or lying in the grass with our legs intertwined, reading books and brushing those curls from his face. It's all the things that weren't the heat, that suddenly make the way he looks at me bloom with new fire. I've missed him. But it's more than missing. It's wanting in a way I was afraid to want him before. A way I wouldn't allow myself to think about him, and suddenly all I want is for him to unfold me.

And he knows that. He can see that on my face.

"I, uh . . ." My mouth goes dry and my fingertips feel hot on the back of his ear. Is it possible that despite two years of unspoken silence, we've *both* been waiting for a second chance? "Abe, I, I—"

A rush of whispers runs through the room and Kurt walks through the doorway. He heads in our direction and my hand drops from Abe's ear so fast I can't control the lack of grace in it. I wish I could hide my panic and not have Abe notice, but Abe notices everything. I wish I hadn't touched his hair. I wish I had more control over the way my body reacts and I didn't see that look on Abe's face, forcing me to admit I have feelings for him.

Only Kurt—

He walks right past us.

And not for a second does he look at me.

Abe lets out a small laugh, like he expected nothing less from Kurt, and I don't want to believe it. I look away from both of them and stare at the shelves by the window, full of graduated cylinders and flasks. Glass things designed to take specific measurements, to catalog a chemical reaction, and measure the invisible.

Kurt flops down at his station behind me and stares up at the ceiling. Abe scowls at Kurt, who leans back in his chair, lifting the front legs from the ground. Tempting gravity.

Anger flushes through me at the fact that Kurt's once again ignoring me. Kurt kissed me and that means something. He can't just hide it under his tongue and forget it. Kisses have effects. They're reagents. They change the whole body of a solution. I won't pretend it didn't happen.

I stand, feeling as uncertain as those legs on which Kurt balances. I feel Abe watching me and I have to push aside whatever I feel about him. The guilt and confusion. I have to face Kurt.

I walk up to him and his gravity shifts.

"Hey," I say, and a split second of panic flies through him. He falls forward, the legs of his chair slamming down.

"Um, hi." He rights himself, brushing down his shirt like he's actually embarrassed. His eyes flick to Abe and something territorial darkens his gaze. Light hangs on his shoulders and my skin remembers the weight of him, against me on that car, and what wakes inside. He's seen and touched so much of me, yet there's always this awkwardness between us.

"So . . . ," I start, hating the quiver in my voice and that this is so public. I hate that Abe is watching, and that there are others, and we're at school. "Do, um . . ."

Heat flushes my ears and I don't know why he does this. Stares at me with those quiet eyes and says nothing, like this is a game. Yet at the same time his look is always mixed with softness, like he's looking for something else. I tuck my hair back with a nervous finger and the bell rings, loudness breaking in, and he clenches his hands like it's the end of a game and the buzzer has gone off.

"Coffee?" he says quickly, and I don't know if I want to cry or scream. Because there's no way I'm going back up to that ridge. I must have been wrong about that kiss, and him sharing his music, and us being—

He grabs my hand.

"No, for real this time," he says, his thumb rubbing my fingers softly. "No, like actual coffee."

Kurt walks out of the gym after practice and his hair is wet from showering. I get up from the curb where I've been waiting and smell soap on him. He looks me over, checking me out, only it's not leering or even sexy. Just a look.

He's unreadable. But somehow unreadable doesn't strike me as unsafe.

I want to kiss him. The cold and the smell of soap have me feeling bold, but I don't know the rules. What does that kiss at Carrie's party make us?

The gym door clangs open and a group of Kurt's teammates come out the door. Laughter cuts the quiet and I see Conner and Tommy look in our direction.

"Do you have a car?" Kurt asks, running a hand through his hair, and I'm thankful he's asking about *my* car and not his.

"Yeah," I say, nodding to where it's parked and leading the way.

Kurt raises a hand to his teammates and their whistles shoot across the parking lot. He flips them off.

"Golden!" The word rings out and I know it's Conner.

I'm certain he said the word "Golden," but I hear *Goldie* in the back of my mind. It curls my stomach with the smell of barbecue and beach peas.

I turn. "Are you sure we should—"

But Kurt's right behind, and we're so close he smacks right into me.

"Shit!" He twists to the left, but our chests connect. I try to catch my balance, but we trip. There's a jumble of arms, and—*smack!*—my elbow cracks against something hard.

I stumble back to see Kurt clutching his chin.

"Oh no! Did I—?"

He grits his teeth together, biting back a surge of pain. I reach out to help, but he steps to the side, holding a hand up that means he needs a minute.

"I'm sorry," I say, giving him the space, and he turns away to spit blood on the asphalt. "Oh God!"

"It's fine," he says, spitting again and wiping his mouth with a sleeve.

"No, it's—"

"Really, I'm fine," he repeats, swallowing with what looks like considerable effort. I don't believe him for a second. "Taylor." His eyes lock on me and I think he's going to tell me to forget coffee. Forget all of this. But then he breaks into a smile, and his teeth are laced pink with blood. "I knew you were trouble."

# Kurt

The Firehouse is crowded, packed with people from school. There are a couple guys from the team who nod when I enter, but I pretend not to see them.

The place is like a cage. Brick walls. Fire poles. Too many chairs.

"What do you want?" Marion asks, and I look at the chalkboard covered with eight hundred menu items.

People stare. People definitely saw us at the party. I've heard the rumors. And the swimming thing is getting around too.

"Coffee, black," I say to the girl behind the counter, and Marion orders some fancy soy double who-knows-what. I taste blood in my mouth.

"That's seven fifty," the coffee girl says, and I nudge Marion.

"Don't you think you should pay for this after busting my teeth?" I joke, but she doesn't get it.

"Sure," she says, pulling out her wallet.

"I'm kidding," I say, nodding to her cash, but she stands there with her wallet open. "Put that away. I got this." I throw a ten on the counter, swallowing back the pink in my mouth. Damn coffee's expensive.

"Thanks," she says, fiddling with her purse and grabbing too many napkins from the counter. I move to put my hand on the back of her neck, to get her to relax, but the guys from the team are watching us. My hand stops halfway between her and me, hanging there like a useless slab of meat.

"Sir? Your change?"

I swing my hand to the coffee girl like it's what I meant to do in the first place, and Marion looks at me funny. I shove the change in my pocket, grab our drinks, and turn to the room.

"Uh . . ." There are no empty tables. "Let's go outside."

"In the back." Marion points to a table crammed in a corner and walks toward it. I pass Hector, from the team, as I follow her, and he gives me a nod. I roll my eyes. He winks with a knowing grin, like he gets it. Coffee first. Fun second. Only that's not how *this* is going to work. And I hate that Hector looks at Marion and thinks it is.

The chairs suck. They're made of cheap metal rods, bent funny and poking in every direction. I sit across from Marion, with everyone behind us, and shift my weight. Only everything's too close and I elbow the dude at the table beside me.

"Watch it!" He shoots me a dirty look.

"Sorry, man," I say, trying to give him some space, but there isn't any to give.

"It's not normally this crowded," Marion says, glancing at the guy. Her eyes fall to her coffee like that might be a complete lie. Red flushes over her neck and I think about how I wouldn't have been able to see that when we were swimming.

"You come here a lot?" I ask, and she hugs her mug close.

"Yeah, with Lilith mostly."

I nod and sip my drink. It tastes like dirt.

She busies herself by pouring sugar into her cup and I try to ignore the doo-wop fifties music coming out of the speakers. Why doesn't anyone play good music anymore? At least jump forward a decade or two and play some Emmylou Harris or Leonard Cohen. I catch her stealing a glance over my shoulder, but refuse to look and see how many of them are watching.

I consider leaving, which is stupid. I want to see her. Just not *here*.

There's light in her hair and I think about her listening to Mom and me. Really listening. That dimple on her cheek, pinching, and then her lips. I've never played that song for anyone. Not even Conner. And the only people who'd remember it are Dad and Josie.

I catch red flushing over Marion's ears again and I know she's waiting for me to say something. I'm not *trying* to make her feel uncomfortable. I just—

I don't do this.

"So, uh . . ." She picks at the edge of her napkin.

"Yeah?"

She sorta smiles, and maybe I'm too eager for her to say something. Her eyes flick over my shoulder again and I gulp down coffee.

"When's your next game?" Little bits of napkin cover the table.

"Thursday," I mumble, and she smiles like that was the most fascinating thing I could have said. Which is exactly why I don't do this.

"You like soccer?"

"I like to run."

"Oh . . ." She squints, and I can tell she's overanalyzing this. "You don't like the passing and shooting parts?"

"No, I like that too, I just—" A giggle comes from behind us and I look back to see—fuck—everyone *is* watching us. "I like the air," I say, trying to ignore them. "The adrenaline. It makes me focus, makes me . . ." I stop. Drops of coffee have fallen from my cup. They pool like brown scabs on the tabletop. Like Josie's scabs.

"Makes you what?" she prompts, but I don't know what she wants me to tell her.

Suddenly talking about soccer seems unimportant, and I want my guitar, and real air. I don't want the coffee machine grinding and everyone staring, and this brick-wall fire-pole bullshit.

I push out my chair.

"Hey, wait, are you—" She stops midsentence as I stand. Clearly, I am.

"Look, I've got—" I start, but I don't know how to finish that. I could lie to her, but I don't want to. "I just—"

I look around the room. It's only people from school. Like at a party. But all I want is the door.

"I get it," Marion says, but her tone isn't snarky. Not like how Vanessa would say it if she realized I was going to bail. Marion says it calm, like this is something she understands, and she's okay with it. She pushes her coffee away and nods to the door, leading the way. I'm so thrown, I just follow her.

Outside, I can breathe again. The air is like an icicle stabbing my lungs. But it makes everything sharper.

"It's October," Marion says. "It's going to be really cold."

I nod, thinking she means the air, but after a few breaths, I realize that doesn't make sense.

"What?" I look at her confused.

She walks to her car and the air is so crisp everything is in hypersharp focus. And yet I swear she motions for me to get in and says—

"You can swim, right?"

# Marion

My bare feet dig into the sand and a chill crawls up my calves. Kurt and I have both rolled up our jeans to below the knee, and I'm cold just looking at the Atlantic. The sun is setting behind us and the purple of evening has begun to shade the horizon.

The water is calm, but the air is fierce, tossing hair across my face. I know swimming in the lake was cold, but swimming in the ocean will be fire. Even summer water is freezing. We're north of the Cape, which sends the tropical currents out to sea. Our water comes from the Arctic.

I'm not sure what I was thinking. I only know that I saw Kurt's face in that coffee shop, ready to bolt, and this all started by running into the water. So perhaps all we need to do is run on in—again.

Kurt pulls off his shirt and goose bumps ripple over him.

"Jesus," he curses, wrapping his arms over his chest. I take in the skin of him, shivering beside me. "You really want to do this?"

"Yeah." I nod. "But I'm not taking off my shirt."

He laughs. "That's fine."

I dig my feet into the sand and run, knowing if I don't do it now I'll lose my nerve. I head for the ocean, full speed, with wind whooping in my ears. There's a loud whistle and maybe a cackle of laughter behind me. But as soon as I hear it, Kurt's running beside me. Fast enough to catch up. Fast enough to pass.

He matches my pace.

Sand kicks up behind us and four seagulls shriek, taking to the air. We pound past their flapping wings and Kurt puts his arms above his head like he's about to cross a finish line. We both yell as the adrenaline surges up from our feet, and we take our first step into the icy-cold water.

Then our second—

And our third—

And leap.

It's a shock—the water.

It's how I imagine dying, with black at my temples and ice in my skin, and the dark current dragging me from the light. Or maybe it's like being born. The type of thing you can only come into screaming. Where every part of you is suddenly, painfully—

Alive.

# Kurt

**We run out of the water and all of me is pain.**

The sky blazes red and Marion shivers with her whole body. She's three steps to my right. Hair snaked over her face. Eyes wild with salt and sting. It makes me laugh.

Wind tears past us and I know we can't stay out in this chill. But the rush, the clarity, makes the pain seem inconsequential.

*This* must be what Mom drank to find.

Marion cuts across the sand and steps in front of me. She backpedals before stopping and there's boldness in her eyes. Her clothes are wet and I can't think straight.

I pull her against me and her mouth tastes like salt. Her hands snake over my chest and I groan, wanting her. She shivers, pulling me close, and I know I have to get her off this beach. There's no way I'm laying her down in the sand.

I pick her up, and her jean-soaked legs wrap around my waist. Somehow, I make it to her car and I lay her down in the backseat. She moans, body arching, and her mouth finds mine. She feels so small in my arms. Delicate, in a way that makes me not want this to go too fast. But she reaches inside my pants.

I press into her and begin unbuckling. Her jeans are so wet they're hard to remove. Our feet scraping against each other and covered in sand.

I pull back and look at her. Blond hair is splayed over the seat cushion, wet and dark as seaweed. She looks straight at me, her eyes dark, and sits up. She pulls her shirt up over her head and leans forward, kissing me lightly.

She unhooks her bra and lies back, under me.

We've been like this before.

In my car.

"Are you—" I start, but she pulls me into a kiss, peeling down my pants.

I throb and want—

But I shouldn't.

Not with *this girl*. Not after the disaster in my car, with her shaking. And no matter how much I want to pretend this doesn't mean anything, I already know that it does. And fuck, I hate that I want it more because it does.

Her hands are all over me and her body seems to want this. Mine certainly does. And this would already be done if—

I pull back and find my coat. It's wedged between the armrest and the floor. I rummage through the pockets for a condom. I find one inside the first sleeve, but pretend to look in all the other pockets—just in case she needs a minute, to decide, or . . .

I look back and she's shivering. Instinct puts my mouth on hers again, and that tremble becomes a quaking in both of us.

I want this.

I want this in a way I didn't know I could want it.

I put my lips to her ear because I have to ask.

"Are you sure you want to do this?" I say.

"Yes," she says, and her hands dig into my back when I enter her. Her throat releases a sharp gasp of breath, and even though I knew she hadn't done this before, it still surprises me.

I slow and move to the sound of the ocean.

I slow till all I hear is the crest of her breath.

# Marion

**Kurt's body is an ocean.**

He feels too good and salt raw and is made of sweat and sliding. My body reacts without permission, stretching at his tenderness as his hips dip.

Rose hips.

In and out of the stream.

And there's too much tenderness. His hands make everything quiver, down to the deep. Down to the dark.

I need this to go faster. Faster, where the way we fit is friction and heat, and none of this tenderness can touch me. Not when I can hear the water—in my ears, in my head—as big as the whole Atlantic. As small as rose hips under the stream.

I bite his shoulder to drive away the smell of meat and gravy.

I bite his shoulder because I don't want to admit this feels good, even though it comes with water and mud.

I dig my fingers into his shoulders because I don't know

how this can possibly be both. Both vulnerable and dark. Both fear and heat. Both wanting him and fearing him and feeling the creek water surface—

Climbing up over my ankles—

Squishing down between my toes.

He holds me after.

We lie in the back of my car, limbs scrunched against each other, wet jeans bunched at our ankles. The arches of my feet press into the damp of his pants and the sky has gone dark.

We don't really fit in this space.

After what seems like too long, I sit up and wriggle back into my jeans. There's sand all over my legs, caught between the skin and fabric, where it will just have to stay.

I open the side door and climb out, letting him get cleaned up without me.

It hurts down there.

Not a horrific pain. Not like I'd imagined it from what Lilith said. More like a dull ache, deep inside.

The water is black now and it's hard to see the line that separates the ocean from the sky. The horizon's completely dissolved. All I know for sure is that we've passed over a threshold and all I can hear are waves rolling over in the dark.

"Hey," he says, behind me, and there are footsteps before his hand brushes my arm.

It's gentle. And yet I fear what gentleness brings.

"Is everything all right?" he asks.

I turn in the dark and find his cheek, kissing the ridge of his stubble, which smells of salt. It's hard to see, but being this close to him, I can tell he's shirtless.

I put two fingers on his shoulder, running them over the smoothness of his muscle. It's not done with desire, but as a question. Like this is a new way in which I'm allowed to ask.

"I took it off before we went in the water," he says, nodding to the beach swallowed in black.

"Right." I remove my hand. "Should we look for—"

"I'll wear my coat," he says, and I'm grateful.

"Are you hungry?" I ask, heading for the car, and I hear him mumble something that sounds like agreement. We both get in the Nissan and I steer us back to town. My stomach grumbles, but I know I won't eat a thing. There's no way I could keep anything down.

# eleven

# Kurt

I expect Marion to take us to a fast food joint. Instead we wind up a hill and stop in front of a large colonial house.

Her home.

"Um . . ." I press my hands into my jeans. "Are your parents here?"

She looks at a car in the driveway, hidden under a cover. Which means it's expensive.

"My dad works in the city," she says, killing the ignition. "He's never home till late."

The sun is set. It seems pretty late to me. "There's this fry place by KFC," I start, but she's already getting out. "Shouldn't we get my car? Or dry clothes?"

"Don't worry about it." She heads for a side door. "I'm sure you'll fit into something of my dad's."

Her dad's!

I zip up my jacket and get out of the car, my pants wet and incriminating.

Her house is fancy on the inside. All wood beams and stainless steel. It looks like a museum. I listen for her parents. Or siblings. Or anyone. But everything's all quiet and just *so*.

She leads me upstairs, which is at least lived in, and her hair hangs wet over her shoulders. I like her hair wet like that. It's private. More relaxed. Not like the girl I see at school trying to be perfect.

She stops in the doorway of what must be her father's bedroom and I see where that perfection comes from. Everything in the room is straight lines and silver knobs. There's even a pair of socks folded at the end of the bed. Just breathing makes me think I'm disturbing it.

"Your dad gonna be okay with this?" I ask as she rummages through the dresser. "You don't have a brother or . . . ?"

"I'm an only child," she says, pulling out a dry shirt, then going through the next drawer.

I look at the family photos on the wall. All the pictures are of Marion and a man with trimmed black hair, who must be her father. There's no one else.

"Where's your mom?" I say without thinking, and she hesitates before laying a pair of pants on top of the shirt.

"Europe," she says, walking to the photos and biting a nail. "Spain, I think. I don't really know anymore. I haven't seen her since I was three."

"Ever?"

She shrugs. "Yeah, ever."

It's weird how calm she is about this. "You mean she could be dead, and you wouldn't even know?" She nods and looks at a photo of her father. "And that doesn't piss you off?"

She adjusts the frame, hanging it straight.

"You can't miss what you don't know," she says, walking back to the dresser. She runs her hand against the wallpaper as she goes, her finger finding a groove in the wall. Her nail digs into the lip where the paper is torn like she's trying to chip away the paint. Only, I don't think she realizes she's doing it.

"That's bullshit," I say, and she turns sharply. "Didn't you ever wonder what it was like to have a mom? I mean, you *have* a mom out there somewhere. Mine's fucking dead."

She stares at me and doesn't move.

I adjust the zipper on my coat, suddenly hot. Afraid of what I just admitted, and how it came out so shitty.

"Look, I didn't mean to lay that on you," I say. "It's none of my business, I—"

"Of course I wonder what it's like to have a mom," she says quietly, walking back to me. She brushes wet hair from my face and leaves her fingers hovering at the edge of my cheek. "I guess . . ." Her eyes go distant, looking through me. "You can't stop someone from leaving you. I mean, I was three, it's not like I could do anything. If someone wants to leave behind their three-year-old, well . . ."

Her voice gets ragged and the sadness in her eyes guts me.

"Hey." I pull her to me, but she puts her hands on my chest, her elbows bent between us so I can't get close.

"You can't miss what doesn't want you," she says, looking down. "I mean, there are people who are *here*, people who—"

"Fuck that! Yes, you can," I say, maybe too forceful, and I hate how much this hurts in my chest. "Trust me, you can miss everything that doesn't want you."

I wrap her close and kiss her, letting that pain meld this space between us. Her arms find their way around me and our lips fuse like, maybe, if we just keep kissing, it will show us the way through this.

"I'm sorry about your mom," she whispers against my lips, and I kiss her words away, because this ache is too big. My fingers clutch the wet fabric of her shirt, then spread over her back to hold her against me.

"It would've been different," she says quietly, and it's more like we're hugging now, not wanting to let anything go. "If she was here and it wasn't just my dad . . ." She kisses me, breathless. "I mean . . . maybe she would have—"

But then she stops and grips me so hard I think she's trying to force together all the parts that are broken.

I kiss her. I kiss her because I don't know how else to make that pain go away. It isn't a lustful kiss. It's something else. Something sad. Something like music, that speaks when there aren't any words.

"Marion?" A male voice comes from behind us and

panic shoots through me. I pull away from her and the separation is staggering. We both feel it.

I fumble my way backward and look out the doorway.

"Excuse me?" There's a medium-sized man in a suit glaring at me in the hall. "Who are you?"

It's the man from the photos.

"Uh . . ." I step back and yank at the ends of my jacket as if the motion will hide the fact that I'm not wearing a shirt underneath.

God, from his angle it must look like I'm—

"Dad." Marion steps in front of me holding her father's clothes. Her shirt is still wet, and from behind, the fabric shows all the way through to her bra.

He isn't looking at her.

"This is Kurt," Marion says, sliding her arm around my waist, and I'm sure she's about to say the word "boyfriend," but instead she stares at her father without explaining why we're wet or standing in his bedroom with his clothes in her hand.

My pants stick to my thighs, itching with sand. He glares at me, but the silence is weird. Something passes between them, like she's waiting for him to ask what's going on. And she might actually *tell him*, if he did.

"Medford," I say, stepping out of Marion's grip. "Kurt Medford, sir." I extend him my hand. "I'm your daughter's, uh—friend."

He doesn't shake my hand.

"We were on the pier," I say, needing to explain this wet

thing. I drop the hand and jam it into my pocket. "We, uh—"

He totally wants to punch my face in.

"It was a stupid dare," Marion says, walking to my side. "You know Lilith."

For the first time he looks at her.

"Lean over the side, Mar-i-doodle," Marion says, pretending to talk in Lilith's voice. "See how far you can go." Marion laughs like she's actually remembering this. "And yeah, we fell in." She looks at me like it was something special and for a second I almost believe that's what happened. Though what *did* happen was—

"Where's Lilith?" he asks, searching me.

"At home," Marion explains. "We dropped her off at the bottom of the hill. Call her if you want." She holds up her father's clothes. "Is it okay if Kurt borrows these? He just needs to change and then I'll take him home."

"You don't have a car?" He scowls at me.

"We took mine," Marion says, and his eyes narrow.

"I don't need the clothes, sir," I say. "I'm fine in—"

"The bathroom is that way," he says sternly, nodding down the hall.

"Really, I don't—"

"Please, Mr. Medford, get changed!"

*Mr. Medford?* Damn, this isn't good! And from the way he looks at Marion, I think he'd do anything to get me out of here.

"Uh, yes, sir," I say, grabbing the clothes even though I

don't want to. I hesitate and check Marion. I don't want to leave her if this is going to blow up in her face.

"We'll just be a minute, Kurt," she says, looking at her father.

I nod and head for the bathroom, but a few steps down the hall I look back and a shiver crawls through me.

I think Marion wanted to get caught.

# Marion

I hear the door of the bathroom click shut and I wait to see what my father will say.

He stares at me, his eyes sad and stern, trying to decide what to do.

He swallows and doesn't move, and I wonder if he can smell Kurt on me. If sex has a stench that men can taste in the air. Like creek water and meat.

What would he do if he knew?

I stand my ground and dare him to put together what is staring him in the face.

It's not hard to see.

Me, in this wet shirt that clings to my chest.

Kurt, all muscle and soaked jeans, in that bathroom getting undressed.

"That boy," my father says finally. "That boy is just your friend?"

I almost laugh.

I want to say:

*"No, that boy is definitely not just my friend. That boy is the one I fantasize about before I go to bed. That boy is the one who took me down to the beach and opened my legs."*

I want to scream at him not to ignore this. I want him to be the parent I need and not treat this like my yellow skirt that was so easily kicked under the bed.

"Yes," I say. "He's just a friend."

My father nods, clutching his briefcase before walking past me into his room, which is straight and perfect and full of orderly things, simple pretty things that come from catalogs and make his life look a certain way. Our life.

"You know, Marion," he says, putting his briefcase on the bed and rubbing the latch like he might say more.

I feel far away. Like I'm on the other side of that stream but he's looking at the water instead of at me. He's left me alone on that log with that man.

"I trust you," he says.

Of course he does.

His eyes jet to the hall where Kurt might return at any moment and we both look at that empty doorway.

It's all negative space.

The purple sky is salted with stars. There aren't any street-lamps on the road, and without them everything is indigo shadow and pavement. Kurt sits in my passenger seat and I can't believe my father let me drive him back to school for his car. But that's the thing . . .

My father trusts me.

The smell of sweat rolls in from the backseat, and I hear the crash of water in my ears. Rolling waves, yearning, and all the things that are new to me. How softness can ache out the past I regret. How skin has a language made of quietness and breath. How Kurt's body is an ocean and it capsizes me.

I don't know if there's a surface or if I'm supposed to learn how to breathe underwater. I only know that there's an underness. A space below, where there's nothing but uncertainty, and I'm not sure who I am anymore.

I turn my wheels into the parking lot and I don't know what sleeping with Kurt makes me. For Lilith, sex is alchemy, gold power and hot. But as I pull the car to a stop and Kurt looks in my direction, I feel that hollow space and what has been lost. That single word that no longer defines me.

Virgin.

And I'm naked without it.

# Kurt

The entire parking lot is empty when Marion pulls into the school, and for a second I think I might sleep in my car tonight. I don't want to see Josie or Dad and have them ruin this. This day was like something outside of my life.

Something better.

I lean over and kiss Marion's ear. Her hair smells of salt water and I want to cut the headlights and take her into the backseat again. I slide my hand around her waist, but her body stiffens.

"Look . . ." She pulls back to face me. "I'll, uh . . . I'll see you at school." She gives me a quick peck on the lips, like a grandma, and nods to my car. I shift in her father's pants, hating that I put them on.

"Do you . . . ," I start, but there's sand on the dash.

Our sand.

I turn back and kiss her. Really kiss her. Her mouth opens for me and my hand slides up her neck. She tastes better than running. Better than air.

"Kurt." She breaks away and threads her fingers through mine. But only long enough to put my hand back in my lap.

"We could—"

"My dad," she interrupts. "I have to . . ."

She lets go of me and presses herself into the shadow by the door. Sand and cold fabric touch my ankle. I look down and it's my jeans wadded up on the floor. Stiff and half-wet.

"Right," I say, bending down and grabbing my pants.

I get out and she does a U-turn and speeds through the lot. I watch her brake lights through the trees.

Red driving away from me.

It unsettles me like I'm seeing Mom driving into the dark. Like there's something on the other side of this. Something she can't come back from.

My mom's eyes were angry that night, glaring at Josie shattering empty eagles into the trash.

The porch light was covered in moths and there was a gash on Mom's face. It was a thin slice below the eye, where her guitar string snapped and lashed hard.

"Kurt, move," Mom hissed, her breath wet with eagle fire as she stumbled on the bottom step and pushed past me.

"The store's not open," I said, running after her.

"At eight o'clock?" She turned to me with a fierce calm in her eyes, black as lake water. Her voice was smooth too, steady enough to mask her unsober. "You owe me." She jabbed a finger into my chest and nodded to the eagles

I'd dumped down the sink. "You're going to pay for every bottle."

"You can't drive!" I said as she marched for the truck.

"Every bottle," she hissed, waving me away.

I barreled my thirteen-year-old shoulder into her leg, taking her by surprise, and her keys clanged against the truck and dropped to the ground.

We both flung to the dirt like animals and I could hear Josie snickering from the porch. I wanted to scream at her, but I had to get the keys first.

My fingers hit metal and I squeezed, my fist tightening around gravel and sharp teeth. I stalked away from the truck, watching Mom still on her hands pawing at the ground, and Josie whistled, like I'd scored a point.

"You going to call Dad?" I yelled at Josie, but she didn't budge.

"Like he'd leave work."

Light flooded over us and I turned into the beam of her headlights in my eyes. How could—? "Silver Wings" filled my ears, coming from her radio, but then Merle Haggard was drowned out by a screech of tires as her truck sped out of the driveway.

Red taillights streaking through the trees.

I opened my hand to see dirt and rocks and a metal chain. It was a bracelet, full of charms that had felt like keys. But they weren't. It was nothing but a fistful of all the things I couldn't do to get her to stay. Just like Marion, speeding away though the dark. Like all I deserve is this. Like there's nothing left for me but red driving away.

Josie's on the couch when I get home. The TV's on, casting blue light over her body. She sits motionless. Like something inhuman. Like something dead.

I take a seat on the couch and I'm sure she can feel my weight beside her, but she doesn't look up. There's an empty bowl in her lap and a spoon in her hand—scraping the sides. Round and round.

There are black lesions on her neck and I don't want to imagine what she thought was inside her to pick those bloody. I follow her eye line and she's not looking at the TV. She stares at an empty patch of the wall, at nothing.

The smell of salt water makes me want to tell her about my day and Marion, but her eyes are sunk so deep in the black hole of her features that the television light can't find them.

"What happened to you?" I say, but it comes out raspy and small.

Her spoon stops moving.

I want to say more but it feels like I've caught her crying, like that night in the hall after Mom died, barking at me and making it clear how much no one needs me. Like I walked in on something I'm supposed to ignore. Something that needs no witness. Especially mine.

It shouldn't be as easy as it is to walk away from Josie and leave her in that empty room. Habit maybe. If you train yourself to look away enough times it becomes a reflex. Only I don't know why Marion is different. Why seeing her cry in my car was something I was allowed to look at. That vulnerability. Fighting to be seen in the middle of all the shit.

I climb onto my bed and think of the beach. How being with Marion makes me feel . . . I don't know, better. Not numb.

I pull out my guitar and play quietly. Not because I need an anchor, or something to hold on to, like Mom. But because I'm tired of the quiet. Because I want the sound, loud and full and possible.

twelve

# Marion

**I can't sleep.**

I lie in bed in the morning with this cavern inside me. A piece missing. The piece that knew how to be the virgin, but doesn't know how to not be one. I don't regret sleeping with Kurt, but somehow I thought I'd feel different—*be* different. That's all Lilith ever talked about. It's all anyone ever talks about. How sex is some kind of transformation into adulthood. How it makes you no longer a child.

But I don't feel grown up. I don't feel Lilith's fire.

All I feel is uncertainty and dark. I'm not even sure what I'm supposed to do when I see Kurt. What does yesterday make us? We aren't nothing, but I don't know that we're something, either. He doesn't know me. No one knows me. Not the invisible parts. And yesterday feels like one more phantom piece of skin.

I get dressed and drive to school early. There's a mist clinging to the leaves, hiding everything. I stand near the east entrance of school, watching the mountain as the fog yawns. It stretches thin with the wind, revealing a blush of maple orange beneath it. Only a moment later the clouds cover that whisper of gold like it never existed.

For a moment it feels like yesterday didn't happen. Or at least, it feels like I could pretend it didn't, and I could sweep it under the fog and go back to who I was before. I texted Lilith and told her to drive to school without me this morning, because I haven't figured out how to tell her. *If* I'm going to tell her.

I'd rather walk into those mountains, where the lips of the fog can eat me.

In the library I sit by the window and pull out my English homework. I can't see the soccer field from my angle, and I wonder if I should go and wait for Kurt. Am I supposed to wait for him before school now? I attempt to read, but my mind keeps drifting to Kurt and yesterday's ocean, of floods, and music, and this empty place inside of me.

"That book must be really good."

I startle and see Abe standing at the edge of my table.

"Oh, it's, uh . . ." I wave the book around, searching for words.

"Riveting, I can tell." His white shirt is pressed and curls hang in his eyes. "You haven't turned a page for about thirty minutes," he says, sliding onto my seat with me and taking my book. He smells like fabric softener and closes the novel without marking the page. "What's up, M? You're never at school this early."

I shake my head and look at the fog.

"What's wrong?" he asks, and I suddenly wonder if I *am* different. If I can't hide this. My eyes feel wet and I grit my teeth to keep it inside.

"I'm fine," I manage, and he doesn't push it. He leans his shoulder against mine and sits there like we're in the grass counting dandelion seeds caught in the sun. The pressure of his shoulder makes me want to unsnap each of his buttons and resnap them back up again. Run my finger over his collarbone. I don't know if it's Abe's collarbone I'm thinking of or Kurt's, just that I want the contact.

I shiver and he looks up.

Is this what Lilith meant? That need for contact. Touch. Like it could hold us together again? I shake myself, not wanting to accept anything Lilith's said, and unsure what to do with this burn in my skin. I can't tell if this heat is really for Abe or if I'm mixed up because of Kurt or if it's stupid hormones.

"Hey," Abe says quietly, keeping his weight on my shoulder but looking out the window. "Did I ever tell you about the first time I shot a gun?"

I pinch my eyebrows at him. "What? What does that have to do with anything?"

"Have you ever shot a gun?"

"No."

"It's freaky," he says, and I laugh a little, but he's serious about this. "I was eleven, and my dad took me to the practice range behind the police station. He wanted to teach me about guns so I'd be comfortable around them, since he's always got one on his belt when he's on duty. Plus there are three more in our house.

"But the second he pulls out that .22, I don't want to touch it. I hate it even more when he forces me to take it and I see how small my hand is holding it." Abe stretches out his fingers and starts massaging his palm. Like maybe he remembers holding the gun.

"I ask my father if it's loaded and *stupidly* I flip the gun over to look down the barrel. He rips it away from me so fast I think I'm a criminal he's disarming. 'Of course it's loaded!' he yells at me, and starts lecturing about how guns aren't toys, which I know, because he tells me every day of my life." Abe crunches his hand into a fist. "So he proceeds to show me the bullets, and where the safety is, and how I'm supposed to hold it with two hands and not one. And then he puts it back in my hand, points me at the target, and asks: 'Are you afraid of it?'

"'Are you afraid of it?'" he says again, tapping the bottom of his fist on the tabletop, each tap punctuating a word. "I'm holding this gun, and even with two hands it's *heavy.* It's nothing like the plastic water toys my friends and I used to run around the woods with. And I want to tell him I'm fine. I *want* to be comfortable with this the way he is. But it's loaded. It has real bullets in it. And as much as I don't want to disappoint him, I tell him the truth. 'Yes,' I say. 'It scares the shit out of me.' I swore and everything."

He smiles for a second, but it drops quickly. "And I'll never forget this: He looked at me with this stone-cold face and said, 'Good. If you're afraid of it then you'll respect it.'"

Abe looks at me, and my pinkie hooks itself in his. It's the slightest touch, but somehow it feels like the right thing to do in this moment.

"Did you shoot the gun?" I ask quietly, and he nods.

"Yeah. It felt like it was going to take my arm off." His pinkie rubs lightly against mine. "I was so rattled I wouldn't even pick up a water gun after that."

"Have you ever shot a gun again?"

He shakes his head no.

"Would you?"

"Not unless my life depended on it."

He leans on his elbows and looks at our pinkies hooked together.

"Why'd you tell me that story?" I ask, and when he looks at me I can feel the energy sparking between us.

"Because you're not the only one who's scared of something."

He's too close when he says that. The silver buttons on his shirt only inches away. I should be angry at him for knowing that and for pointing it out. But that's not what I feel. I feel this tug I don't understand and I'm thinking about buttons again. Undone. Redone.

He smiles, but I *can't* think about Abe this way. I've got Kurt. I *slept* with Kurt. Only, I wonder what it would have been like if yesterday had been with Abe. His curls tickle the edge of his eyebrow and I reach for my book to occupy my hands.

"You want to skip first period and go get coffee?" he asks, and I could burn up from the way he's watching me.

"Since when do you skip school?" I joke to cut the tension, and he shrugs, giving me his dashing smile.

"There's a first time for everything."

I flip open my book and try to find my place. I can't think about first times right now.

"I have to read this."

"Like you haven't read that book three times already," he quips, and my ears burn, loving that he knows that. Only, guilt crawls through my stomach and I look out the window, to the soccer field we can't see.

"I have a thing," I say.

"What thing?"

"Just a . . ." I tilt my weight into his arm, feeling his heat. Why do I want this now when I didn't two years ago? Why, when Kurt is out of sight, does it feel like all bets are off, and every look, every slight touch between Abe and me is heightened? Would things be different if it was Abe in that ocean? Would I be more comfortable with losing my virginity? Is it possible Abe doesn't wake the things that Kurt wakes in me?

"You stopped in the middle of your sentence," he says.

"No, I didn't."

"Yeah, you did." The corner of his lip turns up adorably and I want to blow dandelion seeds into his breath.

"Right." I force my eyes to the window. What am I supposed to do? "It's just there's this thing I said I would do."

"That's a lie."

Abe doesn't say that. It's a female voice.

I look up and Lilith is taking the seat across from us.

"There really *isn't* a thing," she says, leaning forward and tossing her hair to the side. The motion gives us a view down her shirt, which I'm sure was intentional. "She's read that book like eight times. Marion totally wants to skip school for coffee. She's just playing hard to get." I glare at her, but she smiles. "I keep telling her that playing hard to get is *soooo* eighteenth century of her. But hey, the girl's obsessed with Jane Austen."

"There's nothing wrong with a little modesty," Abe says, coming to my defense.

"Well, aren't you a regular Prince Charming." Lilith sits up and winks at him. "Just have her home before midnight, if you know what I mean." She wiggles her eyebrows suggestively and Abe goes red. "Oh, and quick tip, Marion's got this soft spot right behind her ear that drives her cra—"

"Lilith!"

She laughs and leans back in her chair. I hate that her hands know that spot and she's using it as ammunition. Abe's face flushes pink, and I can't help but notice how his eyes flick to my ear.

"You." I point to Lilith and then the library door. "Would you excuse us, Abe?"

I'm up and heading for the exit.

Lilith rises slowly and I look back to see her head tilt toward Abe, pointing out the spot behind her ear.

In the hall, I grip the drinking fountain and gulp down water. Lilith skips up to me in her cherry-red heels and I wipe my mouth and glare at her.

"What was that?" I say.

"You're welcome."

"Excuse me?"

"Mar-i-doodle!" Her eyes sparkle. "I'm not blind. *Something* is going on with Abe."

"*Nothing* is going on with Abe," I assert, but she laughs.

"Oh, I know better."

"Seriously, it's nothing."

"You keep using that word." Lilith swipes an imaginary sword through the air. "I don't think it means what you think it means."

"Thank you, Inigo Montoya," I snap.

"No, thank me after you have coffee." Her tone gets serious and she points to the library. Only, I can't trust her. Nothing she wants me to do is really for me. "That's right, you can thank me later for putting back into motion what *clearly* has been brewing between the two of you for the last two years."

I hate that she knows that. I hate that everything seems so freaking obvious to her.

"You know." She puts a hand on her hip. "I don't know what Kurt did to you. But I like it."

I almost smack her.

"I'm not having coffee," I growl.

"Whatever." Lilith shrugs. "Don't go." She nods to the door behind us. "All you have to do is go in there and tell Abe you're *not interested*."

Cold shoots through me.

"Easy peasy." She leans forward, brushing her lips along the base of my ear. "But you *are* interested, aren't you, Marion?"

"You don't know what you're talking about," I hiss, and Lilith laughs like she knows all the secrets of the world and I'm ridiculous ol' me. I'm furious, and glad I haven't told her about Kurt. That I haven't told her anything. "Why don't you leave me alone!"

"And miss all the fun?" She winks. "You underestimate me."

I roll my eyes and storm away, my head buzzing. I stalk back into the library, but when I see Abe, I know Lilith is right. I *am* interested.

But I can't be. I'm not allowed to be. Not with that boy who was in my backseat, touching parts of me no one has ever touched. I grab my book from the table and pick up my bag. Abe tries to catch my eye, but I deliberately don't let him.

"So, there really is this thing," I grumble, staring at his buttons.

"Okay."

His thumb taps against the tabletop.

"I'm sorry about Lilith." I gesture to the door. "She's mad at me about this, well, this other thing. Just something that—" I grip the strap of my bag. "Something that's none of her business."

"Hey . . ." His silver eyes catch mine. "Do you want to talk about it?"

My eyes fall to his chin. I wish I could tell him everything.

"I have this thing," I repeat, looking at his shirt again and counting the silver buttons. I wish I could go back to the apple tree and freshman year, and start all over again. Redo us, differently.

"Right," he says.

Six buttons.

"Thanks though," I say, selfishly reaching out and tucking one of his curls behind his ear.

Seven buttons.

He looks at me curiously and I hold my breath, watching him longer than I should.

"Marion?"

I grab my things and walk away without saying anything. I stumble through the door, down the hall, and out into the parking lot, where the air tastes of winter and fog hangs heavy on the trees. Plenty of fog hiding golden leaves. Plenty of fog to hide me.

# Kurt

**Josie's still on the couch in the morning. She's half** in a sitting position and half lying on her side, as if she wanted to sleep but couldn't move her legs. I look around for Dad and hear the shower running. It makes me slam the wall.

The door's right there. She could walk right out of it. It's not like the fact that she's home means we can trust her.

Though maybe—maybe she wants to stay.

I start to pace and my legs itch. They want to run. I check the window and it's gray out. Fog. It's the best kind of weather to run in, where you can't see two steps ahead of you. It helps you focus. Forget.

But I don't want to forget anymore. Not with Josie here, and playing my guitar last night, and the scent of almost-gone salt water that I don't want to wash off yet.

I sit in the recliner and watch my sister. Her chest rises and falls as she sleeps. She's so quiet and I don't understand. On TV people go crazy when they detox. They tear shit up.

Sweat like pigs. Scream like the world is on fire. But Josie isn't doing any of that. It's like there's nothing inside her anymore.

"Kurt?" Her eyes flip open like she's a creature in a horror movie, and my stomach rolls into my throat.

"Josie?" My voice is so high it startles me.

"Nothing happened to me, Kurt," she says, her eyes glassy but hard. She's answering my question from last night, but her look has punched me through my ribs and grabbed my stomach.

I want to nod and say it's okay and let that be the end of it. But I can't.

"Something happened," I say, trying out the words again. I have a million questions. Like where she's been and how she got hooked on whatever she's on, and how she got the money for it. Too many bad things crawl through my brain. Maybe I don't want to know.

Why.

That's the big one. Maybe it's the only question that really means anything.

I wait.

She yawns and nuzzles her face into the pillow, lifting her feet onto the couch. Her bony toes dig into the cushion and I see why Dad's in the shower. There's a metal cuff locked around her ankle with a green light that blinks. It's a sensor. Or a tracking device. It's the kind of thing you put on a dog.

My hands ball into fists. This *can't* be the way we deal with her.

I need to be outside. Now. Before I march into that bathroom and pummel him. I'm almost out the door when her voice stops me.

"Nothing happened, Kurt." Josie's eyes peer over the edge of the couch like it's important I understand this. "Nothing happened to me that didn't happen to you."

That can't be true.

She disappears behind the couch, and all I can see is that thing on her ankle, her foot draped over the armrest. I hate the feeling that hits me next. We both grew up in this house. We both had to deal with Mom and Dad's shit. But maybe that's not all of it. She always took me to parties, and drove me to soccer practice before I got my license, and took me out for fries when Mom was passed out and there wasn't any food in the kitchen. She always made sure I got away from all this. And what did I do? I left her on the other side of that wall crying, where I could hear her. But I didn't *do* anything. Maybe part of what happened to Josie . . . is me.

People rush down the corridor and elbows smack into me like I'm going too slow. Maybe I am. I never spend this much time in a hallway.

I look for Marion, but I don't see blond among the

lockers. I'm not sure why I'm looking so hard. I'll see her in chemistry. But then Lilith comes into view and without thinking I wave.

"Lilith."

She turns, surprised, and saunters up to me.

"Kurt Medford. To what do I owe the pleasure?"

"Uh . . ." I drop my hand and shove it in my pocket. The fact that I even called out her name betrays more than I should have.

"She done gone and messed with your head, now, didn't she?" Lilith teases, and I shut up. I can't imagine the two of them don't talk. "Good giiirrrl!"

Elbows graze my back and I almost shift into their flow and forget this.

"Did you need something, Medford?" Lilith fishes.

"I, um . . ."

She laughs and taps me on the chest. "I get it, Medford. You kiss better than you speak. And yes, *if* you're asking, I saw Marion in the library about ten minutes ago. I know, there's nothing sexier than a girl with her nose in a book, huh, soccer man? Threw you for a loop, now, didn't she?" She smiles to herself like that's an inside joke I'm not supposed to get. "I knew that girl had superpowers," she says, tapping my chest again. "I'm glad she's finally using them!"

"What's that supposed to mean?"

"Don't worry about it, Medford," she says, smiling with too much lipstick. "Just have fun."

"It's not like that," I say, and she squints at me.

"Not like *what* exactly?" Her eyes narrow, and I don't want to talk about this anymore. I know what that tone means. I have a reputation. I get it. She opens her mouth to say something snide, but then her hand grabs my shirt instead and there's something protective in the way she grips me. "Look," she starts, her voice getting quiet, and her gaze falls to my shoulder. She pauses, and I'm not sure if she's about to kick my ass or not. The fabric of my shirt tightens under her knuckles and her jaw pinches. A stream of people flies past us, but she doesn't budge. I like that *this* is Marion's best friend.

"Lilith, I—"

"You're gonna break her heart," she says, interrupting me. The fabric on my sleeve pulls tight and she catches my eye—only, her look isn't a threat. She stares at me, matter-of-fact, like this is something inevitable that she thinks I should know. "I'm not saying stop," she says quietly. "You'll be good for her." She lets go and presses her palm against my shoulder, smoothing out the wrinkles. "But you'll also break her."

She starts to walk away and I don't know if that was a warning or an apology. But either way I don't like it.

"Hey!"

Lilith looks back, and I shake my head at her. I want to tell her I won't, but the words can't find their way out.

She smiles weakly and shakes her head.

"You're sweet," she says, then disappears into the crowd.

# Marion

I'm distracted in chemistry class. I can't think straight. I haven't seen Kurt yet and I don't know if I want to. But at any minute he's going to walk through that door and we—I don't know—we're going to have to deal with this. Us. Make it public. Keep it private. Whatever. I can't focus and I don't know which I'd prefer us to be.

I pull out my pen and draw stars on the back of my wrist till there's a solar system covering my arm. I want to connect the dots and make them into something. Invent new constellations. See if there's a way through this skin of stars to the girl underneath.

Abe takes a seat and mumbles something about my inked skin, but I don't catch it because I'm too overwhelmed by the closeness of him. Too warm and confused, and these dark-blue stars suddenly feel like a new way of marking me. His silver buttons sparkle and I can actually imagine myself unbuttoning them. Finding his skin underneath, where I could draw starbursts on his chest, scattered like dandelion seeds. I don't know why I feel brave enough to think that's possible. For me to touch him.

"Are you all right?" Abe's voice breaks me from my daydream.

"Sorry? What?"

"You were kinda off this morning," he says, looking me over carefully, and I don't know what he's searching for. "When Lilith came by and . . ." I flush, afraid he can read everything I'm thinking.

"No, I'm—" I start, but that's when I see Kurt in the doorway.

Kurt doesn't come in. He waits just outside the frame, watching me, and I'm not sure he's going to walk in at all. Suddenly I know I can't face him in this classroom. Not with Abe here. Not with the rest of our classmates watching.

"Marion, are—?"

"Can you excuse me a minute?" I get up and walk away from Abe, not looking back. I don't want to see the disapproving look on his face.

I grab Kurt's arm and pull him down the hall away from the door. I grab him with my star-covered hand, inked with a whole blue universe I want to disappear into.

"Don't we have class?" Kurt says, but he's not really protesting. The slump of his shoulder and the way he opens the stairwell door make me certain he's just as happy to walk away from that room as I am.

The stairwell echoes with the clang of the door, kicking

up dust, and I turn and face him. Fog clouds the window beside us, making his skin look pasty white, and in this light he doesn't look like the gold-kissed boy who was so intangible at the bonfire. Here, he's just a boy. The one boy whose hands know me.

I grip his arm to steady myself, because I'm not sure what I want to ask him. I just need this—seeing him—to happen away from Abe and everyone else. He catches my eye, but I can't read him. His gaze is honest, but I can't see anything new in that look. No secret waiting for me. Nothing to settle this starlight burning through the base of my stomach.

His hand takes my arm and he rubs his thumb over the inked stars, linking one smudged blot to the next. It's messy and lovely, smearing everything I've been trying so hard to keep clean. And then he kisses me. Sweetly. Not hot like in my backseat, or distant like the first time in the car. Just simply, in that weird way Kurt can make something effortlessly simple and at the same time overwhelming. I melt into it, because part of me doesn't want to ask questions or define us.

Part of me just wants to burn.

My heart thumps in my chest as I run around the track in gym class. I close my eyes and listen to the rhythm of it. Body moving. Breathing. Released. I smell the ocean far away and wonder why there can't be more moments like this one.

Just body and breath. Sand and air. No water to drag me down.

I open my eyes, running faster, to see if I can outrun that dark place in the back of my mind. The places that question Kurt and what being with him means.

I look at Lilith rounding the track ahead of me, and wonder if that's her trick. If she turns off all the questions, and exists right here, right now, without looking ahead or behind. Lives in the moment where nothing else can touch her. Is that it? To let go, do you simply have to choose to be free?

"I'll race you to the end."

Abe pulls my attention and I see him jogging next to me. He points to the final lap and smiles, a challenge in the curve of his eyebrow. It makes me feel like a kid, my hair full of wind, and I want nothing more than to play this game.

"Eat my dust," I yell, digging into the dirt and running ahead. Abe's pushing hard behind me, trying his best to catch up to me. Only he isn't Kurt. He isn't fast. I could beat him.

I focus on the track, on the pound in my chest, on the solid lines in the dirt. It feels good to stay between the lines, to follow the rules and race forward without questioning the possibility of what lies outside them. The adrenaline and rush melt all my questions away, and I sprint. That kiss in the stairwell makes me feel lighter, like

I've got wings to fly above this. I can forget Abe behind me and be in this moment, ahead of everything that chases me.

I cross the finish line and my heart feels like it's going to burst. My head is dizzy with exertion. I turn to Abe and we both grab the fence to keep from falling over.

"Okay, you win," he says breathlessly. But I can't talk. I'm out of wind. I half laugh and smile, gulping down air, rather than speaking. And he nods; he feels that too. That breathlessness and clarity. That part where you just feel alive. "Man, I got my ass kicked by a girl."

"Damn straight you did," I say, and he's full smile and laughing.

I grip the fence to steady myself, and my arm is smeared in blue stars. Half-there, half-gone, covered in sweat and fog. Perspiration beads on my skin and I can feel the creek water again, on my wrists and elbows, wanting to drown those stars. It's fleeting, there for only a moment, and I tell myself to ignore it. I don't want it to spoil the joy of running. Of beating Abe. Of momentarily being ahead of everything.

I look at the parking lot beyond the fence. My chest pounds and I swear I see Kurt walking through the cars. Only it can't be him, because there's a dark-haired girl trailing him. Vanessa, I think that's her name. Yes, Vanessa, she's a junior. Only all the joy and air squeezes right out of me, because the guy she's with slumps his shoulder to the side, in the way that Kurt does, and I know it's him.

And then she kisses him.

I flip around and stare at the mountain, not wanting to look back. But I have to, just to be sure. And yes, it really is him, and her, and his car. My fingers and toes go numb. That fleeting feeling rushes back, and there's water up to my chin.

Abe notices. "Hey, are you okay?" he asks, still catching his breath, but I walk away from him and head for the trees. I walk away from Kurt and her, my head swarming with an ocean of things I can't breathe.

"Marion?" Abe calls after me, but I ignore him. Silver reeds slap my shoes, and I walk until the mist smells of cedar and the fog clogs my breath.

A snap of twigs makes me look back, and Abe is following me. It's stupid, but I'm *glad* he's following me. The leaves flutter down around him like orange butterflies, blotting out the school and Kurt and Vanessa and all that, since yesterday, I no longer am.

"Hey, slow down," he says, but I keep trudging forward. "What just happened?"

"Nothing," I say, my limbs aching. "I just need air." I point to the mountain through the trees. "There's a trail up this, yeah?"

"Dorsette?" he asks, confused. "I think so. I hiked it once when I was te—"

"Great," I say, showing him my back and walking deeper into the woods.

He mumbles something that I don't catch. If he wants to go back, he can. I don't need him. But I hear twigs snap behind me and I know he's following. I feel powerful knowing he's coming with me, and I wonder if this is some of that power Lilith has. This spark that's able to lure Abe into the woods after me. I pick up my pace, tromping through the leaves that lie gold at my feet, and wonder if it's possible. Can I be like Lilith and find fire? *Be* fire? Use my skin as a spark? Perhaps *this* is what not being a virgin is. Perhaps this is why things feel different between Abe and me. Because my virginity was the one thing that always kept us apart.

We hike in silence and I can feel Abe watching me. Breathing. Not asking, just coming. We search for the trail for a long time, heading deeper into the mist, and I swallow the salt on the back of my tongue. The taste of Kurt wells inside me and it strikes me that I don't know him. Everything between Kurt and me has been ocean—fast and vulnerable and full of drowning currents. He's a stranger, like that man, and perhaps everything between us dissolves into creek water because I can't untangle them. What if yesterday had been with someone who knew me? Like Abe? With Abe I would mean something. I wouldn't be just another girl lost in the surf.

Abe slogs through the brush, and wet moss squeezes under my feet, soaking through my sneakers. Is Abe the spark that beats the water? Is he the prince whose kiss will undo the bad magic?

"This way," I say, nodding to the fog, but Abe checks his watch.

"We're lost."

"No," I insist, pointing to a pair of birch trees with charcoal knots in their trunks. "I'm sure the path is up here."

"Marion." He pauses to wipe the sweat from his brow. "There isn't a trail."

I spread my hand over the curls of bark. I've stepped off my normal path, with Kurt. I need to keep moving forward and believe there's a path with Abe.

"Of course there is." My thumb peels back the husk of wood. "You said—"

"I said I *thought* there was a trail." His voice is annoyed, and I dig my nail into the tree. "But then you just walked into the woods."

"You make me sound crazy."

"It's not like that, M."

My skin prickles. It's nice to have him call me M. It's familiar, like I'm allowed to touch his hair again.

"You didn't have to come," I say, and my throat pinches, because I wanted him to come. That was part of the lure, wasn't it? Having him come with me.

I look back and he's only a step away.

"Yes, I did."

The white of his gym shirt is damp and his head tilts to the side. But those three words, he's said them all wrong. They've come out pointed and cross, like I'm a child in need of a chaperone.

"Of course I knew there wasn't a trail," I say, yanking at the bark, unraveling its hangnail of flesh.

"That's bad for the tree," he scolds, and I yank it farther to expose the pink.

"It's just a tree!"

"Fine." He runs a frustrated hand through his curls. "You're being ridiculous. I mean, why are we even out here?"

I'm so close to him I can feel his breath.

His eyes flick to my mouth and ice reeds though me. Ice, like the water yesterday, dousing me naked. I wanted him in these woods, but I didn't think I could admit to myself why. And now all I can feel is this red heat raging through me.

Abe doesn't move.

I don't move.

Suddenly I understand that when I told Abe I'd never have sex with him, it was because I didn't think I would ever have sex with anyone. But now I'm this other person—who has—this something new, and all my lines of white and black have become fog, dissolving.

I was the one who stood in the way of Abe and me. And now all this knotted-up heat is unraveling. The flirting. The unfolding looks. Kurt doesn't care about me, his kissing that girl tells me as much. My skin flushes and Abe's fingers dig into the cotton of his shirt. I'm only a breath away from him and the fog is—

"We should go back," he whispers, looking away, and his breath falls against my chin, rolling into the mist.

"We don't have to," I whisper, ferns brushing the backs of my legs. His silver eyes pierce me, blue-flecked, unsure, and all the things I was too afraid to do with him before come rushing through my mind.

The moss beneath us is spongy, full of trapdoors and bog.

"We could . . ." I breathe, watching his mouth, hearing the swollen fog hush through the saplings.

"We're late," he says, turning abruptly.

My throat squeezes, embarrassment lodging itself in my chest and making it hard to breathe. Abe slogs away, back through the tree brush from where we came.

It was stupid of me to walk him into these woods. Stupid to think that there was any of Lilith's power in me. Stupid to think that just because Kurt screws around, I should too.

The orange leaves glitter around us like confetti and I tell myself to forget Abe. To forget the gold spades and this haze inside me, and the two years of missing and wishing

I was brave enough to be the girl he wants me to be.

I have Kurt, and that's all I should want.

Only, I don't have Kurt.

And Abe has every right not to be interested. So why did he follow me into these woods?

# Kurt

After fifth period, I head outside to call Josie. To check in. Make sure she's okay. I lean against my car and pull out my cell. Marion's father's clothes are in my backseat, bunched up and flecked with sand. It makes me smile and think of the ocean. Makes me feel like I'm not covered in ash.

I hear a whistle and look up to see Vanessa walking toward me in a black skirt that shows off her legs.

"Well, well, what have we here?" she says, tossing her hair over her shoulder.

"What's what?" I ask, and she slides those legs between me and my car.

"Empty ride." She runs a finger over the roof. "Kurt Medford." Finger over me. "What, indeed?"

"Can't," I say, stepping away from her.

"It's not a game day," she counters.

"True, but—"

"But nothing."

She kisses me like I'm playing hard to get. I don't kiss back. I just let her do it.

"You gone soft, Medford?" she says, pulling away. I roll my eyes and nudge her off.

"Bad timing," I say, but Vanessa laughs.

"What's her name?"

I shake my head. She throws a hand on her hip and stares me down. It isn't confrontational. She knows I've been with other girls. She just wants to make a game out of it.

"No."

"Aww, come on," she fishes, pressing against me, but I don't bite. Vanessa shifts and black hair flies in my face. I feel her hand in mine and suddenly she's snatching the cell phone from my fingers. "Who you calling?"

"Hey!"

She steps off and looks at the number.

"Josie?" She raises an eyebrow. "Now who might that be?"

"No one."

"Sure, she isn't."

I try to grab my phone, but she hides it behind her back.

"Oh, you've got it bad for this Josie girl!" Vanessa laughs. "I think I'm a little jealous." She's got me pawing all over her to get the phone. "Really, Medford?" She presses her mouth to my ear. "You *don't* want to go for a drive? I doubt Josie would believe that for a second."

I ball up my fists and walk away from her.

"Hey! What's your problem?" she snaps, and I pretend to ignore her and walk to my car.

"I need that phone," I yell back, because damn it, I do, and she cackles, waving my cell in the air like a useless gum wrapper.

"What, this ol' thing?" she mocks, and I've had it. I throw my car door shut with a slam. When I look back at her, she's gone small. One of her arms is wrapped over her chest like I'm dangerous.

"Jesus shit," she hisses, glaring at me.

"My phone," I say firmly, and she holds it up in her hand.

"Fuck you." She chucks my phone over my shoulder into the woods.

I don't move. If I move I'm going to fucking strangle her.

"Well, this is unfortunate," she says darkly, lifting her chin. "You were a good lay, Medford. Too bad your dick has to come with the rest of you."

She stalks off and I turn to the woods. The grass is tall and I didn't get a good look at where my cell landed. Fucking Vanessa!

After a half hour of walking the tree line I admit it's probably a lost cause. Only I don't go back to class. This feels like a challenge. It's like I need to prove to myself I care enough about my sister to find it. That I won't let her down this time. I drop low and look under a few more bushes. Then get up and circle the next three trees. My back feels tight, like I need to stretch. I roll my head and need to run. Clear my head.

And then, just like that—my luck changes.

Next to a string of rocks is my phone, caught in a bunch of grass. I pick it up and start laughing. It's a miracle it didn't hit one of the rocks and smash into a hundred pieces.

Which is when I see Abe—

And Marion—

Walk out of the woods.

# thirteen

# Kurt

I walk straight for them. Abe sees me and slows like he's preparing for something.

Me, clearly.

He nudges Marion and I hate that she looks at him first. He steps to the side and hooks a hand in the elastic of his gym shorts, nodding in my direction. Her face goes pale and I stop walking.

She can come to me.

"Hi," she says, stopping a few feet away with Abe behind her. Her neck red with whatever this is.

"Hi," I say back. But all I can think about is how well she lied to her father and that everything out of her mouth is going to be bullshit.

"We, um . . ." Her lip trembles and that's all she says. I taste blood and salt water in my mouth, and I shake my head with how uncool I am right now.

I spit in the grass and she flinches.

"Look, Medford—" Abe starts.

"Don't speak." I point a finger at him and he shuts up.

"Abe," Marion says cautiously. "Go to class."

He checks me to make sure that's okay, and I stare him down. Ready to pound the shit out of him.

"Abe," she says again. "Just go."

It's her voice that gives him permission, and he speeds away toward the building.

I can't look at her. Everything in me is fists and knots and I'm so pissed I know I should leave. I can't be here. I need to clear my head. Run.

I turn my head and go.

# Marion

**I grab his wrist.**

My heart races and I don't know what he will do. But I won't let him go. His pulse screams under my thumb and he tries to pull away from me.

"What are we?" I ask, and his nostrils flare.

"What the hell was that?" He nods to Abe dashing away.

"Forget that," I insist, and he shakes his head like that was the wrong answer.

He twists, making a show of wanting to be out of my grip. Only he's stronger than me. I'm not the one holding him back.

"What is this?" I say again, motioning to the two of us, but his glare makes the ocean swell in my throat.

"It's nothing!"

"It's not nothing," I say, my voice thin. "Yesterday was . . ."

I try to swallow, but it's the whole ocean. I'm not sure I even know, much less am able to describe, what yesterday was to me. I dig my nails into his arm. I want to throw the dark-haired girl in his face. How I saw him kiss her. But somehow that feels like it will only push him further away.

"Yesterday was important." I cough. "I've never . . ."

But of course he knows that.

He was there.

Inside me.

It was stupid to take Abe into those woods after I saw him with Vanessa. I don't know what I was trying to prove by walking into that fog, but now that Kurt's in front of me I'm desperate to keep him. His lips know me in a way that no one else's have.

"Kurt, I—"

He rips his hand from my grip and his eyes turn dark.

"Do you think you're the first virgin I've ever slept with?" He tosses my hand away, and the tendons in his neck pull taut. "You're not."

He backs away from me.

"Kurt, this—"

"And you won't be the last."

I can't breathe.

The metal rivets of the stairwell dig into my legs. I press the heels of my palms into my forehead, but the pressure doesn't help.

I should go to class. I should get out of these freaking gym clothes. I should pull myself together and get over it.

Only, I'm not sure how to contain myself, how to be

around anyone right now. I suck in air through my teeth, and exhale.

Air through my teeth.

What was I doing?

I pull my hair into a ponytail, twisting the elastic tight. Hair back, twist tight.

Back. Tight.

I should burn this hair off with the stars.

"You can't be here."

I look up and it's Miss Kay, my freshman-year social studies teacher. She has thin eyebrows and hair so straight it gives her pencil skirt curves. She doesn't look angry, but her voice is matter-of-fact.

I nod and wipe my cheeks, which are sore and puffy.

"Go to the nurse," she says, handing me a pass. I take the thin piece of paper. "It's just high school," she says as I stand. "You'll live."

# Kurt

At practice we do suicides and I run till there isn't anything in me but pain.

Legs.

Lungs.

Fire.

Line.

Repeat.

The A-squad finishes and goes to get water. I join the B-squad on the line. I don't wait for the whistle. I run. Pain in my calves.

"Keep up," I yell, lapping them. A few of them curse, and I run over and circle the group. "What was that, you slow pieces of shit?"

They don't answer.

"You're never going to start because you can't fucking run!" I yell, and they glare at me. I speed ahead to the goal line.

Air screaming through me.

There's a whistle, and Coach is yelling, but my ears buzz

and I push harder. I yell at the B-squad and sprint harder. Faster. Lapping them double time.

Harder. Faster.

"Medford! Off the field. Now!" It's Coach, but he's not showing these guys shit. They're never gonna be fast enough if they don't—

Conner grabs my shoulder and knocks me off balance. I stumble. Dig my cleats into the dirt and stay up. For the first time I feel the sweat drooling off my back.

"Knock it off, Kurt," he says, and I smack him away and head for the line. He grabs my arm and shoves his chest into me.

"I'm not kidding, stop!"

"Fuck off!" I push him hard and sprint.

"Medford! If you don't—" Coach's words shoot past, lost.

My heart pounds in my ears.

I bend. Touch the line. Body screaming. Legs pumping.

*Smack!*

Weight steamrollers me. Weight and shoulders.

The ground spins and blood floods my head. My body pulsing from pushing harder, faster, long—

I can't breathe.

Fire shrieks through my skull and my weight shifts.

"Whoa, shit!" I hear Conner's voice and someone grabs me.

I don't fall, pressed against them. My weight hooked on their shoulders.

"God, you need to deal with your shit!" It's Conner's voice in my ear.

"Fffffuu—" I pant, but can't . . .

Someone's swearing. Coach maybe. The voice is far away.

Conner moves under my weight. "Your sister may be gone, and your dad's a prick, but you *can't* take it to the field like this and run till your heart shits out!"

My ears pound and stars prickle at the edge of my vision.

"Do you even *know* what you said to the B-squad?"

I try to tell him to piss off, but there's dirt in my lungs. I need to run. Get air.

"Medford! What kind of fucking stunt are you—" The voice is far away.

"That Coach?" I ask, my voice hoarse.

"You need to sit," Conner says, shifting my weight to my feet. "Can you walk?"

But I don't think my feet are feet. Everything's too light.

"Whoa, whoa!" Conner pulls me back against him. "Okay, forget that, just breathe."

My temples bang and black shoots through my—

"Kurt! Damn it, breathe!"

There's a thud at my back and phlegm coughs up my throat.

"You think you're some goddamned hotshot, Medford?! You think—"

It *is* Coach's voice.

Closer.

But then there's a ringing and lightness and—

"Oh, shit."

# Marion

Lilith corners me at the end of the day.

"Mar-i-doodle, wait!" she says, skipping over to me as I'm on my way to the locker room to get my street clothes. She smiles, pretending everything is normal after our little spat this morning. We haven't really talked since she said all those things in the coffee shop either, but like always, she acts as if nothing is different, that our friendship is everything but negative space. "Why are you still wearing your gym clothes?"

I flash her my pass to the nurse. "Wasn't feeling well."

"Suck-buckets," she says, trying to touch my forehead and fawn over me.

"I'm fine," I say, batting her hand away.

"Good," she says, ignoring my tone and returning to her bouncy upbeat self. "Because, guuurl, Kurt has got it *bad* for you!"

My stomach turns. "Kurt wants nothing to do with me," I say, slipping past her into the locker room.

"Oh, you are *so* wrong about that." She follows me in and the room stinks of towels and mold. A shower is running and the musk of steam makes me gag. "I'm not kidding," she says as I open my locker. "He came up to me looking for you this morning. Kurt, who doesn't look for anybody."

I pull out my street clothes and undress, throwing off my smelly gym shirt and shorts. I stand there half-naked, and I can't ignore how Lilith and I are just like my skin—all surface, years of time and surface.

"Why aren't you more excited about this?" She frowns, tossing a hand to her hip, and I pull on my pants. "Seriously, I thought you liked him."

"You don't know the half of it," I blurt, yanking on my shirt.

She steps back as I struggle to get the cotton over my head. My arms flail and I attempt to punch elbows through holes. Once the shirt is on, I right myself and she's still waiting.

She raises an eyebrow. "So, what exactly is it that I don't know?"

I could tell her I'm not a virgin anymore. That's supposed to be the magical golden ticket that will change us, but I feel further away from her now than ever. I throw my dirty clothes in the locker.

"There's a lot you don't know," I say honestly. She looks at the floor and starts picking at the strap of her purse.

"Well?" she asks delicately. "Are you going to tell me?"

I shut my locker and think about all the inches of skin that would be. How I took off my clothes with Kurt, exposed myself, and that blew up in my face.

"I'm here for you, you know . . . ," she says, looking at me kindly, but Lilith's no longer safe.

"Here for me so you can *what*?" I snap. "So you can run your hands all over me and tell me I'm some kind of touch-hungry pariah? No thanks!"

"It wasn't like that," she counters, but I head for the door.

"I don't know what anything *is like* around you anymore," I say, feeling out of control and needing to be out of this room. But Lilith races in front of me, getting in my face.

"Where do you get off, Marion?" Her eyes blaze. "Do you think tiptoeing around *you* has been a picnic for me?! I don't even know what's going to set you off anymore. You're like a minefield of 'look over here, and don't talk about that, oh, and holy shit, Lilith lost her virginity and I totally saw it, but I'm going to pretend for *five years* that I didn't.' What's that about, Marion? Huh? Tell me, how am *I* supposed to be *your friend*?!"

I can't breathe. Shower steam crams down my throat and everything is spinning. I can't be here. Lilith's eyes are so hard it feels like maybe I'm seeing her for the first time, seeing who she really is.

"You ever think that maybe we aren't friends?" I say

coldly, and it surprises me to see her flinch. "Maybe we haven't been for a long time."

Her eyes water and she purses her chalky red lips together. Part of me wants to hug her and say I don't mean it, but I don't know if that's true. I don't know how to be her friend, or for her to be mine. Just because we grew up together doesn't mean we're supposed to be friends forever, does it? Maybe we're just too different now. Maybe *not being friends* is who we were always supposed to be.

# Kurt

My head throbs, right behind the eyes, like someone cut them out. I blink, and light scrapes pain through my skull.

"Jesus," I hiss, turning on my side, nausea budding in my throat. The paper mattress under me crinkles and I hear Conner's voice.

"Hey, man, are you okay?"

A fuzzy figure moves beside me and what looks like yellow confetti drops from his lap when he stands.

"Did I pass out?" My voice cracks, tongue dry as cement. "Water?"

"Yeah, here." Conner puts a Dixie cup in my hand and I gulp it down. He gives me a second and I drink it, too. "You scared me," he says, his tone serious. I rub my face, and my vision clears enough to see a pamphlet in his hands. It's yellow and wrung-out. Torn to bits. Small yellow pieces litter the floor.

"Nothing scares you," I tease, but he doesn't laugh.

I sit up and twist my legs off the cot. That seemed like a good idea, but the room spins. I grab the metal railing and Conner throws a hand on my shoulder.

"Just chill out," he says. "You're not going anywhere till your dad gets here."

"You called my dad?"

"Coach did," Conner explains. "He had to, by law. You passed out on school property."

The headache pings behind my eyes and the small room comes into focus. White walls. Inspirational posters. Plastic curtains.

"He's pissed, you know," Conner says, refilling my cup.

"Who, my dad?"

Conner's eyes flash at me sharply. "No, Coach."

I look at the ceiling. The fluorescent lights sting like vinegar. "How long have I been out?"

"Only about a minute on the field," Conner says, handing me the drink. I gulp it down and my eyes water from the lights. "But you were so woozy when you came to, Coach called your dad and I took you here. You've been in and out for about twenty." He squeezes my shoulder, and I hear the clanking of the water pipes through the wall.

"I'm fine," I say, and he nods.

"Of course you are." But the look on his face says I'm anything but. "You know . . ." He wraps the yellow pamphlet around his finger. "If you ever need—"

"I know," I say, so he doesn't have to. Of course I know.

The fluorescent lights buzz and Conner stuffs the pamphlet back in his pocket. "Okay, well, if you ever—"

"I know," I repeat, louder, and Conner steps back. He sits down on the confetti-covered chair and I close my eyes. I can feel him staring at me, like after Mom died, when we were in my kitchen the week after her funeral. There were half-eaten casseroles covering the entire table, triple-wrapped in Saran. They probably should've been in the fridge, instead of rotting out in the heat. But I wasn't going to touch them. I refused to eat dead-mom food.

Conner sat at the table, fishing a pinkie through the plastic of one of the dishes, thinking I wouldn't notice. I was making PB and J as he slid a bean between his teeth, and I let him get away with it. I tossed him a sandwich and headed out back.

There was a little patch of grass behind the porch where Mom used to sit, and a green shed with the paint peeling. I ate two bites of my sandwich before I got out the soccer ball and started pounding it against the shed, trying to obliterate the rest of that paint.

Somewhere in the middle, Conner joined in.

I was kicking the ball against the shed, and then he was kicking it, and then I was kicking it, and I don't know if he could tell I was crying, but he didn't say anything.

We just kept kicking the ball.

Bang, bang, bang, bang, bang.

\* \* \*

Dad dangles a cigarette out the open window as he drives me home. It's the first one I've seen him with since he brought Josie home. My head throbs. I lean it against the passenger door and the rumble of the road shakes through me.

"Conner says you were pushing too hard," he says, eyes on the road. I'm pissed Conner told him anything. "You can't do that."

"I can do whatever I want," I mumble, letting the pulse of the tires ring through my ears.

"I wish you wouldn't," he says softly. "I wish you'd realize soccer is a way for you to get to college. To get out of—"

"College didn't do shit for Josie, now, did it?" I interrupt, and he grips the wheel, the veins of his hand bulging.

He takes a long drag from his cigarette.

"When did you get it in your head that you're like your sister?" he says finally, and I don't know what to say to that.

We've got the same blood. Josie. Mom. Me. We're all locked up in this together.

"What is that thing on her ankle?" I say, and he flicks ash out the window. "You got her locked up and you're upset that I ran too hard on the soccer field? Where do you get off?" His jaw tightens. "Huh?" I press.

He chucks his cigarette out the window and puts both hands on the wheel. I think about opening my door. To shake him up. Make him react.

I unhook my seat belt.

"Put that back on," he scolds, and I like the edge in his voice.

"Why?" I say. "Mom didn't? Mom threw herself—"

The brakes *screech* and he spins the truck to the curb. We haven't stopped, but he's grabbed my shirt, yanking me toward him.

"Is this what you want?" he yells, spit in my face. "You want a rise out of me? You want me to hit you?"

"Yes!" I struggle, hoping he will.

His hand trembles and he pumps the brake as the truck rolls to the curb. His face is red.

"Do it," I say. "Hit me for being the only one left."

He pushes me hard against the seat. Fist in my chest. My head smacks against the seat and then his weight is on top of me. Only—

This isn't a fight.

This *isn't* him roughing me up or setting himself up for a punch. This is him grabbing the seat belt and yanking it over the front of me. It's him strapping me in, and clicking it shut.

Like I'm a child.

Like he wouldn't dare lose what is left.

# Marion

I sit in the arms of the oak tree in my backyard. Stars dot the sky above and my bare feet press into the trunk. It's so cold we could have a frost, but all I want is the contact of my skin on this tree.

I run a hand over my name carved into the trunk, not sure my childhood self still exists somewhere under the puckered bark, and I wonder if it's possible that growing up has nothing to do with what you do right, but everything to do with what you do wrong.

"Marion?" Light flashes up the tree and I look down to see my father below. "What are you doing up there?"

The sight of him makes my toes curl and some silly piece of me says—

"Come up."

As if it's an offer he might accept.

I remember the sun dappling this tree, and how the green leaves glowed like stars. The branches were firm underfoot as my seven-year-old self raced higher and higher into the light. My father was below, stomping around the tree and huffing.

"Fee fie foe fum," he called out, hunched over, pretending to be the giant, and I scrambled above, as Jack.

"Come up," I yelled to him. "Come up and catch me!"

"Fee fie foe fum."

He swung into the tree, climbing higher and coming after, and I giggled and squirmed above but didn't go too high. I wanted him to catch me. It was the best part of the game.

Dad's flashlight wavers and the light falls off me.

"Come up and catch me," I whisper, not loud enough for him to hear.

I can't make out his features in the shadows below. There's only the dark stillness of his shape. The light swings again and floods over me and I'm caught, but only by the light of him.

"Come down," he says quietly, pointing the beam to the ground. "Come down."

# fourteen

# Marion

**I get up early and go to school. I** park next to Abe's silver pickup in the lot and look in the cab, but he's not inside. I find him in the library sitting in one of the cubicle desks near the stacks with papers spread out around him, back to me. One hand is in his curls and the other is on the desk with his index finger tapping. I knock lightly on the cubicle, but he doesn't look happy to see me.

"Can I sit down?"

"I've got to get this done, M," he says, but the fact that he called me M means it isn't a "no." I pull out the chair beside him and he goes back to his homework. I sit down and pick up a stack of Post-it notes, pulling off the top note.

"I'm sorry about yesterday," I say, pressing the Post-it to my thumb. "About Kurt."

Abe doesn't say anything, but his pen has stopped writing.

"I . . ."

I run the edge of the Post-it against his desk. It bends and starts to peel off, just like me, flimsy and unable to stick to any of this.

"You were right about Kurt," I continue, jamming my finger against the Post-it, trying to make it stick. "That was—*is*—nothing."

He chews on his bottom lip.

"Why do you even like him?" he asks, not looking at me. "Guys like him are shitheads."

Suddenly I feel the need to defend Kurt, because he isn't like that. I mean, maybe it started out that way on the cliff, but there's more to him. A tender part. A quiet part, like he can see the shadows in all the negative spaces. Like he can feel the sorrow and the weight of the silence.

"You don't know him," I say, but I catch myself. "I mean, *I* don't really know him," I admit. "He isn't what you think."

Abe's reluctant expression turns dark, and I know he's thinking about how Kurt treated him yesterday. I can't deny how he acted. It's not like Kurt said nice things to me, either. But I know he isn't only one thing. Kurt's both shitty and tender. He ignores me, then shares his music. He's ocean and air.

"Look," I say, knowing I can't tell Abe all that, and wishing this was simpler. Only, we can't go back to dandelion wishes and pretending half the seeds won't burn up in the sun. "I want to apologize for the way Kurt treated you. And

I want you to know that he and I aren't anything. Or whatever . . ."

Abe doesn't move. He presses the tip of the pen into his notebook and the dot expands into a small black stain. I drop the Post-it on the table and get up.

"M," Abe says, not looking at me. He taps his calculus papers with his pen. "I have to do this. It's due first period." His pinkie grazes the side of my hand. "But stay, if you want."

# Kurt

There's nothing to look at in chemistry but Abe and Marion.

Her hair is down.

At one point Abe reaches over and touches it and I don't think she even notices. Not like when Tommy's hand was in her hair. Not like when it was mine.

I look out the window and think about the game. I wonder if Coach will even play me. He bitched me out in front of everyone and benched me in practice yesterday.

But I can still run. I *need* to run. Especially if I'm going to have to sit here for another fifty minutes and watch the backs of their heads.

Coach benches me.

I dig my cleats into the grass and bounce my knees to keep them warm. I haven't sat the bench since freshman year.

Time clicks by. I keep looking to Coach. Waiting for that head-nod. But he doesn't look my way.

We're down by two at the end of the third and Conner drops himself next to me. He's the only one holding up the offensive line without me out there. The replacement striker is too slow. He can't keep pace for the whole game.

"Their left fullback is weak," I tell Conner as he squirts water down his neck. "If you drive it up the right you'll have an open shot. I'd set you up if—" I glance at Coach and dig my knuckles into the bench.

"Don't blame Coach for that," he says, tossing the water bottle to my feet. The whistle blows and Conner returns to the field.

The other team scores a goal. We score none. And I don't get up from that bench till it's over.

They're in the hall together. Again. Abe against the locker next to hers. Marion putting her books away. Sun shoots down the hall and I'm not paying attention to her hand on his elbow. Only, my feet are walking. Toward them.

Abe sees me and his grin falls. I step between them and lean my hand against the locker. My shoulder in Abe's face.

"Excuse you," he snaps, stumbling back, and Marion scowls. I swallow hard. I've seen that look before. On other girls. Not her.

"I need to talk to you," I say, and she frowns.

"Then talk."

I shoot a glare over my shoulder at Abe and my fingers curl into a fist against the locker.

"You mind?" I say, and he flicks hair out of his eyes.

"Kind of."

I drop my shoulder and face him. "Kind of? Are you sure you want—"

"We were having a conversation," Marion interrupts, and I look back at her. She's pissed. "If you have something to say, Kurt, say it."

A locker slams behind us and suddenly everything's too loud. I crack my knuckles against the aluminum and roll my shoulder.

"Say it," she says quietly, without the anger of the moment before, and I think maybe she wants to know.

Only, I don't do this.

Any of it.

I drop my arm and I'm gone.

I lean against the brick of the school and kick the grass.

I want a cigarette.

Instead I pull my cell phone out and call home. Maybe Dad will let me take Josie out of the house. Go bowling. Get ice cream. So she's not rotting in that house all day long. So it's not just the two of them. Maybe it's my turn to get her out of that cave.

Students pour out of the building and I see Troy, fighting the crowd with his practice bag on his shoulder. He catches my eye when he reaches the gym door and steps to the side.

"Sucks that Coach didn't play you yesterday," he says, and I shrug, lifting the phone for him to notice.

"Right," he acknowledges, but then he stands there another moment rolling a rock under his foot.

"Coach will get over it," I say. "Especially when he decides he wants to start winning again."

Troy kicks the rock into the grass.

"You should really apologize to the B-squad," he says.

I stare at him and he stands his ground. He's not angry, just matter-of-fact.

The phone rings in my ear, but no one picks up. There's no machine. No voice mail.

Nothing.

"Right," Troy says, stepping off and opening the gym door. "See you at practice in ten."

# Marion

My bag is heavy with books as I head through the parking lot. It's almost four p.m. and there's a flurry of snow in the air. It's nothing more than a handful of flakes dotting the sky, almost invisible, but everywhere.

I look up and see Kurt against my car.

He should be at practice, but he isn't suited up. There's a puff of something white near his mouth and I think it's breath from the cold, but when I get closer I see it's a cigarette.

He takes a drag, and I wonder if he deliberately chose to lean against my backseat door, the one we fell through after the ocean when our skin was salted and wet.

Kurt throws the cigarette on the ground when he sees me and stands upright like I'm a teacher and he's got something to hide. He shifts back and forth, and it's odd to see him uncertain on his feet, when he runs and plays soccer the way he does.

I stop a few feet away, but he doesn't say anything, like the fact that he's standing there should be enough.

"Don't you have practice?" I say, and he looks to the field, where his teammates are set up for a corner kick. One of the players lobs the ball and then the whole group moves as one. Motion, inertia, goal.

"Can we go somewhere else?" he asks, nodding to my car.

"You're kidding, right?"

He stuffs a hand in his pocket and stares at me. I shake my head, because he actually *does* think that's how this is going to work.

"Go to your practice," I say, striding toward the driver's seat, and he steps back as I approach. "Or go find Vanessa."

"I don't like Vanessa."

"I saw you kiss her," I snap. "So, you like her enough."

"I don't *want* Vanessa."

I shake my head and dig in my bag for my keys. "No, you just want to fuck around. I got that."

He looks away, taking that blow, knowing he deserves it. I wait for him to apologize or show any kind of remorse, but he just stands there with his fists balled against his sides.

"Marion." His voice gets low. "I don't know how to do this."

"Then don't," I snap. "Walk away. Ignore me. Do whatever you do with the others."

His eyes cut to the ground and he kicks the asphalt.

"Can't."

I press my palm against the roof of my car. It's covered with a sheet of ice crystals.

"Why not?" I look at him and there's so much emotion in his face I can't even begin to read it. Ice seeps through my palms and there's snow in his hair. "Why not?" I repeat, and he shakes his head. He's close enough that I can see the muscles in his jaw. They're clenched so tight I don't think he could speak even if he wanted to. And for a second, he looks like a little boy. A chill all too familiar reeds through me, shooting straight down to my toes. His eyes are filled with all the things that he *wants* to say. But he *can't.*

*He just can't.*

My feet go cold. Creek-water cold.

I know exactly what it is to want to say something—and not know how.

I turn away from him and lean into the metal of the car. I breathe in the snow. Invisible. Unspeakable. Everywhere.

"Get in the car," I say, opening the door.

He doesn't move because I know he doesn't believe me. I throw my bag in the backseat and point to the passenger door.

"Kurt," I say, tasting snow on my lips. "I don't know how to do this either. Just get in the car."

# Kurt

There's still sand on Marion's dash. Her seats are freezing, but my palms sweat as she pulls out of the lot. The seat belt presses into my neck, anticipating the need to hold me in this seat.

"Where do you want to go?" she asks.

I don't have an answer for that. I didn't think that far ahead. I didn't think about any of this. I roll down the window.

"Just drive," I say, letting my head roll back and closing my eyes.

The engine hums low, then climbs high. It feels like running. Only it's sitting still in the motion of it. It's stillness inside the uncertainty.

It's running and motion and—

She puts her hand on top of mine.

And I want to tell her, *this*—why I can't walk away. Why I can't ignore her. This hope in my chest—

*This* is why not.

# Marion

I drive over the hill and the road opens to the shore path where the ocean crashes against the rocks.

We don't say anything. We drive. We drive and there is music in the silence, the road humming, the rise and fall of his chest. There's music behind the quietness, wind lifting light in my hair, wind lifting light in our breath.

After an hour of driving around aimlessly, I park in front of a brick building with a line of small businesses. Blue awnings hood each window. There's a gift shop, a hair salon, and an ice cream parlor that's only open in the summer. The fourth shop is the reason I drove us here, it's the only shop I know of like this. Kurt leans forward for a better look.

"Have you been here before?" I ask, and he stares out the window before nodding. The blue awning shades a window full of guitars, and a neon sign blinks the word:

*Strings.*

"This place is still here?" he asks, hands perched on the

dash. He looks at me and a smile tugs at the edge of his mouth. "Do you play the—"

"Nope," I interrupt. "Never touched a guitar in my life." I open the door and look back at him. "But *you* play."

# fifteen

# Kurt

A bell on the door jangles and the owner behind the counter looks up. He's got long hair and a goatee, and there are more wrinkles on his face than I remember.

"Evening," he says, his voice full of gravel. I nod, pretending to look at a rack so he can't see my face and recognize me. The problem with living in a small town is there's only one good guitar store for miles. You can't get anything this store has unless you go to the city. Guess that's what I used to love about it. It has everything. Mom used to call it wonderland. "Can I help you?"

"Just looking," I say, turning to Marion like she's more interesting than him. The owner nods, checking his watch.

"We're open for another twenty. Try what 'cha like." He motions to the room and goes back to his paperwork.

Guitars hang from the ceiling and band posters cover the walls: Fleetwood Mac, Dusty Springfield. The whole place is like a time warp and smells of carpet desperate to be cleaned, but I like that about it. It's real. I head for the back, where the acoustic guitars line the shelf.

I pull one down and feel its weight. Solid neck. Light body. The strings feel good under my fingers. A radio behind the counter dribbles out an old country tune and I brush against the strings, but the twang still echoes through the store.

Too loud.

And at the same time, not loud enough.

Marion leans against a rack of sheet music, chewing on her pinkie. She pulls out a Steve Winwood book from his Blind Faith days and pretends to be interested in it. I adjust for pitch, turning the knobs. Not sure I want an audience. But the shy way she waits for me to play, just giving me the space, makes my chest clench in the best possible way.

A smile tugs my lip and my hands remember. The chords. The songs. How to fingerpick. Strum. My foot starts tapping and we have music. Music that I haven't played in four years. Music I was sure I'd forgot.

I don't worry about making mistakes. I just play, and Marion doesn't ask me about the song. She bobs her head like maybe she's remembering the one I played her on my iPod. Only this one's different. More raw.

Hair falls over her face as she tilts her head, watching me. It makes me nervous, but I like her here, listening. Like someone's supposed to hear this. I smile at her, which makes her neck go red, and we both start laughing.

My cheeks hurt from smiling and that fist in my chest,

that knot, it's easing. I tuck my chin down and hunch over the guitar and play the song. Music fills the whole store. Mom's music.

When I'm finished, I walk over to Marion and put the guitar in her hands. She shakes her head and puts her arm up in protest.

"Oh, I don't—"

But I move behind her.

"Don't worry, it's easy," I say, wrapping my arms around her waist to show her how to hold it. I trace my fingers over hers and press them into the strings, mapping out the chord. "One, two—" Adjust her pinkie. "This one goes here. Okay, now strum."

She laughs nervously and brushes the strings, the sound wavering.

"Not bad." I laugh. "That's a G." My head nods against her neck and I move her hand to the next position. "Okay, this is a D7."

I show her the pattern of notes. Repeat them. Smell her neck and tell her to strum like she means it.

I leave my hands on her hips and she plays the pattern on her own. It takes a few tries before she gets it, and then she laughs, rocking back into my chest when she realizes what song it is.

"'Mary Had a Little Lamb'?" she asks.

"It's a classic," I say, stepping back because I'm way too turned on by this. I move around so I'm facing her, and tell her to play it again. She repeats the phrase, slowly growing more confident. Adjusting her shoulders so she's got room. Finding a posture that feels good.

Raindrops start to tap on the other side of the ceiling and I close my eyes. I want everything to be like this. Rain. Music. Possible.

The water starts to stampede and thunder claps, making me laugh. Marion slides her hand over my arm and nods to the front of the store. Right now, all I want is to take her into that rain.

I put the guitar back and we turn the corner to see the front window streaked in pink, water flooding it as the neon sign flickers.

"So much for snow," Marion says, but I'm glad it's raining. Rain feels just right.

"Hey!" the shop owner says, and we both stop in our tracks. His brow scrunches when I look back and I see that searching look on his face, like he knows me but he isn't sure how.

"Aren't you . . . ?" He squints and shakes his head, hoping I might put it together for him. That's not going to happen. Marion glances at me curiously and I wave the man off.

"You have a nice night," I say, reaching for the door.

"No, wait," the man says. "Aren't you Lane's son?"

I cough.

I can't believe he just said her name—out loud, like it could be anyone's.

"Yeah, Lane Medford. She used to come here all the time. Play songs in the back like that." He nods to the acoustic section. "Your name is what—" The owner pinches his goatee. "Craig?"

Lightning flashes, followed by a clap of thunder that makes all the guitars shake.

"Kurt," Marion says in the rumble, and I almost think the owner misses it. But then he tosses a finger in the air.

"That's right, Kurt."

Rain slams against the window and the radio crackles in search of a signal.

"I never got a chance to tell you how sorry I was," he continues, shoulders slumping as a frown turns over his face. "About your mum."

Marion's eyes are on me. But all I can do is stare at this guy.

"I haven't heard one of your mom's songs in a long time." He nods to the back corner. "It's nice to know you still play them."

I wish I hadn't.

He's about to say more, but his eyes cut to Marion.

"Well, it's nice to see you," he says, hitching a pair of glasses onto the end of his nose. "I hope you come back." He grabs a stack of receipts and starts punching buttons on the register.

I don't look at Marion as I walk out.

I don't care that there's rain.

# Marion

Kurt stands next to my car with the rain pouring over him.

He waits for me to unlock the door and doesn't say a word. I get in the driver's seat and for a second I don't think he's going to get in the car at all.

I roll down the passenger window and reach through it to grab his hand.

"Get in."

# Kurt

The windshield wipers beat furiously and water floods the street. Pine trees tower on both sides of the car and Marion drives slowly. She maneuvers us past a large puddle and I grip my seat belt. The cops said if Mom had worn her seat belt that night she might have survived her accident. Of course, it wasn't really the seat belt that was to blame.

The rain becomes fists. The windshield turns into a sheet of water and I almost say something, but Marion pulls off the street.

"I can't see," she says, and the car tilts when she finds the shoulder. She pulls the brake and cuts the engine.

We sit. Nowhere to go.

I turn up the heat and aim the vents toward my drenched shirt, and she turns on her hazards. The windshield floods red from the flashers blinking.

"Did you know that man?" she asks. "At the guitar store?"

I shake my head. "I don't *know* him," I say. "We used to go to that store. That's all."

I squeeze the water out of my shirt, but there's so much it makes a puddle on my stomach.

"Was he a good friend of your mom's?"

I don't know how to answer that. They were chatty. Always talking music. I don't know if that makes them friends. I press my shirt into the puddle to sop the water back up.

"You can take that off," Marion says, but she catches herself. "I mean, not like *that*." Her cheeks flush and she looks out the window. "You can put it in the back." She nods behind us. "Let it dry." Her face is angled away from me. But after a second her cheekbone lifts with a smile. "It's not like I haven't seen it before."

Her whole neck goes pink.

"Oh?" I can't help but smile. "In that case . . ."

I pull off the shirt dramatically and throw it behind us. Her ears go scarlet. I wait for her to steal a glance, but she purses her lips and deliberately stares out the window.

"What?" I egg her on. "You've seen it before."

She shakes her head, trying her best not to smile.

I want to lean over and kiss her neck, fish out that smile. But somehow—

*This*—

Not leaning over. Not kissing her. This, that is us, just sitting here.

*This* is better.

I wrap my arms over my chest and recline the seat. I

think she looks over, but I keep my eyes on the ceiling. The rain pounds the metal above us. It pounds into the silence until all I hear are guitar songs and downpours and humming in my brain.

"We used to play together," I say. "Mom and me. That's who the other guitar was in that song on my iPod."

I crack open the window and smell the earth outside.

"She would have loved this rain." I look at the road. A river of water divides the lanes. "She would have run right out in that. Into the street. She would have taken her guitar and bet on her life that nobody would come around that bend."

The road is empty. No one has passed us since we pulled over. It would have been a good bet.

"That guy in the store," I say, thinking of Mom buying strings. "He must remember us." I think of Mom's chipped nails plucking songs out in the back part of that room, wedged between the sheet music and the dust. "It's nice," I say, realizing the store owner was just trying to be kind. "That he remembers."

Marion's hand slides over my shoulder and the cold of her fingers feels good.

"My mom was an alcoholic," I say, looking at the pavement. The water screams outside. "She got drunk. She got in her truck. She . . ."

Rain floods.

It floods everywhere.

We sit for a long time in that rain-pounding silence. Her

hand on me. And I keep imagining Mom's truck barreling around that corner in front of us. I imagine myself running into the road to stop her, but Mom's too drunk. She drives right over me. I imagine it again and again, running into the road, knowing she's gonna hit me. But each time there's this hope that she'll look up in that last second and see what she's doing.

I put my hand over Marion's, to keep it on my shoulder. I squeeze her fingers and something in me . . . starts talking.

"I was the one who always cleaned her up in the morning," I say. "I wiped the vomit from her hair. Fed her aspirin. Hummed the songs her fingers weren't strong enough to grip her guitar with. Not Dad. Dad was always at work. It was *me*.

"And I'm the one she chose to play her songs with. And writing those songs meant the whole damn world to me. It was the one time it felt like we were free. And sure, I don't know when that bottle started showing up on that bottom step. I don't know if she always took swigs between the songs, or during, or all through, or if it was something I only noticed when I got older. But *yes*, the booze was part of it. Part of what made her music—hers. Maybe I knew that. Maybe we all did.

"All I know is that when she didn't have the booze, she was awful. An animal, like—"

I grit my teeth. I can't say this out loud. *Like Josie padlocked behind that door.*

"She was filled with this . . ." I ball my hands into fists, not sure how to describe it. "This rage or . . . something she couldn't get out. Like she wanted to leave her marriage, or blame her shitty career on having kids, or that this—our life—wasn't the one she had planned. But it was the one she was stuck with. And she kept telling me she loved me, but somehow she couldn't get her head above it. I poured all her damn bottles into the sink but she still went out for more. That's all she ever wanted. More. Like maybe she never *wanted* to get her head above it. Like maybe she *wanted* to drown."

That comes out ragged, and Marion trembles—like it strikes a chord in her. This is all confused as shit and Marion doesn't say anything. She holds my shoulder and listens and lets me sit with this. I open the window and the rain hits my face.

"Who does that?" I ask, and I don't know if I'm asking Marion or God or Mom. But I ask, because *I* need to know. "Who *chooses* to drown?"

# Marion

I squeeze my hand on Kurt's shoulder, but the motion feels wrong.

Mechanical.

The rain pounds and yet this is quieter. *This* is more intimate, more naked, more upsetting and tender than being in that backseat with him.

He wipes his face, and his words, his secrets—

My hand on his skin—

Gags me.

I want to comfort him, but this is too vulnerable.

I want to swallow and pull my hand away and pretend I don't see this. Pretend I don't know the weight of what he's sharing with me. Stuff it in my mason jar with the dead bugs and hide it in my closet. Ignore the weight of what I *cannot* share with him.

I force myself to keep my hand on his shoulder.

Force myself to listen. To grip his shoulder.

To swallow.

Swallow it down.

# Kurt

**It's still raining when I sit on the back porch step** after Marion drops me off. My bare feet press into the wet scraped-away wood, where Mom's feet used to tap.

Out in the dark the rain drizzles against the shed and somewhere a dog barks. I want to go find that dog and bring him in out of the rain. But I can only hear his voice, far away.

*Her* guitar is in my lap.

I haven't touched it since she went in the ground. Not once. Not even after I begged my dad not to bury it with her.

The strings are out of tune, and it takes a little force, but I twist the knobs unstuck. My reflection gleams in the dark-red wood that looks almost black, and I only make enough noise to tune. Then I listen to the darkness and the rain.

If Mom were here, she'd make up her own song. She'd start with one note. A single note. The first note she heard in the rain. Then she'd match it with a chord and a harmony, and all the other things that only music can find.

My first note is a G.

Not anything special. Just a simple, solid G.

Because this isn't Mom's song.

This one is mine.

# Marion

I slump in the bay window of my bedroom and stare out at the backyard. My hair is matted damp on my neck, and I try to breathe as the rain picks up again and floods the rooftop. Raises the level of the stream, dragging the rose hips under.

The oak tree is barely visible with the porch light, and its thousands of branches tangle—

Wet as thick worms.

I hear Kurt playing that song in the back of my mind. I hear him whispering his secrets and asking why one chooses to drown. How darkness can consume us. How . . .

I cough—

I gag.

Like I've swallowed all those branches and I'm choking them down.

The creek water squished between my toes.

Mud in my toes as he unzipped his—
Dirty mud in my toes.
Dirty, dirty mud.
Worm in my mouth.

# sixteen

# Kurt

**The grass in the backyard is still wet from the rain.** A breeze drifts through and everything smells fresh, like rainwater and metal. I tune my guitar and I'm not sure I want to play this morning. But I want to sit here, next to that spot that was Mom's. Take this one note at a time.

"Was that one of Mom's songs you played last night?"

I turn to see Josie sitting on her windowsill. She's in her bedroom with the window open, leaned up against the screen.

"You heard that?"

She nods, scratching her arm. "Yeah, it woke me up. I thought Mom was out here for a minute. Thought maybe I was dead." She catches a scab with her nail and a glint of blood colors her skin. "But then I saw it was you. I should have known. It was too pretty, that song. That's not how I remember Mom's songs."

"No?" I ask. "How *do* you remember them?"

"Not like that," she says, picking at the blood. "Sadder."

"Mom's songs weren't sad."

"Yes, they were, Kurt. They were awful."

I grip my guitar and turn the knobs, the pitch out of whack. "Then why didn't anyone *do* something?"

Josie lets out a weak laugh. That's the million-dollar question, isn't it? There's a hundred things we think we should have done—now, after—only if we went back in time . . . would we have done any of them?

"Well . . ." Josie's voice gets bright and cheeky. "We could have locked her up!" She wiggles her ankle bracelet at me. "That might have been fun."

I frown at her and that bunched-up feeling tightens in my chest. The sarcastic tone in her voice says she meant that as a joke, but of course it's not.

"Josie, I—" I pluck the A string. It's out of tune. Am I supposed to apologize? Tell her I know how fucked-up this is? Of course I want to get that thing off her ankle, but where would she go if she was free? That's the part that scares me. What if I never see her again?

She gets quiet and doesn't say anything, and maybe she feels that. Or maybe this is just another one of those moments with walls between us, with her on that side of the screen and me on mine.

"Play me that song," she says, breaking the quiet. "The one from last night."

"It's not anything." I shake my head. "It's not one of Mom's."

"Good." Her cheek presses against the screen and I can't

read her eyes, gray mesh hiding them. "Play it," she says, her voice getting strong. "This house needs music. Fuck the dead."

I smile at that. *That* sounds like my sister.

I brush the strings. It really isn't a song yet. It's just a bunch of chords still trying to find. I work through the mess, and there's something in it—a rhythm, a phrase, something I can feel, and I want to trust it. That's all I know. I want to believe in the possible.

"What do you think?" I ask when I'm done, but Josie's looking past me to the trees. "Hey, Jos." I try again, but she's in some other place in her mind. It reminds me of how she used to watch Mom and me from that window ledge, wanting to be out here with us. Only, Mom kept the music for just me, and selfishly, I liked it that way.

"I'm sorry Mom never taught you how to play," I say, but she stares into the trees. Her tongue jets into that empty space where her tooth should be, still looking for what's missing, knowing something should be there. And I hate the feeling that crawls through me, because *I* can see that tooth is gone, but *she can't*. And it scares me to think we're both searching for something that isn't there anymore. It scares me to think how blind we must be.

# Marion

Before first period, Conner Aimes stalks up to me and slams himself into the locker next to mine. He tips back his Red Sox hat and glares.

"Conner . . . ?" I say cautiously.

"You the reason Kurt skipped practice?" he snaps.

"Excuse me?" I swing my locker open, noting how he's positioned himself so I can't hide behind the door.

"You heard me."

"Isn't that something you should ask him?"

"I'm asking *you*." He leans in and I can smell hot dogs on his breath. I pull my notebooks out of my bag and stack them carefully on top of each other.

"What do you want me to say, Conner?"

"I want to know if he was *with you* or not."

My skin crawls with the way he says that, like I'm meat, distracting Kurt with the parts of me that are far less important than a soccer ball.

"Fuck you, Conner." I slam my locker and stalk away.

The hallway has too many elbows. I can't get far enough, fast enough. Conner's hand slaps onto my shoulder and I whip around to face him.

"Seriously, what do you want?"

The crowd parts and people stare. Conner angles the brim of his hat between himself and the onlookers, nodding for us to move into the stairwell. I don't oblige.

"Look," Conner hisses, trying to keep his voice down. "Kurt's never missed a practice in his life, all right. In his *life*. You get me?"

Conner stares at me, but his feet do an impatient dance below him. He glances around, unsure how long I'm going to make him stand here, and the pressure of everyone's eyes makes me nervous. He nods to the stairwell again, and this time I concede.

"Look, Kurt doesn't talk," Conner admits, stopping under the stairs. "I just need to know what's going on. I'm not trying to get into your shit or—" He makes a half-obscene gesture.

"You want me to walk away again?" I snap.

"No! Look . . ." He yanks his hat off and strangles it between his hands. "Just level with me, okay?"

I stare at him, ready to demand an apology, but I can't ignore his unsettled expression.

"Okay," I say, stepping back and waiting for a freshman who's slowed at the bottom of the stairs to pass.

"So?"

"So, we went for a drive."

"And?"

"And then we went to a guitar shop."

"A guitar shop?"

"Kurt plays the guitar," I say, eyeing him. "I'm sure you know that." He frowns, and I can't tell if he does or not, which completely blindsides me. Are Kurt and Conner not that close? Are they like Lilith and me? Age-old friends, but everything is half-truths and secrets, buried so deep it's hard to know where to begin.

"And?"

I adjust my bag. "And then we got stuck in the rain." One of Conner's eyebrows rises slightly. "Seriously?" I snap, sick of his innuendos.

"Fine, fine." He waves a hand like a white flag, but I can tell what I've said isn't satisfactory. Not because Kurt and I didn't get rain-happy, but because it doesn't add up for him.

"That's it."

"That's it?" he echoes angrily.

I think about my hand on Kurt's shoulder and that ocean of rain. Of the things he started to tell me, and the things I will never tell him.

"I didn't know skipping practice was abnormal for him," I say. Conner shakes his head and his sneakers squeak against the floor. "Conner, that's it. What else do you want—"

"Whatever," he says, twisting that hat and ducking out from under the stairwell. He's almost gone when I call after him.

"Hey, do you know—" I pause when he looks back, not sure if this is the right time to ask. Not sure there is *ever* a right time to ask. "Do you know when Kurt's mom died?"

Conner's muscles tense and the hat in his hand goes still.

I've crossed a line. "Forget it," I say, turning to go. "Never mi—"

"He talked about her?" Conner eyes me, but his tone isn't angry.

"Well, sort of." I tilt my head so my hair falls in my face like a shield. "He talked about her drinking."

"Was this yesterday?"

I nod, but it feels wrong to admit that to him, even if he is Kurt's friend. "You know, I shouldn't be talking about—"

"He was thirteen," Conner interrupts. "And you're right, you shouldn't." His stare scolds me, but his tone is kind. "He doesn't talk to *anyone* about her."

Conner watches me as footsteps bang up the stairwell over our heads; his stance is defensive, his body rigid with jealousy. But something in his expression is sad. He stares me down, but there's a tinge of hope in that look. And that's when it hits me, what that look actually is—it's respect. His lip tightens and he puts his baseball hat back on.

"If Kurt's going to skip practice," he says, "he should tell me first. Got that?"

"Okay." I nod.

The bell for homeroom rings, but he doesn't leave.

"Did he talk about Josie?"

I shake my head. "No, who's Jos—?"

"His sister." His gaze hits the floor. Voices and movement rush past us as the crowd heads to class. I feel the pull to join them, uncomfortable with all that Kurt has trusted me with.

"Did she die too?" I ask.

"No," Conner says, shaking his head, but then he stops. "Well, maybe." He looks at me then. "You should ask him about her."

# Kurt

Marion walks ahead of me down the hall. I watch the small of her back. Her hair. The slight tilt to her shoulders, hitched to the right. She bends with the weight of her bag and moves through the crowd.

I don't want to be blindsided by her. I want to keep this hopeful feeling.

I follow her until I can't stand it anymore and I slide up beside her. She doesn't know I'm there until I slip my fingers into her hand. She startles, then calms as I squeeze her fingers. It reminds me of her hand on my shoulder. Of her and me . . . Learning how to do this.

She squeezes me back and I pick up my pace and let go. I walk through the crowd ahead of her, because I don't want this to be a scene. This is just the quick brush of a hand. *We* aren't something everyone else has to see.

Conner walks with me to the practice field, matching my stride even though I'm faster than him. Our cleats dig into dirt. He says nothing. Not even a joke.

"I covered for you," he says finally, eyes trained on the field.

I didn't ask him to do that. But I knew he would.

"I told Coach it was a stomach bug. That you were throwing up." He rolls his shoulders, not liking the lie. "It's your deal now. Got me? You gotta convince Coach not to bench you."

"What, you can't hold the offensive line without me?" I joke, but he stops in his tracks.

"I do fine without you." He squares his shoulders. "The question is, what are you going to do when I stop cleaning up your mess?"

I stare at him, shocked.

"Con, I—"

"We're late," he says, showing me his back. "Keep up."

At practice we run and do drills and I try to get him to ease up. I set him up for shots. Pass him the ball. Wait for him to return the favor or make a joke. But he makes his plays with Troy and Andy instead.

Ignores me.

# Marion

I lean against my car in the parking lot and stare at the mountain tipped in sunlight. I can't see the soccer field from my angle, but I didn't want to be too obvious by waiting by the field. The air is crisp and I can't keep my mind off yesterday's rain. Off floods and Kurt's music and mothers drowned in 80 proof or lost on the other side of the sea. Is it because my mom is gone that he felt I might understand? That I'm trustworthy?

What makes anyone ready to spill a secret?

A sparkle of gold sun sits on the edge of the mountain, a single glare of light flickering vibrantly. It's a grain of sand in my eye, with the whole sun hidden below it. You're not supposed to look directly at the sun. Not in the daylight when it's exposed and scalding the sky. Looking at a star that close will burn out your eyes. It's only meant to be seen half-shadowed, with the whole body of the earth to protect you.

"Hey! You hungry?"

I expect to see Kurt, but it's Abe. I squint as he leans

into the sunlight next to me, orange light tangling his curls. I have to look away and not let my eyes linger.

"I'm fine," I say. "And I have a thing."

"Right," he says, scuffing his shoe against the asphalt. "Of course you do."

He says it quietly, drumming his fingers against the metal of my car. Everything about him seems sad, like he's giving up and I'm that ridiculous girl on the Ferris wheel again, always striking matches and pretending I know how to play with fire. My palms press into the metal of my car, and my pinkie finger falls against his. He stills at the touch and I want to explain to him that I'm not that girl anymore, that I *do* think about him like that. I just . . . I'm not allowed to. Not with that soccer field just out of sight. Not with the secrets I'm supposed to keep.

But one secret always spills into the next, and before I know it Kurt will expect more of me. He'll see the mud in my toes and the rose hips that don't allow me to speak. But not Abe. Abe is different. He isn't a minefield that wakes the secrets in me. Abe is starting again.

"Okay, well . . ." Abe pushes off the car to leave, but I hook him with our pinkies. Warmth spreads through my chest when he looks back at me.

"I'm sorry," I say, but it comes out wrong. It sounds like a good-bye, when I'm desperate for him to stay.

"Don't be," he says, annoyance in his voice. "I get it."

"No, I mean the carnival."

That stops him.

It stops me, too. I want to be brave and apologize for how I ruined us. Clear the air. But the way our pinkies hook together feels uncomfortable, like being in my car with my hand on Kurt's shoulder. Something I can't take back.

"I mean," I say quietly, trying to find my breath. "I mean, how I broke up with you."

Abe is so still that his thumb is not tapping. We've never talked about this. His eyes hit me and it's clear he's been waiting a long time to hear this.

"Okay," he says, and my tongue goes limp.

"I, um . . ." I try to gauge his reaction, but his expression is stone. "I was a stupid girl." I unlatch our fingers and bite the edge of my thumb, pressing the nail into my lip. "I didn't know what I was doing and I didn't know how, how to . . ."

My words are hot, caught and thick.

"You," I stumble. "You were my first kiss. My first . . ." I drop my hand and gesture awkwardly to my chest, and the parts of me he's touched, because I don't have a word for that. Then the first that is Kurt, aches through me, and I don't think I can do this.

"Uh-huh?" he prods. He wants the rest.

"I care about you," I whisper, my hands shaking. "I just . . . I just didn't know how to be *with* you. Or how to talk to you . . ."

I look up and his eyes are kind. Thank God, they're kind.

"I didn't know how to let you . . ." I feel the ocean on me. "How to let you"—waves breaking over and under— "touch me."

He stands silently, rigidness all through him.

"I was a stupid—"

"You were never stupid, M," he says. "You were just scared."

My cheeks pinch and I purse my lips tight. It seems so obvious when he says it out loud. I look at the ground, feeling that sick-blue pinch of sugar at the back of my throat. Cotton candy I couldn't swallow.

"Maybe." I look up, trying to salvage us. "Maybe I'm not scared anymore."

His eyes go dark. Desire dark. And there's no more sun.

"Marion." He moves fast, stepping so close to me that I can smell the soap on his skin. His closeness is disarming and the edge of his mouth brushes the hair on my cheek as he moves it to my ear. "There's a point when you're going to have to decide what you want," he says, lingering there too long, and my whole body clenches. "And when you decide what you want, you're going to have to ask for it."

He steps away from me and the mix of cold and heat between us leaves me tingling. His silver eyes sparkle and I feel paralyzed and more confused than ever.

"Enjoy your *thing*," he says, walking away without another word, and I don't know what to do with the heat he's left rippling through me. He gets into his pickup and drives away, and I jam my wrists against the silver door handles of my car. I let my hair whip around my face in the swell of the breeze, and I'm glad Abe's gone because I don't know what to do with him. With this craving. I close my eyes and breathe in the air that smells snowy and fresh like white linen and pearl buttons and—

A soft palm squeezes mine.

I want to melt into him. I don't care who this heat is for, I just want to burn.

"Your car or mine?" Kurt asks, but all I want is his mouth.

"Mine," I say, handing him my keys.

Once we're in my car I crawl over and kiss him long and hot. His hands slide around my waist and up my shirt, and our mouths fog the windows.

"Where?" he asks, breathless.

"Anywhere," I say, kissing him again, and he turns the ignition.

# Kurt

I take Marion to my house. It's a bad idea. Josie will be home. Dad will be home. Not to mention Josie looks the way she does. But I'm tired of the car.

Dad's truck is gone when we arrive, which seems too lucky, but I'll take it.

I try not to notice the look on Marion's face when she takes in my concrete house. My overgrown yard. The chain link between our lot and the next. This is exactly why I don't take anyone to my house. But her hand slides into mine and she nuzzles herself against me and all I want is the bed.

"My sister," I say. "She's gonna be home."

"Josie?" she asks, and I'm surprised she knows her name.

"Do you remember her? She graduated when we were sophomores."

Marion shrugs, like she doesn't want to admit she's paid any attention to my life. It makes me kiss her until it's hard to breathe.

I get out and walk her to the front door.

"Look, Josie's been gone awhile," I say, trying to prepare her as I get out my keys. "She looks . . . different." I hesitate with the key in the lock. "I'd appreciate it if you didn't tell anyone about her or . . ."

Marion kisses me so lightly my whole body throbs.

Inside, the house is a mess. It looks normal to me, but to Marion . . . I've been in her house, and it doesn't look like this. Dirty bowls on the coffee table. Ratty old couch. That cigarette smell imbedded three inches thick.

I don't see Josie anywhere.

I consider opening a window, but I lead Marion to my room instead. Down the hall it's dark, daylight glowing faintly behind three small curtains, and Josie's door is closed.

"I think she's sleeping," I whisper to Marion, nodding to my sister's door.

Everything's quiet.

Too quiet.

I wonder if I should go check on her. Or look to see if Dad's left a note. But Marion kisses my cheek and her salty smell makes me forget them.

My room doesn't have a lock. I jam a chair under the knob, which takes a couple tries, and Marion pretends to be interested in the trophies over my desk.

"Those are from soccer," I say, messing with the chair. "But a few are from middle school, and track."

Tiny flecks of gold reflect from the trophies onto the

wall. They catch the light from the window over my bed. The sheets are rumpled. Half on. Half off. Left that way from this morning, because I didn't expect to have—

"Sorry about the mess." I pick up a stray shirt and chuck it into the hamper and straighten the sheets. "Just give me a—"

"It's fine," Marion interrupts, her voice right behind me. Hand on my back. I turn and her mouth presses into mine. I wrap my arms around her and our bodies find the bed. Sheets tangle with the smell of her. Of us. Of clothes being removed, and sweat, and me in—

Her body arcs and this is *not* like in the car. It's not closed windows and feet against door handles and bunched-up jeans half-off and wedged. There's room for both of us in this bed and I'm overwhelmed by the space of it. There's space for elbows and arms. There's space for legs and limbs. And I want all of it. I want every inch.

# Marion

**I tremble and want this moment.**

I want it to hold me. To burn me. To sear me with his breath, and his words, and his him.

I want to hang on to his touch and his scent and the brush of crisp-soft sheets against my toes and shins.

I want this to keep. I *don't* want this to dissolve, like it did the first time, into rose hips, and creek water, and unspeakable skin.

But he's tender. Too tender. And everything frail and soft and vulnerable—

Turns into mud.

# seventeen

# Kurt

SEVENTEEN

**The sheets stick to the sweat of my legs and Marion** rolls off me.

She turns, clutching her hair, and leaves me to look at the white of her back. Her shoulder blades arch and her body trembles. I've seen her like this before. That first time in my car.

The sheets tangle over us, but we don't touch. I put a hand on her shoulder. But she shakes it off.

"Please don't," she whispers.

My hand hovers over her. Useless. I ball it up into a fist and stare at the ceiling. Stare at the gold flecks from my trophies that are spit over the walls, a hundred tiny pieces broken in the light.

I hate what I'm hearing. Marion's crying sounds like when I could hear Josie through the wall. But I was too scared to knock on her door, because she was going to tell me to fuck off. And this is just like Mom coming home obliterated and me not asking why. Hoping she knew how to figure it out herself. Hoping she knew how to hang on.

This sounds exactly like that. Just as far away. Just as close.

And I'm sick of it.

I roll over and pull Marion against me. I wrap her in my arms and refuse to ignore it. I hold her tight and promise not to let go. She tries to shake me, just like Josie did with her fuck-you glare, but I won't let her. I'm not walking away from this.

I'm going to see this.

Hold her through it.

I won't let her find some other way to chase the pain— music, booze, whatever. I'm going to sit here in it.

With her.

It takes a minute for Marion to realize I'm not letting her go. But when she finally does, her shoulders release, relaxing into a new quiet, and then they heave and she sobs.

Sobs with her whole body rocking against me. Sobs about something I don't know, and maybe I can't know, and maybe I will never know.

I want to understand, but maybe I don't *need* to. Maybe all I need is to be here, and that's what fills the void. Maybe all I need is for her to understand that she doesn't have to do this alone.

# Marion

**He holds me so tight it feels like something new** breaks in me. A flood that I didn't know was in there. And I'm tired. Of holding it in. So he holds, and I cry.

I cry for all the things I can't say. For the loss, and the naked parts of me, and the shame. For the tenderness of his touch, that may never do anything but bring the darkness to wake. For being a child.

When Kurt finally releases me, the sheets are a puddle beside my head. He touches my shoulder, my spine, my hip, and then lets me lie here in the sheets. I stay still, breathing, for what seems like an hour, and the shadows grow dim.

Then there's music.

Fragile acoustic music. It comes with the brush of his arm on my back. Soft. Meant to comfort. It comes with his heart, and his secrets, and his him. And I should love this. I *want* to love this.

But I can't.

Love means trust, and trust means letting it rise—the

silence that I don't talk about, the invisible that is only allowed to be shimmering half-truths and not really seen. He's not allowed to make those parts of me become solid in the light. I won't let him. I won't let him coax it out of me. It's too dark and black, and all the oceans and rain can't wash it out. My shame is too messy, and love is supposed to be clean.

"I have to go," I say, sitting up and collecting my clothes.

Kurt stops strumming, and I have to turn away from his concerned eyes, wanting all of me. The room goes quiet and I slide on my shirt. My jeans. My socks. The sun is almost gone and a tiny bow of orange is all that's left rimming the window.

His hands press into his guitar strings and the tiny vibrations cut out.

"Are you sure?" he asks, as I walk to the door, my whole face puffy from crying. I look back, and for the first time he looks naked—vulnerable—with only his guitar over his lap. His knees press awkwardly together and his toes dig under the sheets.

"You don't have to tell me," he says, running a hand over his arm, covering his chest. I unhook the chair and move it back to the desk. "Whatever it is," he insists. "You never have to tell me."

But that's not how this works. Of course I have to tell him for this to be what he thinks that it is. For us to be what he wants. My hand falls on the doorknob and he's up.

Guitar left behind him on the bed.

"Don't," he says, putting his hand on the door, and I can't ignore the way my body reacts when he's as close as he is. How my skin knows his skin.

"Kurt . . ." I barely get the word out. All of this caught in my throat. I step away from him, needing distance. Everything too near the surface.

"Stay, please," he says. "I *don't* have to know."

I glare at him, anger slicing through me, furious at him for wanting me to pretend. The fact that he knows there's *anything* to tell, is the problem. Nothing real, nothing important can start like this! Not with this secret sitting between us. And the fact that he wants to pretend it isn't there—like Lilith, like my father—infuriates me.

"I have to go!" I say, whipping my hair off my neck.

"You don't." He presses himself against the door to keep it shut. "You can—"

But his voice drops out and gets raspy, unguarded in a way that scares me more than anything else about him. I can hardly breathe and the room smells like sweat and dust and I wish he had something to cover himself with.

"This . . . ," he says, his voice trembling. "You, me . . ."

He struggles for the words, fidgeting with his hands, and his eyes flick to the bed, like he wants the sheet to cover his legs. But he looks at it for so long, it scares me to think perhaps I'm the only one he's ever taken to that bed. That everyone else gets the car and the ridge.

"Marion, I . . ."

My chest squeezes and I know what he's going to say before he says it. Only, I don't want to hear it out loud, because it's not true. It can't be true when he doesn't know all of me. Not with the shame and shitty parts that are filled with mud and darkness.

No one can love those parts.

"Marion, I lo—"

"I'm not your mother!" The words splinter out of me. It's a low blow, and it scares me with how harsh it comes out. But I needed something to stop him—anything. I couldn't hear him say it.

I cough, and try to glare at him like I mean it.

"I'm not some girl you're supposed to save," I say, and everything about him goes rigid, the softness in his eyes turning to ice.

"Fuck you." His glare hits me hard, and the sun is gone. His words are pained and angry, and I know I've used something he's trusted me with. A secret. But he should never have trusted me with it. He shouldn't have told me about his mother. Sharing those parts only makes him vulnerable, gives other people ammunition. People like me. Only, I know it was shitty and I shouldn't have used it.

But this is what I do when I'm backed into a corner.

Shame crawls through me and I can't bear to face him. I reach for the doorknob, my knuckles brushing his side, and he jets away from me. He stalks to the far end of the room and yanks the sheet off the bed to cover himself.

I stare at his back, knowing I've broken something. I wanted to walk out of this room unscathed, but that isn't the nature of things. Lake water or ocean, if you touch the surface, it will ripple. If you dive under, it will never be the same.

There's only one way to fix this. But I can't give him that grenade. No one's allowed to have that part of me.

I get in my car and drive. Drive away from Kurt's house. From his arms. From his skin.

Away.

Away from what knowing too much of me brings.

I roll down all the car's windows and the cab turns into a whipping air-tunnel of night and hair. It slashes around me uncaged. And I need this wildness out of me. I need to believe I'm not this person, this mean and angry girl, lashing out.

Kurt is all wrong for me. He's been wrong from the beginning. No one starts a relationship half-naked and crying. Not like on the ridge. That's not how anything important is supposed to start. Love stories begin with daydreams and wishes, and sweet kisses on the back of your hand. Not mud. Not sand.

I press the gas, and black trees streak past. Too close. I need someone else. Someone whose touch doesn't dissolve into rose hips and beach peas and feet drowned in the sand. Of course Kurt wakes those things. How could he not? Our first kiss was on the ridge, with his hands in my hair, wanting nothing but to take things from me, and force—

I hit a pothole and my car swerves. Metal rattles and the weight of this threatens to swallow me. My knuckles grip. I smell burned rubber and my instincts kick in, realigning the tires between the double yellows and the white.

I drive, trees blurring on both sides of me. Hair blocking my vision.

I need to believe that skin can be skin and nothing else. That skin can be silent, and not wake with memories that pull me into their current to drown. I need to believe there is another side of this, where you can have a relationship with someone who doesn't need to get that close to you. That there can be clean slates, and apple trees, and beginning again.

So, I drive.

Because there's only one person who's supposed to be my Prince Charming. One person who will release the bad magic. The person who knows me. The person I can trust. The one who started all this as my friend, and liked me because I was smart, not because of my pretty blond hair.

So, I drive.

And I don't stop until I'm at Abe's house.

# Kurt

My trophies are dark above the desk. I sit on the
bed and pull my guitar onto my lap. Shadows fall over the
neck and the maple wood sticks to my thigh. Everything
in this room is small.

The window.

The bed.

Me.

I keep seeing Marion's eyes slicing through me, red and
wet and—

Nasty.

Like Mom's.

Like she was pissed at me for—I don't know—being
here. For not letting her out that door. For seeing her at all.

This *wasn't* about Mom. And fuck her for thinking it
was. Only there was no air in this room, and there still isn't.
And I don't know how to get any of them to stay.

Isn't it *enough* that she doesn't have to tell me why she

sobs like that? Isn't it *enough* that I'll be here for her no matter what? That I love her. That—

My chest hitches, air caught.

I pluck one string on my guitar and wish I hadn't. The note fills up the empty room, and it's hard to breathe.

But I keep plucking that one string anyway.

G and—

G and—

G.

Because it hurts.

But the quiet hurts more.

"Who was that girl?"

I look up and Josie is standing in the doorway. I pull the sheet up over my guitar and legs.

"Well, I'll be damned," she says, smiling and showing off that empty space where her tooth is missing. "Good for you, little brother."

Her voice is so warm, she almost sounds like herself again.

"It wasn't like that," I say, swallowing back the ache in my chest. How good it was. How it's gone.

"You like her, huh?"

The brightness of Josie's voice echoes through the room with everything else I can't hold on to. I look down at the guitar in my lap—an awkward lump under the sheet. Shapeless and too large.

Josie leans against my door frame and I want to tell her about Marion. I want to tell her that I don't just *like* this girl. I want Josie to sit at the end of my bed and listen, with that toothless grin on her face. I don't want to explain it. I just want—

The phone rings. Not mine, but the house phone in the kitchen.

Josie jolts up, pushing herself off the door frame and toward the kitchen with an energy I didn't know that she had.

What's she—?

I move out of instinct, tossing my guitar to the side and pulling on my pants.

The ringing has stopped and I find Josie in the kitchen with Mom's phone cord wrapped around her. Receiver up to her mouth.

"Tina? Yeah, hey!" She coughs into the receiver.

"Who's Tina?" I ask, but this crazy smile spreads over her face like she just won the lottery.

"Yeah, yeah. Hold on," Josie says into the phone, finding a pen and scribbling an address on the inside of her arm. I try to sneak a look, but Josie holds a finger up telling me to wait. She listens to whatever the person on the line is saying. "Kurt." Josie caps a hand over the receiver. "You have a car, right?"

"For what?"

"To meet." She nods to the phone.

"Meet who?"

"My friend."

"Who's going to give you *what*?"

That slap-happy grin falls from her face so fast you'd think I killed a puppy. What the hell is up with this day? First Marion, now Josie? All I want is to walk out of this damn kitchen and forget them. Only Marion broke something in me, and I can't ignore this.

"All right, slow down," I say, her sad face cutting into me. "Give me the phone. Let me talk to them." She hands me the receiver and her fingers feel like twigs. "Who is this?" I demand, untangling Josie from the cord, and there's a silence on the other end that makes me squirm. "Hello?"

"Josie?" The voice is female and far away.

"Who is this? And why are you calling my sister?"

"Is she all right?"

"What would you know about it?"

"Probably more than you," the girl says bluntly, and I don't like it. "Can you put her back on the phone?"

"No. How about you tell me who you are and what's going on?"

"Kurt!" Josie snaps at me. "She's an old friend."

"Hi, old friend," I say way too snarky, but I want to cut through the shit. "What are you going to give my sister?"

"Fuck you, Kurt!" Josie tries to grab the phone but

I won't let her have it. She gives up after a second and throws her hands in the air. "You think all I need is you and Dad and to be locked up in this hellhole? You think *this* is a life?! Don't delude yourself into thinking that just because I'm home I won't slit my wrists or hang myself in the shower!"

I feel like I've been kicked in the gut. Josie rolls her eyes like I should have seen that coming.

"God, Kurt, there's a hundred ways to check out of here that have nothing to do with Mom's truck."

"You wouldn't do that."

"Wouldn't I?" That angry, dead-eyed Josie is back. "Give me one good reason not to."

My gut's in my throat. This isn't happening. Not after—

"You wouldn't do that to Dad and me," I choke out, but the glare in her eyes says otherwise.

"Right," she says, that eerie hoarseness returning to her voice. "After he kicked me out. After you did—what? When have you ever cared about me, Kurt?"

"I, I—" I rack my brain, and it horrifies me when I can't think of something to say. My mind is spinning, and this is happening too fast. It's possible I didn't do enough, but I didn't do *nothing*. "You were gone," I say, but the words feel so damn small.

"No, I wasn't." Her eyes get glassy. "*Mom* was gone, not me. You were so ready to save Mom. But you didn't give a shit when I needed you, Kurt! Dad checked out, but God, you didn't have to go with him."

"I am *not* like Dad."

Josie shakes her head. "You're exactly like Dad," she says quietly.

"I'm *nothing* like—" But my lip trembles and I don't want to see it. The cord to the phone is wrapped so tight around my arm, my hand is red.

"Can I talk to my friend?" She nods at the phone.

I lift the receiver, not sure if anyone's still on the other end. "Hello?" I say into it, feeling like Marion and Josie's bloody punching bag. "Hello? Tina?" I ask again, but the following silence is so big I don't want to tell my sister her friend's not there.

"Yeah, hi," the small voice says, and it's stupid how relieved I am to hear it.

"Tina?" I grip the phone.

"I'm still here." Her voice sounds like an arrow shot through all the dark. I don't know who this person is, or what she knows about my sister, but I can see the desperation in Josie. Her skin is gray, dried up with lesions that all the lotion in the world can't make smooth again, and her eyes are scared, like if we don't do this—

She's got nothing left.

When Josie lived here, I heard her crying on the other side of that wall. Crying every night. And I ignored it.

I can't do that again.

"Give me one good reason to trust you," I say into the phone. "I lost my sister once. I don't want to lose her again." Something warms in Josie's expression, but that alone isn't going to make me okay with this. In fact, I haven't a clue what this Tina person could possibly say that will make me want to take Josie to see her.

"I saved your sister's life," the voice says. "Twice."

Except maybe that.

# eighteen

# Marion

Abe's father answers the door. He isn't in uniform but the cruiser sits in the driveway. His mustache is trimmed and even though he's in civilian clothes his presence is impressive.

"Marion?" He gives me the cop squint.

"Hi, Mr. Doyle. I, um . . ." I cough and wipe my chin. "Is Abe home?"

He stares at me a second, like he's trained to do that, to wait for a confession. I tuck my hair back and he straightens the left side of his mustache with his thumb.

"Abe's up in his room," he says, stepping back. "Would you like to come in?"

"No." I ignore the warm lights of the hallway. I don't want to remember Abe's house from before, the sweet balsam of the wood furniture, or the flannel blanket over the love seat. I want this to reinvent myself.

"I can wait here," I say. "If you don't mind sending him down."

He straightens the other side of his mustache.

"Are you all right?"

I look to the forest. Somewhere in the trees I can hear branches fencing with the wind, their thin gray fingers grasping against the air.

"Of course, sir," I say, pulling away the strands of hair that stick to my face. "If this is a bad time I can—"

"No." He checks his watch. "I'll get him." But he doesn't move, eyeing me instead. "Please." He motions to the hallway again. "You're not wearing a coat."

I look down and he's right. My arms are covered in goose bumps and all I'm wearing is a thin T-shirt with no bra underneath. I pull my hair forward to cover my chest and step into the foyer.

"Thank you," I say, and Mr. Doyle closes the door. The warmth covers my arms and I breathe in, remembering this house and its rustic smell of wool and soap.

"Would you like a hot drink?" he asks as I cross my arms.

"No, thank you, sir. I'll wait here. "

"There's hot tea in the kitchen."

"I'm fine."

He hesitates, looking me over again, before heading for the stairs.

"I'll get Abe."

I nod and wait, hearing his footsteps on the second landing. I imagine Abe up in his bedroom doing homework on his plaid comforter. The same comforter that lay under us two years ago when our relationship changed from apples and dandelion wishes to something more physical.

I can do this, be with Abe. I'm supposed to be with him. He was always the one. Everything will be different with him. It has to be.

The fireplace in the living room snaps, shooting a cough of ash against the grate. The warmth of Abe's house is suffocating. What if being with Abe isn't different? What if I really am this girl, lost and on fire, and full of darkness?

I hear footsteps on the floorboards above. *What* am I doing here? I can't just show up on Abe's doorstep and expect him to fall into my arms and want me. That's insane.

I shouldn't be here.

I turn and walk out the door.

I invite the invisibility and the wind as my hair tangles everywhere, over my face and neck. There's wildness inside me, reckless as the cold outside.

"Marion, wait!"

Abe jogs out of his house as I unlatch my car door. He skips on one foot when he gets to the grass, his feet bare, responding to the ground that's damp. After a moment, he gives up on keeping his feet dry, and speeds through the grass.

"What's going on?" He puts a hand on my car. "What are you doing here?"

"I'm not here," I say, letting the wind fray my hair. I stare at the woods beyond my car and think about climbing a tree, wrapping myself in its tar shadows and climbing up so high the thin branches won't be able to hold me.

"You *are* here." He frowns, and I notice his curls are wet, freshly showered.

"It's nothing. I just—" Over his shoulder, Mr. Doyle is standing in the open doorway. Abe follows my gaze and waves off his father.

"It's fine," he hollers, but it takes a minute for Mr. Doyle to retreat into the glow of the house. "What's wrong?" Abe rests a hand on my shoulder and I feel the warmth of him through my shirt.

"Why does something have to be wrong?" Wet pricks my eyes and I turn into the wind. He's not allowed to see this broken part of me, it will ruin everything. His hand falters, a nervous finger fluttering at the hem of my skin.

"Okay, what's *not* wrong?" He steps back and runs a hand through his hair. "What's . . . what do you . . ." His arms drop to his sides. He looks at me—plainly.

Heat stretches through, under, and in, and I'm dizzy with it. I can do this. I can. Everything with Kurt is secrets and messiness, mud and shame, but with Abe, Abe will be lighter. Easier. Clean.

Abe won't bring the creek water.

"Can we get out of here?" I ask, eyeing the windows.

He looks over his shoulder and I step in close, wanting his nearness, wanting his heat and his smell of freshness and soap. When he turns back, he's startled by how close I am.

"I, um . . ." His breath hits my lashes and he swallows. His eyes dip down my neck to the cotton that barely hides what's beneath. "I might have to—"

"Get in," I say, tugging open the car door and stepping away from him. His body follows me unconsciously.

"Wait, I should—" His eyes dart to the house.

"Get in." I drop into the driver's seat and turn the ignition.

"Hold on, let me—" He looks back, about to cross the lawn for permission.

"Abe."

He looks at the seat beside me and shoots around the car, taking the passenger seat. His toes curl against the sand on the floor, his feet wet and bare. The dirt sticking.

"Where are we going?" he asks, and I pull into the road.

"You'll see."

I roll down my window and air rushes over me. Air rushes over my neck and under the cotton of my shirt. My hair whips around me like ocean waves crashing, and Abe smiles, getting wind drunk with me.

This is possible. I can feel it. It's already lighter.

More joy. More surface. More wind.

I press my foot to the gas and drive us past the seashore, and the firefly fields, and the apple orchards—

To the forest—

To the turn where the trees part and the dirt road winds up to the ridge. To the place where people go, to do, what you do, in cars like this one.

# Kurt

I put Josie in an oversized sweater and hat. We go outside and she's so thin she starts to shiver. I wrap an arm around her and there's so little of her under that sweater, I can grab a whole fistful of the sleeve before I find her arm.

My foot hits something. That *thing* on her ankle. I shake my head, because I haven't got the key.

"Do you need a coat?" I ask Josie, knowing the second we leave the property Dad's going to know something's up. He'll be pissed. But that's something I'll have to deal with later.

"Where's the—" Josie inhales sharply, and I look up to see what she sees.

"Fuck!" I kick the ground.

The driveway's empty. I took Marion's car here. Not mine.

"Hold on," I say, pulling Josie close to get her to settle. "Give me a minute, I'll solve this."

I take out my cell and dial. I smell old yarn as Josie burrows her head into my shoulder. It's the hat. Something Mom bought at a yard sale when we were kids. I want to forget the phone and just hold her, but Conner picks up.

"What do you want?" he snaps, still pissed.

"Con, look, I've been an ass," I say, rubbing Josie's back. "I get it. But I'm in a bind. Can you pick me up at my house?"

"For what?"

"I need a ride."

"You have your own car. Drive it."

"It's at school. Look—" Josie shivers next to me and I know the only way this will work is if I tell him the truth. "It's Josie." I hear him suck in a breath. "She's here at the house. I need to take her somewhere, but my car is at school."

There's a long silence and I see headlights through the trees.

"Josie's there?" Conner asks, unsure.

"Yeah." My voice cracks. "You know I wouldn't joke about this."

"Conner, is that you?" Josie leans into the receiver, speaking in a voice I don't think he'd even recognize. I watch the headlights come closer to our house and hope it's not Dad.

"Conner, please."

The headlights shoot past.

"Okay," he says. "I'll be there in ten."

*  *  *

Conner can't hide his shock when he gets out of his SUV and sees Josie. Even all bundled up he can see her sunken face. The lesions. That missing tooth.

"Hey, Josie," he says uncomfortably.

"Conner!" Josie skips up to him, fake-happy and putting on a show. She pulls him into a hug. "Thanks for helping."

"Yeah, sure," he says, not touching her. Instead Josie hangs on him awkwardly. He looks over her shoulder at me, and I can tell he didn't even recognize her.

"I know," I mouth to him, stepping up and pulling Josie back. "My car's at school in the lot," I say, noting Conner's face, which is almost as pale as my sister's. "You can drop us—"

"No." Conner shakes his head and opens the backseat door. "Where are *we* taking her?" His expression is firm and I know there's no talking him out of this. Not that I want to. I squeeze his shoulder to say thanks.

"Okay," I say, helping Josie into the backseat and asking her for the address.

"Thirteen Five Bishop Street," she says, wiping her nose with her knitted sleeve.

"There isn't a Bishop Street in Emerson," Conner says after climbing into the driver's seat and punching the address into the GPS. "Are you sure it's not—"

"It's in Stoneham," Josie says, interrupting him. "Not Emerson."

"Stoneham!" Conner looks at me. "That's an hour away."

"I said my car's in the lot. You don't have to—"

"No, it's just—" Conner frowns. "Are you sure about this?"

I shake my head. "No."

Conner steals a glance at Josie. His body is angled away from her like he doesn't want to see behind the shadow that's swallowed her eyes.

"Still," I say, wrapping an arm over Josie. "Gotta do this."

"All right, Stoneham it is." Conner turns the ignition and pulls into the street.

Josie kicks off her shoe and starts to mess with the tracker on her ankle, revealing dark scrapes where the skin has rubbed raw.

"Hey," I whisper, taking her hand in mine. "Stop."

She grunts in frustration, but then leans into my chest. I kiss the top of her head, and it feels good to be getting her out of the house. To be the one helping her for once. Conner turns onto the highway and I look down to see the green light on the device has stopped blinking.

It's changed to red.


We turn onto Bishop Street and that good feeling in my stomach crumples to ash. Bishop is packed with telephone wires and narrow two-story houses. The streetlamps flicker, revealing abandoned porches, and one house has particle board nailed over the windows. The rest have metal bars and grates.

House 1305 has a throw blanket over the front window instead of a curtain. It doesn't work very well, light poking through the tiny openings of thread.

"This is it?" I ask.

Josie nods, unhooking her seat belt, and I exchange a glance with Conner. This is bad. We both know it. But Josie is already getting out of the car.

"Hey, Josie, hold up," I say as she hobbles through the lopsided gate toward the steps. A shadow moves over the blanket in the window and Josie speeds up. "Hey, wait!"

Conner and I race out of the car after her, barely reaching her side when the front door opens. A shirtless man stands in the doorway sucking on two cigarettes. Bags of skin hang from his face and uneven whiskers cover his chin. He inhales deeply and his two cigarette embers glow.

"Josie." He smiles, wrapping a bony arm around my sister. "We missed you." His eyes narrow at Conner and me over her shoulder. "Tina missed you."

I taste blood in my throat.

"That's my brother and his friend," Josie says, as Cigarette Guy ignores us and walks Josie into the house.

"And you are?" I ask, following them into a living room that smells of pot and rotten eggs.

"A friend of your sister." He flicks ash at me, his bruised arm still hooked over Josie's neck.

I ball up my fists. I could take this guy. Conner and I could. No problem. But he's not the only one in the room.

Someone sleeps on the floor to our right on a bare mattress. And I hear two voices down a hall with no windows. Conner grabs my elbow. He wants me to be cool right now, but I don't think that's possible.

"Tina's in her room," the guy says, rolling his arm off Josie in a grotesque motion that makes it look like he dislocates his shoulder. She ducks under his arm and turns down the hall.

"Hey, Josie!" I call after her, and she looks back at me, her eyes bright in the dark.

"It's fine, Kurt," she says, her voice solid, like she doesn't need me. "We're just gonna catch up, okay? Give me ten."

I move to follow her, but Cigarette Guy rams a hand into my chest.

"Tina doesn't know you."

I shake him off. "I don't care."

"Nope." He shakes his head and blocks the hall. "That's not how this works."

Conner tightens his grip on me.

"I don't get to meet Tina?" I snap.

Cigarette Guy blows smoke in my face. "Nope."

Conner steps in front of me before I have a chance to punch this guy.

"How *does* this work then?" Conner asks, holding me back with his weight. Cigarette Guy glares at both of us. He grabs a metal chair and drags it in front of the hallway. Black bruises run down the inside of his arm and I remember seeing something like that on Josie's legs, when she was getting into strange cars. Going to parties.

"You wait here," Cigarette Guy says, taking a seat. "Or you wait in your car. She'll be back in ten."

"There's no way we're—"

"We'll stay here, thanks," Conner says, cutting me off, gripping me with both hands.

"This is bullshit," I say, but Conner shoots me a look. He's scared and I know it. I shouldn't have dragged him into this. Who knows what's at the end of that hall.

It was stupid to come here. I know that. But I was tired of ignoring Josie's eyes. And maybe that's who Tina is for Josie, the one who stood by her, when Dad and I were gone. Even if Tina does lives in a shit hole like this. Maybe that's what real families do. They get down in the shit with each other. See these places. Walk through it. The thought tightens my gut and I can't help but think about Marion. Walking out my door. Pushing me away. Like maybe she's caught in one of these places you're not supposed to find your way out of alone. And I let her leave.

I look to where the shadow has already swallowed Josie and there's a small red light near the floor, where her feet would be. It's the first time I'm thankful for that tracker. Only she's another red light walking away from me.

How do you know when what you're doing is going to help? How do you know it's not going to send them further into the dark? Like dumping out Mom's bottles? Like ignoring Josie? How far am I supposed to walk into the shit with them? How far before they have to turn around and choose to walk back to me?

I look up to call after my sister, but that red light—

It's already gone.

# Marion

My headlights carve a small tunnel through the trees. Ahead of me is the dirt road with a foot of saplings running along each side. Somewhere in the dark, beyond what I can see, is the ridge.

Abe sits quietly beside me, his thumb tapping on the door frame, and I have to remind myself that he always does that. That he's not nervous. That he wants to be here with me. I drive slowly because the road is pitted, and there's no more wind. No more laughter and speed. The heater hisses between us, coughing out thick air, and it seems like forever before the trees open up to reveal the cliff.

My stomach tenses, remembering Kurt and this ridge, remembering only hours ago Kurt in his bed. But Kurt brings out the worst in me. He doesn't know my favorite color or my favorite book. He only knows my skin.

I pull into the clearing and cut the engine, wondering if Abe has ever been up here before. Probably not. He doesn't do things like Kurt does. Abe is a gentleman.

I look out at the view and there's no moon. No land-scape below bathed in soft light and stars. Only a spray of clouds dotting an otherwise blackened sky.

"My dad is going to be pissed," he says as I unbuckle my seat belt.

"You can call him," I suggest, and he fidgets in his pockets.

"I don't have my phone. I don't have anything."

"Here, you can use my mine." I reach into my purse and pull out my cell. His fingers drum along the side of his jeans, but he doesn't take it, and I can tell now that he *is* nervous. Not like Kurt, who's always so sure of himself, with that grace. I tell myself it's a good thing Abe's nervous, that it proves he won't be the same.

"We don't have to be here," I say, hoping the offer to leave will make him want to stay. "I can take you home."

I put the phone on the dash, and he stares out the wind-shield. *I* want us to stay. I need to know what we can be. I lean over and smell the Ivory soap on his neck, fresh and clean.

"Forget your father," I whisper, unlatching the buckle on his safety belt, and the nylon zips over him with quick release.

"Marion, I—"

But my mouth is on his, kissing him, soft and hot and sweet. His lips open to kiss me back, and he doesn't taste one bit like Kurt. Which is good. He tastes more saccha-rine. More gentle. More teeth.

I thread my fingers through his curls and we kiss for a long time, folded together. His lips soft and polite. And I remember this about him, his tentativeness. His sweetness. It's folded with fragileness, and for a moment I feel like that girl with blue cotton candy dissolving on her tongue.

Only this needs to stay cotton candy. It's not allowed to turn into mud.

I press against him, wanting more, to show him I can be the girl I wasn't before. But his hands don't stray from my waist. I twist, my hips rolling against his lap, and he pulls away, panting.

"Hey," he whispers, his breath on my ear. "Slow down."

Panting.

Breath on my ear.

My stomach squirms and the smell of barbecue fills my nostrils. My skin tenses, because he's not allowed to wake my skin. Not like Kurt does. He's supposed to be different.

I need this to be us—just us—just me and him. Not like with Kurt. Not hands and memory, and mud under my tongue.

I need skin to *only* be skin.

I take his hands and slide them up under my shirt, over my breasts, because this has to move faster. I need to be ahead of it. Ahead of the dark, and the wet skirts, and the dirty—

Abe groans, and we are mouth and mouth again. His

fingers glide over the front of me, but his touch is so gentle, so soft, so hot—

I shudder.

It shoots an ache through me that trembles deep, touching places I don't deserve. Places that he and Kurt and *no one* are allowed to find.

And it hits me—it's not the fact that Kurt doesn't know me that wakes what's within, it's his tenderness. It's the soft way his hands explore. It's the way he learns to speak with my skin. He's fast and hot, but always gentle, always slowing, and pulling back, and listening. And it's not my favorite color or my favorite book that Kurt's trying to find. It's me. The real me. The invisible part that's naked and afraid and searching for a connection.

It's the vulnerability that wakes the water.

It's admitting that the water is part of me and worth seeing.

I press into Abe—hard—because I can't have this softness. Because slow and tender lets the darkness seep in and I can't let this be vulnerable like it is with Kurt. This is a clean slate. This is surface. Only surface. Only skin.

This can't mean anything. Not if meaning wakes the water beneath. This is only allowed to be burning and heat.

"Marion?" Abe pulls away, sliding his hands off my chest. He pants, his lips bruised with my taste. "What . . . What are we doing?"

I kiss him hard, yanking open his shirt and scattering

his buttons over the floor. I slide my shirt up over my head and press skin to skin. Drink his lips. I feel him through his pants and he groans and when I'm sure he can't get enough of me, I take him into the backseat.

"Marion, wha—?"

I take his collar and pull him against me. There isn't time for talking.

"What *is* this?" he insists.

"It's nothing," I whisper. "It's everything." I breathe hard, my lips at his ear. "It's whatever you need it to be."

Abe's weight is on top of me and we've become a mess of tangled clothes and limbs. His mouth is uncertain on mine. Too tender. Maybe second-guessing this.

"I want you," I whisper, but his hands stay at my back. I push them toward my jeans and repeat, "I want—"

"I heard you," he says, pulling his hand away and kissing me so gently it rocks the darkness inside. His kisses, like Kurt's kisses, let the creek water seep in. They're too soft and vulnerable, too—

I pull him hard against me.

"I need—"

But he resists.

"Slow down," he whispers, but I shake my head. This has to be faster.

"Abe." I squeeze my legs around him, needing his weight over me, on me, like the ocean. "Two years ago when I said I'd never sleep with you . . ."

I know now what slow and tender brings, and I want it the other way—

Where he takes me down—

Takes me under—

Lets me drown.

"I lied."

I pull him against me, smashing his lips against mine. Needing him to pull me into the hard dark that is the other side of this. Needing to believe that this can be surface and unwaking. That it's possible to do this and not taste the rose hips.

If tender brings the dark, then hard must bring the light.

But he doesn't want to.

He won't.

"Marion, stop." He pushes me off him and moves to the other side of the car, wrapping himself in his white shirt. He holds the fabric closed with his hand, ignoring his pearl buttons covering the floor.

"I thought you wanted this?" I say, covering my chest.

"Not like *this* I don't," he says, shaking his head, like he has no clue who I am. "I mean, God, Marion, what the hell are you doing?"

I stare out the windshield at the night, empty of stars, covered with too many clouds. I want the water to take me. Because soft or hard, cold or warm, Kurt or Abe, no matter *who* it is, or *how* it is—

The silence is winning.

In the back of my mind I hear Kurt's words, in that flood of rain, talking to me about his mother. And I hear him asking—

*Who chooses to drown?*

I look at the hurt in Abe's eyes, and the shame takes me. The fear.

The part where I walk into the creek water and take part. The piece of me that doesn't know how to say no, even when hands grip me and force worms into my mouth. The rage that is silence. The silence that is shame, and the person that hiding this shame makes me become.

Drowning happens in the quiet. It happens slowly, till I'm too far under, and the surface is too far away, and I can't speak anymore, because everything is water and I've swallowed it all down.

I look at Abe and realize Prince Charming is a fairy tale and nothing about being with someone is simple. He clutches the sides of his shirt and I understand now that bringing him here was never about proving to myself he wouldn't wake the creek water. I brought him up here to kill my last breath of hope.

I brought him up here to prove that he would.

# Kurt

**My watch clicks past five minutes and I'm antsy.**

I look at the guy passed out on the mattress. He's really out. Hasn't moved since we got here. I'm not even sure he's breathing.

Minute six ticks by and I want back in that room.

I tilt my watch to Conner and his eyes dart to the exits. To all the corners in sight. There's that guy passed out on the mattress, a couch, and an unlit fireplace. There's only one window and the floor is covered in trash. Cigarette Guy has the only advantage—a metal object, his chair. The lamp in the corner is too far away.

Conner starts to pace, gauging our next move.

"You got somewhere to be? Settle down," Cigarette Guy says, getting out of his chair to block the hallway. He stubs both his cigarettes out on the door frame where the wood is covered in burns.

"It's been ten," I say, and he scratches his beard.

"So wait longer."

"*You* said ten. Josie said ten." I kick a fast-food box on the floor and his back goes straight.

"Well, maybe ten means twenty." He pulls a blade from his pocket and Conner stops in his tracks.

I catch Conner's eye. His fists are clenched and I know he doesn't want to rush this guy. But he nods, letting me know he will if he must.

"You know," I say, stepping away from Conner and crushing another fast-food box with my foot, "in my book, ten is ten."

"Yeah, well, your book don't—"

I run.

I rush him like he's the ball. His eyes flash wide and he tries to swipe that knife. But I'm fast. Low. Under him before he has a chance. I slide tackle him, smashing into his feet and crashing him to the ground.

Something clangs on the floorboards. The blade maybe. I don't have time to look. His legs tangle with mine and—

*Crack!*

Pain splinters up my shin. I grunt, scrambling away from his kicking leg.

There's a scream.

Conner's pounced. The two scrabble, scratching arms and legs, when—*bam!* Cigarette Guy connects with Conner's jaw. Only, Conner wrestles and Conner's mean, punching him back as fast as he came.

I look for the knife. Cigarette Guy's hands are empty.

They're balled into angry fists that pound at Conner.

I see it. Just out of reach to their left.

Adrenaline surges and I scramble on my elbows and knee. I try to put weight on the injured leg, but pain shears up the bone. I knock the blade away just as Cigarette Guy sees it. It shoots across the floor, sliding under the mattress.

I check the passed-out guy. He hasn't moved. And fuck, it looks like he's dead, but I don't have time to check. Nails dig into my ankles. I twist, kicking Cigarette Guy's hands, and it distracts him long enough for Conner to get the upper hand.

Conner pins him, digging a knee into his back. He yanks the man's arm behind him, twisting the wrist like one of those martial-arts badasses. He leaves the fucker's free hand flapping against the floor like a dying fish.

I recheck the mattress. No movement.

Cigarette Guy whimpers and Conner nods that he's got this. My chest pounds and I gasp for air, realizing I've forgotten to breathe.

"Go," Conner says in a raspy voice, nodding to the hall. I cough back the pain and limp toward the shadows. This visit is over.

I bust through the door and the back room smells like puke. For a second I don't want to see what's inside, but I have to get my sister. Then a second smell hits me, like burned metal or glass, and there's a candle in the corner that cuts through the dark.

I see a bed with Josie on it. Not wearing her sweater. Not wearing her hat. And there's a man on top of her.

He's—

I ram my shoulder into him, pushing him onto the floor and pounding him till he's broken. He doesn't put up a fight, and when I look at his face, I see he's already half-gone with whatever's stripping his eyes dead. Meth or fucking dope.

I turn to see who else is in the room. Find Tina. A dark-haired woman is in the corner sitting on the floor, her head rolled back against the wall.

"You told me you were going to help her!" I bark, but the woman doesn't look at me, her eyes glassy and glued to the ceiling. She doesn't care that I pounded the shit out of that guy. She doesn't care what he was doing to Josie.

My sister's on the bed—not moving. She lies limp, a pipe in her hand, her head bent in my direction.

"Josie!" But she doesn't react. Her eyes are vacant, looking right through me. Like she's dead. "Jesus, fuck!" I climb on the bed and shake her. "Josie! Goddamn it! Josie!" She doesn't respond, her body heavy as lead. "No, no, no!"

She isn't breathing. I blow air into her mouth then press on her chest. Rhythmic beats. Like they teach at school, to get air in the lungs. Air in the lungs.

"Josie! Goddamn it!"

Her chest lurches, sick bursting up her throat, and I turn her head to the light as bile drips from her mouth. "Josie?"

I shake her, but she doesn't respond. "Oh, God, please!"

Her chest jerks again and her mouth foams with slime. I grab her sweater and pull it down over her, scooping her into my arms.

"Hold on, Josie, hold on. Conner!" I yell so he knows we're coming. She moans, but her body is deadweight against me. Pain stabs my shin as I run down the hall.

Conner curses at the sight of us. "Is she—?"

"We have to get to a hospital. Now!"

I'm out the door. There's a *thwack!* behind me. It's probably Conner, punching out Cigarette Guy. I don't care. I drag myself down the steps, and Josie feels too heavy for someone so small.

I get us into the backseat and lift her head so she doesn't choke on her spit. Sour bubbles from her mouth and I can't take this—

The vomit in her hair. Her body limp in my arms. The fact that—Jesus, fuck!—she looks *exactly* like Mom.

Conner busts out of the house and slams into the driver's seat.

Drool oozes from Josie's lip.

"Drive," I say, which he already knows to do, but I yell at him anyway, because I need to yell at someone, anyone, to keep this from being real. "Please, Conner!" I pound on the back of his seat. "Drive! Faster! Now!"

# nineteen

# Marion

**I need air.**

I grab my shirt and pull it down over me. Abe sits on the far side of the seat with his clothes rumpled and his lips pink. Blond hair falls limp over my shoulders and I have a choice. Walk out of the creek water—

Or fall in.

Choosing to drown would be easy, slipping under the water into the silence, leaving only the light babble of the stream. No more fighting, or hiding. Drink the water and no longer breathe.

"I don't know what I was thinking," I say quietly, and Abe doesn't look at me. None of this is fair to him. His fingers fumble with the strings from the broken buttons of his shirt and he closes the fabric over his chest. "We should go."

He punches the remaining button of his shirt through its hole, his pinkie finger fishing it through the tiny opening before he looks up.

"Did you ever like me?"

His whisper fills the car and I can't look at him. My throat tightens with how impossible it is to answer that. How liking him, how even loving him, is not enough. How it alone cannot shield him from the razors of this secret. How caring about him doesn't mean I won't tear him to shreds.

I look out the window and the sky is black and starless. I wish there was one—just one—single star. Or maybe even an outline like the stickers on my bedroom ceiling hidden under all those layers of paint.

But the night is seamless and dark.

*Yes*—I want to tell him. *Yes, I like you. I've always liked you.* But—

"I'm sorry," is all I manage. It's what I really mean. There's nothing else I can say that will fix this.

Abe gets out of the car and walks to the edge of the cliff. His white shirt billows like a ghost against the seamless horizon. I can't see where the sky ends and the land begins. There's only flat surface and endless dark. No separation. No space with which to divide this. No way to blame this on him, or Kurt.

This is all me.

Everything since the creek, all the canyons of silence slung between me and Lilith, my father, Kurt, Abe—I can pretend it's them. But that's all it would be. Pretend. And all that does is leave them in the dark at the edge of this cliff, hating me.

*I've* made this divide. All this silence and darkness—
Is mine.

It was me who chose to drown.

I drive us out of the woods, and Abe sits beside me in silence.
I don't blame him. He's earned this quiet space, which is
private and not for me to see.

The road bumps and I think of Kurt and the first time
I was on this ridge. My body was screaming—not hot, but
sobbing—because there are things it can't keep holding in.

And if I keep pushing it down it will drown me.

And I can let it.

Or I can reach for the surface—for words, for breath,
for the air that can make all this silence take shape again. So
I can become visible.

I pull up to Abe's house and my stomach turns when I see
my father's car parked out front. Abe's dad is a cop. Of
course he called my father when I drove off with his son.

I grip the steering wheel, but it's slippery in my hands.
My front bumper hits the curb and metal scrapes against
pavement.

"Jesus," Abe curses, opening the car door before I've
even stopped. I slam my foot against the brake.

"Wait," I say, pulling the emergency gear, and he glares
at me. "Wait, I'm—" I shift the car into park, but grab the
wheel again, needing something to hold on to. "I wanted to

say—" I squeeze the wheel, barely able to speak. "I'm sorry. I'm awful. I didn't mean to hurt you, and I can't believe I—"

"Don't!" His voice slices out my air. "You don't get to be the victim in this."

His words lodge in my throat.

Unswallowable.

His furious eyes bore into me, and I deserved that.

"I . . ." I whisper. "I'm—"

"Just don't." He leaps out of the car and slams the door shut. He stomps up the lawn with his bare feet pounding into the grass. It makes me think of my broken flip-flop as I raced through the reeds, needing to get away.

Abe disappears into the house and a moment later my father replaces him on the lawn. He's angry—my father—in a rage I've never seen. Heading straight for me.

# Kurt

The nurses swarm us at the emergency room. They take Josie out of my arms and put her on a gurney. They yell for wires and pumps and bags of fluid. They roll her away, behind the glass. And I can't follow.

The fluorescent lights buzz and I'm left with empty air.

With nothing.

A lady behind the counter waves paperwork at me. She asks for my name. Josie's name. Insurance numbers. For my parents. They ask if I know what kind of drugs she was on, and Conner tells her whatever he can answer.

I can't breathe.

There are other people in the room. Watching us. Sitting in plastic chairs bolted to the floor. Waiting, like us, for whoever they have behind the glass. And it's quiet. Too quiet. Especially after the yelling and commotion and strapping her down. I try to breathe but—

Oh God, what if I lose—

I swallow. Press myself into the counter and try to get my legs to remember how to hold me up.

"And where did you find her?" the lady behind the counter asks as I suck down the sterile air that tastes like vinegar. Her pen stops writing and she looks from Conner to me.

"A friend's house," I say finally, my voice hoarse. "She needed to see her friend Tina. That's where she was. Tina's house."

"You're kidding me, right?" The lady gives us a smug look, and I want to knock out her teeth.

"No, he's not kidding," Conner snaps, and she cuts him a look.

"You *do* know that Tina's the street word for methamphetamine, right?"

My knees go out.

Conner tries to catch me, but I'm on the floor.

"Wow, okay," I hear the lady say. I think she picks up the phone to call a doctor or someone but "He can't be on the floor" is all I catch.

"He needs air," Conner says, trying to get under my weight and help me to my feet. But I don't want to get up. I don't need air. I don't want air ever again.


Conner sits next to me on the curb, and we wait for my dad. Light from the emergency room glows behind us, and I hang my head between my knees. Somehow, through snot and spit, I breathe.

"I messed up," I say, my voice ragged. "I messed up."

Conner takes off his coat and drapes it over me. His hand stays with the coat, against my back.

"I thought Tina was a person," I say, and Conner nods.

"Of course you did. Who knows a thing like that?"

There's a crack in the asphalt under me. A hairline crack that's so thin it's almost not there. It's the kind of thing you can pretend not to notice, until it guts you in half.

I raise my head and feel dizzy. The blood draining. I look at Conner and I know there's snot and vomit all over me, but he doesn't look away. He's always been here. Right here. Next to me. No matter what. It hits me that he's doing exactly what I did for Mom. Being here. Seeing. Not looking away or judging. Just picking me up. There are things you're not meant to carry by yourself.

"Con, I've been a shitty friend," I say, adjusting my leg, which is still throbbing, and he shakes his head. Pats me on the back.

"Don't worry about it. It's fine."

I look up at the sky, not sure if Mom's up there. Not sure if Josie's on her way to follow.

"It's not fine," I say. "None of this is fine."

There's water on my face. Dripping down over my chin and hitting the pavement. Finding those hairline cracks.

"I'm sorry," I whisper, and he rubs my back. Lets the tears fall.

"I know," he says, and we sit there. Him and me. No matter what.

My father storms into the ER sucking on a cigarette and stomping so loud everyone turns to look. I get up from my plastic chair, but he doesn't see me.

"Medford, Josie," he barks at the attendant behind the desk. "Where is my daughter?"

"You can't smoke in here, sir," the attendant says, and he curses at her, looking for a place to stab the thing out.

"You got a trash?"

The attendant points outside. "There's a receptacle by the—"

"Screw your receptacle! Where's my daughter?"

"Dad." I walk toward him and he turns violently. Ash litters the floor. "They don't know anything yet."

Two steps and he's on me. Clutching my shirt. Teeth in my face.

"What the hell did you do?" he spits. "I leave the house for three hours and—"

"Sir!" The attendant's voice is sharp. "Do I need to call security?"

He lets go of me.

"No, *you* need to find out what's going on with my daughter!" He points behind the glass.

"Sir, I don't appreciate your—"

"I don't care!" He glares at her. "I'll be waiting out by the *receptacle* when you have an answer." He grabs my shoulder and pushes me toward the door. Conner gets to his feet and the attendant picks up the phone, both of them eyeing me. I wave them off.

This is between Dad and me.

Out by the trash can, Dad takes three long drags of his cigarette and starts to pace.

"You better start talking," he says, flicking his ash. "You better start telling me why my only daughter is in the ER, ODing on some shit she isn't supposed to have!"

"Because she's a meth-head, Dad!" I kick the trash can and pain splinters through my leg. White flashes in my vision and I have to grab the can to keep from falling over. It's the same leg that Cigarette Guy smashed.

Dad flinches but he doesn't offer a hand.

"I fucked up," I say through the pain.

"You're damn right, you fucked up." He points his cigarette at me and I grip the can, wanting to pull it off its bolts and chuck it at him.

"*And* she's a meth-head!" I say, glaring at him. "She just wanted more. I didn't know that, but that's what it was! That's all it ever is."

His face is stone. He doesn't want to hear it.

"She's *Mom*!" I yell. "She's just like Mom."

He's on me then, grabbing my shirt. Smoke in his nostrils. My leg throbs and I can barely stand. I lean into him, shaking my head.

"I dump it out. I try to keep her away from it. But she still goes out looking for more. That's it. She's Mom."

"Don't disrespect your mother like—"

"Mom was a drunk!"

His knuckles press into my chest.

"And Josie's a meth-head! And they *both* just wanted more."

He yanks me close and I taste the ash on his breath. "Your sister is—"

"Why didn't *you* stop Mom?" I interrupt, razors scraping up my leg. It hurts so much I can't see straight. Fire at the edge of my vision. "*You* were her husband. Why was *I* the one pulling vomit out of her hair and dumping the bottles down sink? What did *you* do?"

He's grips me so hard, I think I stop breathing, and I can't see his eyes. For a second I think he might be holding me up, because I can't possibly be standing on this leg.

And I see it all now. How it isn't one thing I could have done, but a hundred little things. Looking left instead of right. Knocking on my sister's door. Asking Mom to talk to me instead of playing our guitars. Maybe it's as simple as watching a movie with Dad and learning to stand in each other's presence. We might be able to make it if we did that. If we could all be like Marion with her hand on my shoulder in the rain, listening, seeing, despite how uncomfortable it is.

Uncomfortable but *choosing* to stay.

"I fucked up," I whisper to Dad. "With Josie, yeah,

you're right, I made a bad decision. But *you* fucked up too. Where were you? Where have you been the last four years? It's like both of you died when she got in that truck. I don't know how to carry this by myself. Yes, I fucked up, Dad, but *you* fucked up too!"

He pushes me away and I have to grab the trash can to keep my balance. It doesn't matter; I hit the cement anyway. Pain streaks up to my groin and I see him stalk away to his truck. The cigarette falls out of his hand. Red embers on the pavement.

Burning out.

He unhooks his tailgate and then slams it shut again. At least that's what it sounds like he does. He's too far away for me to really see what he's doing. I rub my eyes and think maybe he's just standing there. Gripping the back of the truck. Fuming. He stands there for way too long and I'm sure he's going to get in that truck and drive away. Sure he's going to leave me alone with this mess.

Again.

I get up.

There's fire in my fucking leg, but I get up.

I limp over to him and it takes forever with the bones twisted wrong and scraping against each other. But I walk.

I put my hand on his shoulder and he's shaking. Shaking like he might never stop.

"I don't care that you fucked up," I say. "I care that you stay."

He rams the butt of his palm into the tailgate. It slams like a gunshot. He rams his hand into the metal again—

And again—

And I wait there with him, until he stops.

"Josie and me," I say. "We won't make it without you."

# Marion

My father is furious. He races toward me with the light of Abe's house blazing behind him.

"That man is a cop," he growls, throwing a finger toward Abe's house. "You think I like cops calling me in the middle of the night? What the *hell* were you doing?"

Hair blows in my face and he stops at the curb. He takes in my rumpled clothes, my bra-less shirt, my tangled hair.

"Jesus Christ," he hisses through his teeth, realization forcing him to turn away. Both his hands ball up and all the muscles in his neck tense. I hate that he can't look at me.

"Give me your keys and get in the car!" He points to the Lexus, and I do as I'm told. My keys jangle too loudly as I put them in his palm and we peel out into the street.

I see my car getting smaller in the rearview mirror and my stomach turns knowing Abe will have to see it in front of his house in the morning. I hear his ragged voice in my head, pissed at me, with his buttons all over my floor. Buttons I scattered.

Cold crawls up my legs. Squishy and mud-water cold.

My father grips the steering wheel so hard his knuckles are white. I lean into the armrest and hold tight, trying to keep steady, to breathe, swallow.

"I'm sorry Mr. Doyle had to call you," I say, and he scoffs.

"No, *I'm* sorry he had to call me! *I'm* sorry my daughter can't be a respectable young adult."

"We didn't do—"

"I don't want to know!" His lips jam together and his eyes bore into the road. He huffs, nostrils flaring, like there's water rising inside him. "Jesus," he growls, almost to himself. "And who was that *other* one? The other day? Your *friend*."

I taste salt and the ocean.

"Kurt."

"Right." Saliva flings from his lip. "How many—" He cuts himself off, grinding a palm into the wheel.

"Just the two," I admit.

"Stop talking."

"I didn't sleep wi—"

*"Stop talking!"*

Silence razors between us. Silence thin as ice. It's toxic. It lumps with rose hips and worms in my throat. Ramming quiet. Ramming down. Ramming shut. How long can he ignore me? How long can we pretend not to see?

"You're grounded," he snaps, but all I hear is the clang of belt buckles and the sizzle of raw meat on the grill.

"Do you remember the barbecue?" I wheeze.

"This discussion is over."

"Do you remember the barbecue?"

He speeds up and tightens his grip.

"*Your* company barbecue," I insist. "The one where I got sick?"

"I said you're grounded! I suggest you think long and hard about the type of girl you've be—"

"What type of girl is that?" I snap, and he stares at me, his eyes scared.

He doesn't say it. He goes silent, and yellow road signs flash by us in a blur, threatening caution and dark.

"I cut my hair," I say, my voice sand-caught and harsh.

"What are you talking about?" he whispers, his arms locked on the wheel.

"The Fourth of July barbecue. The day I cut off my hair." I grab a clump of my blond, wishing I could razor it off. "All of it. Gone! And you barely noticed. You didn't care!"

"I thought—" He looks at me, and his face goes white. Something naked and afraid floods his expression and his eyes snap back to the road.

"What?"

His Adam's apple presses against his throat. It moves like a marble pressed hard against the skin, thick and impossible to swallow.

"What *did* you think?" I press, but he refuses to look at me. "You're upset I'm out late with a boy my own age, but you didn't care about *that man*!" I dig my feet into the floor and it isn't solid anymore. It squishes like dirty mud in my toes. "Do you *remember* that man, from your work?"

His hands tighten, and *I know* he knows.

"He played horseshoes with me?" I cough. "You remember?"

His head shakes slightly and my pants stick to my thighs.

"*That man* who took me for a walk."

"Marion, stop."

"That man—" It catches in me. The water. The current.

"Stop."

It swells.

"That man who kissed me."

He frowns and shakes his head.

"That man who put his . . . put his . . ."

Rose hips jam in my throat. Worms and rose hips and—

"He put himself in—"

I choke. I gesture.

"Goddamn it Marion!" Dad pulls the car over, banging his trembling fist into the dash. "What's wrong with you?"

I gasp for air.

"Why would you say that?" he yells. "Why would you—"

I gasp—

"You were *fine* after the barbecue." He's so loud. Louder than I've ever heard him. Ocean loud. "You were sick!"

I gasp and choke, trying to dislodge the rose hips and the water. I gasp and hack and roll down the window and spit out the snot, and suddenly he isn't yelling anymore. He's grown so still beside me it's like he isn't even there.

But he is.

He stares at me in the dark. In this pitch-black dark, as I cough and wheeze. Spit dribbling down my chin. He stares at me. His little girl: hair tangled, water stung, grown-up. Too grown-up.

He looks at me, for real.

"You were . . ." But he can't finish that sentence because he's crying.

My father is crying.

Because I'm not invisible anymore.

# twenty

# Kurt

Tubes wrap Josie's arm and there are needles in her wrist. IVs drip whatever they're giving her and the machines beep. She lies on her side, curled in the fetal position, wearing a paper gown. She's asleep. She's breathing. Thank God, she's breathing.

I sit down beside her and see short spiky hair, visible on the left side of her head. I touch the fuzzy strands next to her scalp, brushing my thumb against the tender area where the hair grows from the skin. Always growing. Always trying again.

Dad sits down on the opposite side of Josie and takes her hand, pressing her bony knuckles against his lips.

"I'm sorry, Josie-girl," he says quietly. "Stay with us."

I watch him. His face is covered in wrinkles. Hard work. Seams. Regret maybe.

He looks up and it strikes me—how scared he is. How certain he was—when he walked into this hospital, flinging ash and fire—that she wasn't going to survive this. His chin trembles against her fingernails and I'm not sure he believes, even now, that she'll keep breathing.

"Don't let go," I say, picking up Josie's other hand, and I don't know if I'm saying it to her, or to him, or maybe even to me. But this is my family. And I want all that we have.

# Marion

Lilith agrees to meet me outside her house and I wait by the sidewalk. There's a small dust of snow on the grass and frost-etched crystals paint the curb. Winter is coming. Real winter with real cold.

Lilith walks out in her boots and scarf, and before she can say anything I put the blue mason jar in her hands. The one with the stars punched into the tin lid. The one with the dead bugs inside. I think her lip falls open, but I'm already walking toward the path in the backyard.

"This way," I say, and she follows in silence as we walk to the firefly field. It's barren when we get there. The grass is dead and the goldenrods have shriveled to fists. Reeds hang low on the powder-sugar ground, and the air is crisp as our feet crunch on snow.

"You're right, I saw you," I say, taking the mason jar from her hands and unscrewing the lid. She looks at me and then at the blue glass holding the tiny bugs and their tiny legs.

"I know," she says quietly, reaching into the jar and taking out one of the flies. She balances it on the tip of her finger, black and fragile against all this white.

"Did that boy rape you?" I ask, barely above a whisper, and the wind whisks that bug off her finger and into the sky. My lip begins to tremble.

"What?" Lilith looks at me sharply. "No! No, he didn't— is *that* what you thought?"

I look at the jar, the cold glass ice in my hands.

"Why would you think that?" she asks, and I can feel the wet on my face. I breathe deep, standing in the cold and the quiet, and I know I can be louder than this silence.

"I cut my hair?" I say, looking up. "Do you remember that? How I cut my hair?"

She nods slowly.

"That was the same summer," I say. "Before I saw you . . ." I tip the jar over and the bugs drop out, catching the wind, falling to ground. "There was a man—"

Understanding washes over Lilith.

"Oh my God!" She grabs the jar and tosses it to the ground, grabbing me. Hugging me. Hugging me so damn hard, like she'll never let me go, like she could melt all the snow.

I tell Lilith everything.

About the creek.

About Kurt.

About Abe.

We walk back to her house and sit on her porch, wrapping ourselves in blankets and warming our hands with cups of hot chocolate. Sunlight streams through the trees and makes the frost sparkle, a hundred tiny glints of truth all caught in the light. I can hide from the sun all I want, but its starlight is everywhere.

None of this is easy to tell her. But the more I give it breath, the more I'm able to breathe.

"Why didn't you tell me?" Lilith asks, her head tilted down and away, and I shake my head because there are too many answers to that question.

"Because you never asked," I say, thinking of how easy it's been for all of us to pretend. "No, that's not really fair," I say, not wanting to lay the blame. This is mine to carry. "I never *let* you ask."

I think of her sitting beside me on my front step with that mason jar in her hands. Of all the things she's silently wanted to talk about and I ignored, allowing them to fall into the negative space between us, as if that much emptiness wouldn't tear a hole in our world and invade.

"I never listened when you asked," I say. "Because I thought I could push it all away. You were right about the touching. I liked it. I needed it. You were the only one I'd allow that close. I thought that would be enough. I thought if I never said anything out loud, if I left it in the quiet, it would evaporate."

But nothing truly evaporates. Water changes to steam,

but the clouds catch it. The clouds hold it till it's time to rain. And when it rains, the rain comes to drown.

I reach out and take Lilith's hand and draw invisible circles over the ridge of her thumb.

"You feel it, but it's invisible," I say. "It doesn't leave a trace. But it's there, under everything. And it wakes."

Lilith shakes her head like she doesn't know what to say.

"If I'd known . . ." Her gaze gets faraway, like she's thinking about all the years we've known each other. And perhaps she's thinking about all the possible signs, the maybes, and the way I slid the sun into a shadow and covered it with paint.

"I'm sorry about the virginity thing," she says finally. "I was pissed. I *knew* you knew about the guy in the firefly field, and I was pissed you wouldn't talk to me about it. I kept testing your boundaries. I thought that after a while . . . If you, you know . . ."

Her eyes flick to me, cautious.

"If I lost my virginity?" I say.

Lilith nods, wrapping her arms around her front, oddly uncomfortable in her skin.

"I guess, I thought if you finally did it, it wouldn't be this thing you avoided all the time. And I resented you for avoiding it. *I* needed someone to talk to, Marion . . ."

Lilith's pinkie trembles against the side of her hot-chocolate mug, and her defenses crumble. The light slants and for a moment Lilith doesn't seem like invincible fire.

She looks like a girl. Plain, and oddly ordinary. Fighting her way forward, just like me.

"I can't believe this happened to you," she says, looking out at the field of frosted dew and sun.

"It did," I say, because I need to hear it out loud.

Over and over.

I need to give invisible words breath and sound, to make it real and solid.

"It did happen."


Lilith drops me off in front of Abe's house so I can get my car.

I climb into the driver's seat and see Abe's buttons scattered over the floor. I collect the tiny white disks, carefully, cradling them in my palm.

My chest tightens and I know this is the end of a friendship. Maybe this was never a friendship in the first place. I liked Abe, I always have. But somehow I've always been looking backward, to that first kiss, to the promise of what might have been waiting out there for us. Of what I hoped we could be, but we never were. Like a childhood princess wishing for her prince. But I can no longer live in that space where you never show who you really are. And I'm out of dandelion wishes.

I look up the lawn to Abe's house one final time before driving away. I don't know how I will face him at school. He'll never forgive me. And he doesn't have to.

I drop the buttons into my cup holder, counting each

shell-colored snap as it glints in the morning sun. They're tiny as pearls and deserve more than this plastic holding place. But I want them here, next to me. To remind me.

To remind me of the apology that I will give, which will never be enough. Of how the quiet doesn't discriminate. Of what I'm capable of, and how I've already been given my second chance. Of how sometimes all you're left with are seven small buttons.

# Kurt

Dad walks with me through the two silver front doors. At the desk we check in with the nurse, and she gets her keys. The place is nice. A little like a cheesy hotel with bad art. But I'm not going to complain.

The nurse leads us down the hall and looks back curiously at the cases I'm carrying. One in each hand. But she doesn't say anything. When we get to 15B, she knocks before letting herself in.

"Josie?" she sings. "Josie, you've got visitors."

There isn't much inside the room. A twin bed. Some furniture. A few of Josie's things. All I care about is that this room has *her* in it.

Josie comes out from behind a kitchenette and smiles. She's looking better. Her hair is thin and that tooth's still gone, but her skin has color. They let her go shopping so her clothes are new, and today she's wearing something flowery and yellow. It makes her look like spring.

"Is that what I think it is?" she says, eyeing me, and I nod. "But why two?"

I lift up the guitar cases and put them on her bed, and run a hand over the brown leather of the one on the left.

"Because this one's for you."

She frowns at me.

"I don't play."

I undo the latch and the smell of sour opens with the case. It's a dark smell, but I like that it's in there. It's what Mom smelled like and I don't want to forget it. I pull out the guitar with its red wood and I hand it to her.

She shakes her head, not sure she can take it, but I insist. Finally she gives in and takes it reverently, sitting at the edge of the bed and cradling it in her lap. She runs a finger over the strings and they let out a small whispering sound.

"You're giving me Mom's?" she says quietly as I unlatch my own guitar.

"No," I say. "I'm giving you *yours*."

Her eyes go soft, and I think of all the times she lingered behind that window screen, watching Mom and me making songs without her. How I knew she wanted to be out there with us, but we never gave her the chance.

"I don't play," she repeats.

"That's okay," I say, sitting down beside her and moving her hands to show her how to hold it. I tilt her hand so she can strum, so she can hear the music, and we can find a way to get through this alongside each other. Because the music isn't going to save us, but it *will* give us a reason to spend time together. And that's the part we need.

"Mom taught me how to play on this guitar," I say, lining her fingers up with the strings. "And now, I'm going to teach you."

I watch Marion in the hallway. I watch her every day. Watch her get out of her car, put her books away, talk to Lilith. We haven't spoken, but I know she sees me.

I make a point to walk past her. Catch her eye. Brush my hand against hers. I'm here. She knows I'm here. Even if she doesn't need me. I'm watching.

If I've learned anything from Josie, it's that I can't look away. So I don't. But it's also not my choice. I can't save her. I can only make sure she knows I'm here, and I see.

I can read Marion's eyes now. And there's something in them that says she just needs space.

So I find her. I touch her hand. And I find her again the next day.

I remember her standing in the trees after she cried in my car, that first time on the ridge. She stared into the forest wanting to walk into the dark, and I didn't know how to take her hand and walk her through it.

But I do now. Uncomfortable as it is. I just am a presence, touching her hand, every day. Letting her know she's not alone. And when she's ready, if she's ever ready, she'll walk back to me.

# Marion

**It's afternoon and I'm walking to class.** The sun flares and I look up to see Kurt down the hall eclipsed in light. For a second, all I see is gold and I'm not sure if it's actually him.

But then there's a quiet brush against the back of my hand.

I turn from the glare and he's there, not saying anything. His knuckles brush mine, he gives me a sideways smile, and I'm about to go my way—

And he go his—

When I take his hand.

I squeeze it, and he squints, not sure what to make of me.

"Firm handshake, remember?" I say, not letting go, and he smiles.

"You were always surprising," he says, but there's sadness in his eyes.

Dust fills the sunlight between us and suddenly I am certain that nothing—not even a ribbon of light—is ever clean. Everything is full of tiny particles. Full of skin, and dirt, and sand. But it is that dust that shows us the invisible. It is the dust that creates the shape of the air.

I squeeze his hand tighter and nod to the hallway door.

"Will you . . . ," I start, leading him to come with me. "Outside? Away from all of this." I nod to escape the buzz around us, the hallway, the people, the roaming stares.

He shifts toward the door and follows me outside, where I kick off my shoes and walk through the frozen grass to the trees. I keep his hand in mine the whole time, until I find a tall sturdy maple. Its branches low enough to climb.

"Marion?" He looks at me confused, and I test a branch to make sure it can bear my weight. The bark is rough and cold against my fingers. I climb onto the first bough, getting a firm grip before leaning back and extending a hand to him.

"Come up," I say.

The breeze flirts with his hair, spins it in tiny spirals, and he looks so cautious and unsure.

"Remember being a kid?" I say. "When the best thing in the world was climbing a tree? When nothing seemed more scary, or challenging, or important?"

He looks past me at the branches above, naked and reaching for the sky, having shed all of their autumn stars.

"Remember how everything looked completely different from up there? Only it's still the same landscape, except you can see farther."

His cheeks relax into a smile and he takes my hand. We

climb. Fast, careful, beside each other, our feet and hands weaving over silver branches and pulling us higher as we head for the sky.

We don't look down.

The branches grow slim and we have to balance, toe to toe, close to each other to keep our gravity centered near the trunk. And the sun touches every branch. Every inch of bark and skin.

When we reach the top, the branches are so thin there seems to be nothing but air beneath us. It's the point where there's nothing left but to trust the fragile whispers of these limbs. Trust or let them snap beneath us.

I tell him.

I tell him everything, like I told my father and Lilith. And when I do my lungs open up, like the wings of a butterfly, learning to catch the lightness of flight. And I don't tell him because I want us to be together, but because he needs to see me for real, and know who I am. And then he can decide what he wants. If he even wants to be friends.

We sit in the tree and he tells me about his sister. Tells me how she OD'd, and that he's teaching her guitar. We cling to the delicate twigs and find words, no matter how difficult. No matter how spare. And I close my eyes and feel the touch of the sun. And for a moment it feels like the water can no longer touch me, and all around me there is nothing but air—

And air—

And air.

# Acknowledgments

So much love goes to the two ladies who loved this book from the very beginning: my editor, Sara Sargent, and my agent, Melissa Sarver White. Thank you for believing in me and this story. Along with them, I want to thank the amazing staff at Simon Pulse and Folio for your support of *All We Left Behind*.

I will forever be indebted to the teachers who've helped me hone my craft. I'd still be struggling to find Kurt and Marion's voices without the classes, mentorship, and compassionate criticism of Amanda Jenkins, Shelley Tanaka, Mary Quattlebaum, Laura Kvosnosky, Ross Brown, and Patty Meyer.

I could not imagine a more supportive and brilliant community than the students, faculty, and alumni of the Vermont College of Fine Arts. Particularly my Dystropians. I love you all, and yes, it's happening!

I also want to thank everyone who read snippets, drafts, and revisions of this project. This book was shaped immensely by the insights of Sheryl Scarborough, Melle Amade, Steve Bramucci, and Ellen Regan.

Thank you to my parents for always supporting me, even when I chose a career in writing, or I dyed my hair hot pink. And lastly, a big shout-out to my rock, Russell Gearhart, for his patience, love, and unwavering belief in me.